Briley Van Campton

A. Henry Moen

This is a work of fiction. Names, characters, places, and incidents are products of the author's imagination or are used fictitiously and are not to be construed as real. Any resemblance to actual events, locations, organizations, or persons, living or dead, is entirely coincidental.

World Castle Publishing, LLC
Pensacola, Florida
Copyright © A. Henry Moen 2018
Hardback ISBN: 9781629898889
Paperback ISBN: 9781629898896
eBook ISBN: 9781629898902
First Edition World Castle Publishing, LLC, March 19, 2018
http://www.worldcastlepublishing.com

Licensing Notes

Cover: Karen Fuller
Editor: Maxine Bringenberg

Table of Contents

Dedication

For the Dreamers.

Chapter One: Hooky

Briley had never wished as hard as she was wishing this very instant. Her eyes were all scrunched up and her forehead creased. *PLEASE!* she screamed in her mind. *PLEASE just let school be canceled!* She could feel her ears turning red with the effort and in her mind, Briley could feel the planets falling out of alignment from the force of her wish. But when she opened her eyes, Briley was still riding the bus. Mandy Jones sat next to her blabbering on about her stupid science project that her stupid dad had helped her on all year long. Mandy and her show off know it all dad had created a robotic dinosaur from scratch.

"I'll probably get first place, that's what Father says!" Mandy chimed. Then Mandy asked the question Briley had been dreading since stupid Mandy opened her big fat stupid mouth. "So what is your science project all about?"

Briley didn't dare tell Mandy that she had forgotten all about it. She had to think quickly and usually, thinking quick wasn't one of Briley's strong suits. Today was no exception.

"Well...." Briley's heart thumped in her chest when she saw the school in the distance. "You see, it's very quite top secret! In fact, it's so secret that the Smithsonian Society has sworn me to secrecy, and right now as we speak, the FBI has my science experiment, but they won't let me talk about it."

"I don't believe you." Mandy retorted without blinking an eye.

Then Briley heard the telltale squeak of the bus brakes. Her body moved forward, then back as the bus came to a shuddering stop and she gazed out the window at the Piedmont Public Elementary school. Children were laughing and joking with each other, but Briley felt like she was dying inside. She tried wishing one more time really hard, but it was no use. She had had two whole months to work on her science project, but something more important always seemed to pop up.

Briley watched as Mandy bounded to the front of the bus with her bright yellow pigtails bouncing. "I hope your pigtails catch fire today!" Briley whispered.

Then, slowly, grudgingly, like leftover broccoli, Briley exited the bus. She was going to be the first child ever in the Van Campton line to ever flunk out of school in the fifth grade. Briley's brother Harrison was older than her, and he gave her a noogie as he passed by her. He always sat at the back of the bus with all the other older kids trading Castor Cards. "Come on, Sis!" her brother yelled. "Get your game face on!" And then he put his fingers in his mouth and pulled his cheeks out so Briley could see all of his teeth. It always freaked her out when he did that.

"I'm coming!" Briley called out, and took a step toward the school. She watched Harrison enter the school, and then she stopped walking. All around her children ran toward the school doors, but Briley just could not get herself to do it. And then almost against her will, Briley walked backward into the parking lot, across the street, and into the buildings that made up Piedmont's downtown.

Brilianne Amelia Van Campton of the Van Campton family, who ran the Van Campton Inn and the Van Campton Bank and Trust, had just skipped school. Briley was pretty sure her mother was going to murder her when she found out. Briley was going to be the youngest victim of murder in the history of Piedmont. "And so...," Briley reasoned, "I'll just have to make sure she doesn't find out!" A plan started to form inside Briley's head. She just had to come up with a science project and complete it, and then get it to the school before anyone reported her missing. "OK! First stop! The library!" A man looked at Briley funny as she announced her destination, so Briley stuck her fingers in her mouth just like Harrison had done to her and showed him all her teeth. The man shuddered as he walked away.

Piedmont was a small town tucked away from the rest of the world. The downtown is not very large, consisting of a dozen or so shops. Briley's brother often joked that you could cover the whole of downtown Piedmont in the time it took to fry an egg. So it took almost no time at all for Briley to run past all the shops. She shot into the library and headed straight to the science section of adult books. She ticked off the books one by one. "Paleontology, biology, chemistry...ah...astronomy!'

Briley had always loved the stars and constellations, and she reasoned that since she was working on a very strict time frame, the simple solution would be best. She opened the book and thumbed through the pages, finally settling on the planet Mars. An essay would be easiest. It was no secret that Briley was not a science genius, so as long as she had SOMETHING to turn in, her mother wouldn't murder her. She began to read about Mars, and to write about Mars and the moons of Mars, and it was really no wonder at all that Briley fell asleep, because all of those words about Mars were really very boring.

***

"Psst!"

Briley tried to lift her head, but her cheek was glued to the astronomy book.

"Psst!"

She looked around with her eyes, but could not see who was pssting her.

"Little girl!"

Briley freed her cheek from the book and looked up. Mr. Trugorn was standing above her, frowning rather severely. When she looked him in the eye, he recognized her instantly.

"Ms. Van Campton, the library is closing. Time for studious young girls to head home."

Briley smiled at Mr. Trugorn, then looked down at her essay on Mars. She was about half done, so she had plenty of time to finish. Then his words sunk in.

"What? Closing? What time is it?" her heart thundered with a panic.

"Quarter after six!" Mr. Trugorn said matter of factly. "You're lucky I checked the back stacks — I nearly locked you in. I've shut down all the computers, so I can't check that book out to you. But I can hold it for you if you'd like."

Quarter after six? School was three hours over, and more than likely sometime in the night, Briley would be murdered by her own mother. "Uhm, no, that's all right." Briley smiled innocently. "I've got all the information I need. I can do the rest at home."

Mr. Trugorn smiled and put the book away, and escorted Briley out the door of the library. Briley started walking past all the closed up little shops of Piedmont, wondering how on earth she was ever going to explain away all that had happened. As she passed the curio shop, she caught her reflection in a tall freestanding mirror. Everyone always said that Briley was "cute as a button," but she had never really figured out why buttons were cute. She had hazelnut hair and round blue eyes. Her hair was darker than the rest of her family, who were all very blonde, but as far as Briley could tell there was nothing remarkable at all about her reflection. In that instant, Briley felt very much like a button, though. "It's like I'm sewn on to someone else," she said aloud. "My insides don't match my outsides." Briley wasn't sure what she meant by that, but she walked away from the curio shop feeling very much out of sorts.

Her home was at least two miles away, sitting atop one of the many small hills that decorated Piedmont. It was going to be getting dark soon, and Briley didn't relish the idea of walking home alone in the dark, no matter how safe Piedmont was. The school year was winding down, but spring had been slow to come this year, and summer seemed like a distant thing. She was dressed in a blouse and skirt, but had forgotten to bring her jacket with her. Briley sighed aloud, pulled her backpack tight to her back, and set forth. Maybe if she walked quickly enough, she would get home before it got too dark out.

Once she was past the downtown shops, Piedmont opened up to an assortment of small parks and homes. There weren't really any neighborhoods in Piedmont. The houses were kind of like chocolate chips on a cookie…close enough to mingle, but never touching. The people of Piedmont were often like that as well. They all lived close enough, but never really melted together. At the thought of cookies, Briley's stomach rumbled. How long had it been since she'd eaten? She couldn't remember,

9

but it made little difference. Briley walked past the parks and homes that made up her town, trying to figure out what she was going to tell her mother when she saw her. Her father was out of town on a business trip, at least. No doubt he too would be furious at her for playing hooky, but he would be gone for at least another week.

As the light slimmed down and the stars peeked out from the darkening sky above Piedmont, Briley traced her fingers along one of the many hedge rows that bordered the manicured lawns of a Piedmont park. Her mind wandered from excuse to excuse. So far, Briley had discounted kidnapping, temporary insanity, and medical emergencies as plausible explanations for her skipping school.

The hedge she traced her fingers on had thorns in it, and Briley pricked her finger on one. She immediately brought her injured finger to her mouth, but the pain didn't last long and within moments, she found herself following the hedge row with her hand outstretched again. For some reason she found it comforting, and started counting the blooms she saw on the hedge. She was nearly at the edge of the hedge row when she heard giggling behind her.

Briley spun on the spot, ready to confront whoever was following her, but there was no one there. She squinted and used her hand to shade her eyes, but still didn't see anyone. "Just your imagination!" Briley told herself. She often let her imagination get the better of her, and more than once had been scolded for daydreaming in class. Briley turned back around and started to step forward again, but as she reached toward the hedge with her hand, she heard the giggling again. "It's not funny!" Briley cried out, turning round so fast there was no chance of anyone escaping her eyes. But there was still no one there. "I said it's not funny!" Briley cried out, and it was then Briley heard a tiny voice reply.

"Oh, but it tickles!"

Briley spun in circles, looking for the source of the voice, but couldn't find one. She was either totally going mad or deep in a dream. Briley hoped she was dreaming. Maybe she hadn't actually played hooky, and maybe she still had time to finish her science project. She pinched herself hard and did a few jumping jacks to try and wake herself up, and the giggling sound came again, only this time it was followed by the sound of clapping. Briley turned to the hedge, and then she saw him for the first time.

He was the strangest creature Briley had ever seen. Even in her wild imaginings, she had never invented anything like him. The man seemed to step right out of the hedge. His skin and hair and even his eyes were all different shades of green. The creature smiled, and Briley saw that even the inside of his mouth was green. He had leaves enfolding his body instead of clothes. Vines grew from his head instead of hair. He was short for a man, and he chuckled as Briley backed away, her eyes wide.

"Oops!" The man chuckled good naturedly "You weren't supposed to find me!"

Then just as quickly as the man had appeared, he walked backward into the hedge, disappearing from view. Briley rushed to the spot where the being had been, feeling all along the hedge, but there was no sign of him. "Wait!" she cried out "Who are you?" But it was no use. The man was not to be found. Briley was determined to find him, and so she plunged headlong into the hedge, thorns and all. She felt several pricks as she stumbled through the dense plants. When she came out on the other side of the hedge, she looked around. But she was still in Piedmont.

In fact, she was reasonably sure she was standing in the Yarrows' yard. They ran the curio shop she had stopped by earlier. The house and the grounds were all dark. Briley looked up and the night sky was filled with bright jewels. The stars seemed closer to her than they ever had before, and Briley reached out, imagining she could catch one in her hand.

She was amazed to feel something soft and tiny in her fist, wriggling against her fingers. Briley cupped her hands together tightly and peeked in between her fingers. Whatever she had caught in her hands went for the opening and poked Briley rather hard in the eye. "Ouch!" Briley cried out, smashing her hands together. She emptied her hands, expecting a grasshopper or beetle to fall out, but there was nothing in her hands except a little bit of glitter. Briley heard the sound of applause again, and she spun around looking for the man made of vines.

"What is going on!" she cried out.

As Briley looked around, she saw the world around her as if it were see through. The yard and house that the Yarrows lived in looked like a thin film laminated on top of another, more lively world. Just for a split second, it looked like there were little fairies darting back and forth across a pale blue sky.

Instead of being scared, Briley was fascinated. She ran toward the cloud of fairies and smacked her head on the outside of the Yarrows' house. She had only a split second to cry out in pain before her vision faded, and Briley slumped to the ground right then and there.

***

Argon moved from the hedges and stood over Briley, frowning. He placed his green hand to her cheek and sighed aloud. As usual, Candice was hovering over his shoulder.

"Will she be all right?" Candice asked him.

"For now she sleeps." Argon traced his fingers along her jaw. She was so pretty, it made his heart lurch to look at her.

Candice flitted from his shoulder and hovered above Briley's brow. Her wings flitted so fast it was impossible to see them. "I will send her good dreams." Then Candice landed atop Briley's nose and kissed her on the eyebrow. Candice was tiny, even for a sprite. Argon had saved her from a hungry spider so many seasons ago, and ever since, she had never left his side. Candice flitted to Briley's ear and whispered so low that Argon doubted even crickets could hear her. When Candice was done, she returned to Argon's shoulder.

"Is she the one you were looking for?" Candice asked.

"No," he sighed deeply. "But she has the sight." Argon looked down. It was always so tempting to bring humans beyond the Hedge. But it was against the rules of their kind. "We will have to keep looking for the other."

"So…what do we do now?" Candice asked.

"Nothing yet," Argon chuckled. "We return and wait!"

Chapter Two: Pixie Bites

When Briley opened her eyes, she was quite startled to see a pair of soft green eyes staring right back at her. Briley screamed, and then the owner of the eyes cried out. He stood, banging his head on a hanging lamp, and then tripped backward over a coffee table. Briley laughed aloud, looking at Mr. Yarrow sprawled across the floor of his own living room and rubbing his aged bald head. Just then Mrs. Yarrow walked in with a tray laden with sandwiches and tea and orange juice and fresh fruit. She placed the tray on the coffee table. "Oh Reggie. I hope you didn't scare the poor child!" she said.

At the sight of food, Briley forgot all of her manners and grabbed a sandwich with each hand, shoving them into her mouth. Reggie stood and Mrs. Yarrow sat in a grand easy chair across from her. "Help yourself, dear," Mrs. Yarrow said as if Briley hadn't already started devouring the food before her. The sandwiches were delicious, with baked ham, tomato, and a sharp cheddar cheese.

"Thank you!" Briley said in between bites, trying not to spray crumbs everywhere. "Thank you ever so much!"

Reggie took a seat next to his wife and smiled at her. His teeth were stained all yellow, but he had kind eyes. "She certainly has an appetite, Nora!" he said in a friendly tone "Should we keep her?" He winked at Briley in a grandfatherly way. She decided on the spot that she rather liked the Yarrows.

Briley started to feel full and finally slowed down on her eating frenzy. She put down her plate and sipped on a glass of orange juice.

"Feeling better, dear?" Nora smiled at her.

"Oh yes! Very much so, thank you!" Briley managed to recover her manners and folded her hands in her lap. It was only then that she gazed down, noticing the state of her blouse and skirt. Her clothes were covered in dirt and ripped in places. Briley noticed she had several scratches on her legs and arms, and she remembered her adventure with the hedge and the strange green man.

But neither Reggie nor his wife acted as if anything was out of sorts, as if they found little girls in their garden all the time. That thought brought a flutter of fear to her heart, but Briley squished it right then and there. The Yarrows were so nice; and besides, their family had lived in Piedmont for ages. "I should probably call my mother," Briley said. "Could I use your phone, please?"

"We've already talked with your mother, dear." Mrs. Yarrow smiled. "She said she was on her way."

"Oh," was all Briley could think to say. Then she thought of a word in her head that she knew if she said aloud would get her grounded for certain.

Reggie started clearing the dishes away. "Let's see to those scratches, shall we?" Nora asked.

15

Briley nodded and followed Nora to the bathroom. The house was filled with knick knacks of all kinds, but there wasn't a spot of dust anywhere to be seen. The house was expansive and neatly kept, but everything seemed placed as if it were on display.

"Do you have any children?" Briley asked before she could catch herself.

Nora stopped mid stride, with her hand hovering above the bathroom door knob. "We did, once. Reggie and I don't like to talk about it."

"Oh. Uhm. I'm sorry I asked." Briley examined the carpet between her torn shoes.

"Nothing to apologize for, dear. Come on. Let's get you fixed up a bit, yes?"

Nora smiled at Briley and she tried to smile back, but the joy had left Mrs. Yarrow's eyes, and Briley could not help but feel it was her fault. Nora helped Briley get cleaned up, and she had a gentle hand with the hydrogen peroxide. Briley desperately needed a long hot bath and a fresh change of clothes, but aside from that, she felt much better after eating and getting most of the dirt from her arms, legs, and face. After that, she sat in the living room. Reggie and Nora Yarrow taught Briley a card game called cribbage that she rather liked. They were laughing and smiling, and Briley could not help feeling sorry that the Yarrows had lost their children. They must have been excellent parents. Then the doorbell rang, and Briley remembered that her own mother was expected. Briley gulped. She really didn't want to be murdered.

***

The car ride home had been silent. But now Briley sat at her kitchen table. Her mother had used her middle name at least six times already.

"Brilianne Amelia Van Campton!" her mother cried out.

"What on earth were you thinking? You could have been murdered!"

Harrison stood in the corner of the kitchen. Occasionally Briley would link eyes with him and Harrison would mock their mother, waving his hands around silently and mouthing a lecture. At least she could count on him being on her side. Their mom was thin and tall with long blonde hair. You might look at her and think a gust of wind would knock her right over. But when Briley's mom was upset, she seemed to grow two feet taller and thicker than an oak tree.

"Sneaking off, skipping school, staying out who knows where for who knows how long!" Briley's mom was pacing in front of her, and as she turned her back Briley locked eyes with her brother, who chose that moment to stick a finger up his nose. If there was one thing Mother couldn't stand, it was a nose picker. Briley couldn't help but giggle. Her mom rounded on her instantly.

"Did I say something funny?" Her mom's face was red like a tomato about to pop. Briley cowered in her chair.

"No. I'm Sorry. I—"

"Three days, Brilianne! Do you have any kind of idea what can happen to a girl your age in three days?! With no word? No phone call? And you say you forgot? For three days?!"

Briley was pretty sure that her mom's eyes were about to shoot straight out of her face and splatter against the wall. But wait. Three days? The Yarrows said that they had found Briley that very morning, and Briley just couldn't believe that they would lie about something like that.

"But I—" Briley began.

"No buts! I've had the police scouring all of Piedmont for you! For the love of Mike, Brilianne! Your father had to end his business trip early, and he will be back tomorrow to deal with you. I am at an utter loss! I know you are absent minded, but this is just beyond anything I can put a finger to. Grounded!" her mom shrieked. "Room! Go!"

Briley had never seen her mother so furious. She caught Harrison's eyes, and he too looked frightened by the level of their mother's anger. There was nothing to do but go to her room and wonder how she had lost two days. Could she have slept in the library that long? But no, that was ridiculous.

Briley cautiously exited the kitchen, as if afraid to wake a lumbering giant snoring in the next room, and tiptoed up the stairs. She replayed the previous day in her head again and again. It must have something to do with the strange creature she had met near the hedge row. If anyone would know what had happened during those two missing days, it would be him. Quietly as she could, Briley crept up the stairs to her room, pulled out her bathrobe, and then went to the bathroom and began drawing a bath. As she watched the water fill the tub, Briley tried to recall all the details of the hedge and the green skinned man she had met and the fairies she swore she could have touched, but it was all very foggy.

***

The bath stung worse than Briley could imagine, but it felt good too to get all the grime off her. Usually she just took showers, but for deep down dirt there was nothing like a good hot bath. Besides, it gave her time to think as she poured an extra dose of bubbles into the water. Her mother wouldn't dare intrude on her while she was bathing. "It just isn't proper," she would say. The Van Camptons had a reputation to keep, and Briley so far was not very good at it. She was eleven years old. "On the brink of womanhood!"' her mother would say. But to Briley, being a grown up didn't seem to have any advantages at all.

"I'm never getting married," Briley said aloud into the bathwater. "I'm never having children." Briley's theory was that people who had kids had to behave themselves to set a proper example for their kids. "So if you never have kids...." Briley giggled. She had had this argument in her mind with her mother several times. "It doesn't matter how you behave!"

She splashed the soapy water around for a little while and then climbed out of the tub, toweling off and examining her scratched up body. It was then she noticed the little round red marks on her forearm, near her biceps. They formed a perfect ring, and looked kind of like she had gotten attacked by sixteen giant mosquitoes in a perfect circle. Briley felt along the red marks. They didn't itch or burn. In fact, to her fingers, it felt like they weren't there at all. Briley applied ointment to her many little cuts, and figured it couldn't hurt to put the ointment on the red bumps as well.

After that, Briley crept into her room and sat at her desk, which she had placed right against the window. Briley gazed outside. It was already past midday. Their house set atop a little hill, so from Briley's window she could see her school and part of the downtown. Now that she was looking for it, she could see the Yarrows's house and the hedgerow that ran between it and the park next to it. If Father was going to be back tomorrow, she would have to go back tonight, grounded or not. Of course, she didn't want to go alone, which meant including Harrison on at least part of her adventure.

Briley sighed, got up, and packed a backpack with some odds and ends from her room that she might need, like a flashlight and a change of clothes. Briley opened her closet and dug around until she found her pocket knife. Then she grabbed pretty much anything she could think that she might need and stuffed it into the backpack. Briley shoved the pack under her bed just as her mother opened her door. Briley jumped about five hundred feet in the air and flopped onto her bed.

"You scared me!" Briley let out breathlessly.

"Briley." Her mother sighed, and then closed the door. Her mom's eyes looked rimmed with red, as if she had been crying for hours. "You scared the utter life out of me running away like that. What is going on?" Her tone was quiet, almost a whisper.

Briley didn't know how to answer. She hadn't run away, but telling her mother that she had no idea where the time she lost had gone was just going to start another round of shouting. But Briley really didn't like to lie either. She wasn't very good at it, and most of the time it just made her tummy feel yucky inside.

"I wasn't really thinking, Mom." Briley looked down at her shoes. "I didn't want to face school because I totally forgot about my science project." She sighed. "I headed for the library to finish up my project. But then I went for a walk in the woods. And then I got lost and couldn't find my way out of the woods. At first it was a kind of adventure. But then I got turned around and it was really scary." It was as close to the truth as Briley could think of without her mom thinking she was crazy. When she looked to her mother's eyes she saw tears on her cheeks, and her mother put her arm around Briley's shoulders. Briley hugged her mom hard and she began to cry too. They sat that way on Briley's bed for a while without saying a word. After a time, her mom kissed her on her head and stood. She straightened Briley's bedsheets and left the room.

"I love you, Briley," her mom said.

"Love you too, Mom." Briley wiped her eyes and her mom closed the door.

Briley Van Campton

***

Briley's house had been in the Van Campton family for generations. It was built atop one of the many little hills that dotted the landscape, and it was originally a very cheery yellow color. The cheery yellow paint had faded with each year and been touched up when needed, but because of the rains they often got in Piedmont, the colors never quite matched up. The house was six stories tall, including a wide finished basement that had been dug into the top of the hill. From afar, it looked very much like a mismatched castle that had been built by color blind goblins.

Within the house, there were more bedrooms than Briley could count. But her favorite feature of the house was the air ducts. Built into the floorboards of each room were small openings to the air ducts, and after years of exploring the house, Briley had finally chosen her bedroom not because of its size or the color of its walls, but for the very fact that she could hear everything that went on in the house from the ducts connected to her room. Her brother Harrison had shown her the grates when Briley was small, and they had devised a system of communication.

Her mother was still awake, but the sun was setting over Piedmont. Soon her mother would prepare dinner, and then they would all settle in for a quiet night's sleep. But Briley was still determined to find out where her two days of lost time had gone before her father came home and turned Briley into Van Campton stew. Briley tapped on the opening to one of the ducts in her room with a screwdriver in a pattern only Harrison would recognize, and waited. She didn't hear a response, so she tapped on her grate again.

This time, Harrison answered. They hadn't come up with a complex enough system to have whole conversations, but enough to conspire together. Usually it was Harrison who wanted to sneak out in the middle of the night. Together, she and Harrison had explored most of the wooded areas around Piedmont with some of the other children.

What? Harrison responded
Adventure tonight, Briley tapped
No way!
Have to!
No way.
Give you two weeks' allowance.
OK. Fine. When?
After dinner.
Just you and me?
Andersons? Briley asked, hoping for some back up.
Grounded. Wendell and Grace?
OK! Plan?
You fake sick at dinner. I get back up and meet you at the stump.
Good idea.
Better be good, Sis.

Briley heard footsteps outside her door and tapped a quick reply. *It will be!* Briley straightened from the grate just as her mother opened her door again. Her mother smiled. "Dinner is ready, Briley."

Briley smiled back. "OK, Mom. I'll be right down."

***

Harrison Danforth Van Campton stood outside Wendell and Grace Ashford's house window and put his trumpet to his mouth. He needed to time this just right. He had made the mistake of texting them with his cell phone once, but both of their parents had found out and his mom had taken away his cell phone for two solid weeks. Harrison watched as the lights went out one by one in the Ashford house, and then he let out a shrill blast on

22

his trumpet like what a cat might sound like if its tail was stuck in the garbage disposal. His duty done, Harrison ran for the tree stump. The stump was just inside the woods. All the kids of Piedmont used it as a meeting ground if there was adventure to be had. Aside from the ice cream parlor downtown, there wasn't much to do in Piedmont. So mostly the kids explored the woods, played midnight in the graveyard, or walked down to the stream for a swim just to have something fun to do. When he got to the stump, Briley was already waiting for him.

"Wow. You made fast work of Mom," he panted.

"Yeah," Briley grinned. "I think she wore herself out today with all that yelling. She went out like a light."

Harrison laughed and plopped his pack down on the ground next to Briley's. They both sat on the stump, which was at least ten feet wide. He had no idea how old the tree was that had grown there. It must have been huge. Harrison had tried to count the rings once, but lost track.

He had to give it to his baby sister...she sure was gutsy choosing the night after her disappearance for an adventure. He didn't want to admit it, but he had been just as worried as their mom. Maybe even more so. And Briley hadn't told him anything about what had actually happened.

"So what's this all about, B?" he asked.

"Can you keep a secret?" she asked him. Harrison almost laughed out loud. Between the two of them, they had enough secrets about each other to shock the hair off a mountain goat. "I don't know what happened!" she said. "That's what I need to find out."

Harrison guffawed, but then she started to tell him exactly what she'd done, about the science project and the library, and then the weird green man in the hedgerow. He knew his sister had a vivid imagination, but he could tell when she was making up stories. Briley was a horrible liar.

"So I want to go back there tonight and talk to the creature I met. I know it sounds crazy. If we don't find anything, you can lock me up for good!" Briley's eyes were locked on his.

Harrison still wasn't sure if he believed her or not, but he nodded solemnly. "All right."

Then Wendell and Grace raced toward the stump with their own packs. Grace was a year older than Harrison, and Wendell a year younger than Briley. Being around Grace always made Harrison feel awkward at first. She had bright blonde hair and freckles. Usually at school, Grace wore dresses or skirts, but she and Wendell both came running up in jeans and long sleeved shirts. Grace smiled as she ran, and her purple and pink braces practically glowed against her teeth.

Grace got there first and jumped atop the stump triumphantly, letting out a whoop. Wendell came up afterward. "What is the adventure tonight?" he said, ignoring his sister's victory dance upon the tree stump.

"We're going through a hedge!" Briley announced. Both Ashfords looked a little crestfallen, but Briley didn't give them a chance to complain. She outlined in detail where they were headed, and by the end of it, all four of them were getting excited about sneaking through the parks and yards of Piedmont. It was a different kind of adventure than what they usually went on. The risk of being discovered got them all talking about different ways to move quietly, and how to look for a proper hiding spot.

In the end, Harrison was elected as leader because he had the best eyesight. He set off, moving quietly with the other three close on his heels. He decided to take the most direct route he could think of, which would mean crossing through four yards before they got to the Yarrow's house.

"Flashlights off!" Harrison called out as they got to their first obstacle of the night. They all stood outside Mrs. Kerrington's fenced in yard. Their lights all winked out, and the only light came from the stars and moon above. Luckily the moon was full. He crouched down and the other three all gathered around. "OK," he said. "Grace, you'll go first. I'll boost you over the fence. Then I'll climb over. We'll unlock the gate and let Briley and Wendell in." He looked from face to face as he talked, and everyone was nodding. "Then we just have to sneak across to the other side of her yard. We can let ourselves out the front gate. I'll lock the front gate and then climb over."

"What if we get caught?" Wendell asked.

Harrison sighed. Of all the Piedmont kids, Wendell was the most nervous. He was small for his age, even smaller than most girls. "Well, just don't get caught, OK?"

Grace took Wendell's shoulders in her hands and looked him in the eye. "You'll be fine! Just be quiet and quick, that's what you're good at." Wendell seemed to grow taller as his sister talked confidence into him.

"OK, ready?" Harrison whispered.

Nobody said anything, but he looked around and they were all nodding in unison. Harrison bent down and cupped his hands. Grace put her hands on his shoulders, then her foot into his hand, and Harrison felt his face grow hot. He was pretty sure he was blushing, and was thankful for the darkness around them. Grace was lighter than he thought, and when he stood she laughed, springing lightly from his hands. He hadn't meant to toss her, but she didn't complain.

Grace landed without a sound on the other side of the fence, and then Harrison scrambled over. He landed softly next to

Grace. She helped him up and then they were both scanning from side to side looking for the back gate. Grace spotted it first and tapped him on the shoulder. Harrison looked where she pointed and nodded. They matched strides.

Briley and Wendell met them at the back gate. Grace opened it for them, cringing when it creaked, and they were all silent and still for a good thirty seconds before Harrison shut the gate quickly. It closed noisily. Everybody cringed, but no lights came on inside the house.

"OK," Harrison whispered. "Now let's get to the other side."

Nobody said anything. He looked to Briley, who nodded. She grinned at him with excitement in her eyes. Harrison took the lead, stepping quietly and keeping close to the house. Mrs. Kerrington was well known for her dislike of young children. He had no doubt that if they were discovered she would call the police on them quick as lightning, and with his father coming home tomorrow, it was definitely something he wanted to avoid. Still, he couldn't dispute the sense of adventure that lingered in the air. They had never gone sneaking through neighbors' yards before.

They made it safely around the house and Harrison peeked around the corner. Mrs. Kerrington had her porch light on, but the rest of the house was dark. He looked behind him and saw Grace had taken up the rear of the pack. Behind him was Wendell, and then Briley. He motioned with his fingers toward the front gate, and then started forth.

He was only about three steps past the corner of the house when he heard a low growling sound. Then everything exploded into chaos. Grace shot past him like a flash, her sun yellow pigtails flying behind her. "Run, stupid!" she cried out, and Harrison looked behind him. Briley and Wendell were following on

Grace's heels, but he just stood there dumbstruck looking at the giant dog that was bounding toward them. The dog was HUGE! Harrison stood there wondering how Mrs. Kerrington could ever walk such a thing. Then the dog snarled and his instincts finally kicked in. Harrison ran all out toward the gate.

As he ran, he had his eyes glued to the front gate. He watched Grace fumbling with the latch. Briley was trying to help her, and Wendell was actually squeezing in between the slats of wood. Harrison really hoped Wendell didn't get stuck doing that. The dog was growling behind him. Harrison didn't know if it was his imagination or not, but he swore he could feel the dog's hot breath on the back of his knees. Grace finally got the gate open, and she and Briley were through like a shot. They pulled Wendell through, and now Briley was beckoning Harrison on with her arms. Grace was braced behind the gate, ready to slam it shut.

"Harrison! Watch out!" Briley cried out to him.

Harrison's blood was all in his ears and his reflexes must have been working overtime, because out of the corner of his eye he saw just a flash of black and Harrison leapt suddenly to the right. The dog was thrown off balance by his leap and rolled in the grass. Harrison pumped his legs and dove through the gate. Grace slammed it shut, and none too quickly. The dog was snarling at the gate, and they all saw Mrs. Kerrington storm out onto her front porch with a flashlight.

"Who's out there?" she screamed. "I hope this taught you hooligans a lesson!" She was marching toward the gate with her flashlight weaving back and forth. They all cinched up their backpacks and ran. "I'm calling the police, I'll have you know! Next time you come, there will be three dogs! Maybe four!"

But her words were lost on Harrison and the others. They ran for the nearest park and hid in the trees, out of breath. Briley was pulling at a water bottle while Grace comforted her brother. For himself, Harrison was panting with his hands on his knees. "When did Mrs. Kerrington get that giant beast?" He tried to laugh, but it came out more like a wheeze.

"That was a big dog!" Grace said in awe. "Did it get you?"

"No. I'm good. But I think I might pass out." This time Harrison managed to laugh.

"I think we need to add a dog whistle to our adventure packs," Wendell said.

They all burst out laughing. Briley laughed so hard water squirted out of her nose. Their revelry didn't last too long though. In the distance they saw the red and blue flashing of police car lights, and they moved deeper into the trees bordering the park. Mrs. Kerrington really had called the police. Of course there were only three officers in Piedmont.

"I think we should head home," Harrison said.

"No way!" Briley spouted off. "When Dad comes home tomorrow, I'm likely to be grounded for the rest of the year. I want one good adventure to remember before I have to spend the rest of my life sweeping that giant house."

Harrison couldn't help but smile at that.

"All right," he said. "But one more vicious Doberman and we call it quits. Deal?"

"You got it!" Briley said.

***

After the adventure with the dog, Briley was pretty sure she never wanted to own a dog ever again. When she was little she used to beg her parents for a puppy, but not after seeing that monstrous beast almost bite her brother.

Once they were a safe distance from Mrs. Kerrington's, they decided to take a break. There was a small circle of stones just the right height for sitting on, and Briley chose a rock and opened her pack. Grace sat on the rock next to her, and Wendell sat next to his sister. Harrison seemed jumpy though. He dug a sandwich out of his pack, but scanned the woods about them. He didn't even come into the circle, standing instead at the edge of the ring of stones.

"Is Harrison OK?" Grace asked Briley as she opened a bag of potato chips.

"He's just shook up, I think," Briley said. "We've never come that close to getting caught on our adventures before."

"Where are we heading anyway?" Wendell asked.

Briley munched on her sandwich and passed around her bag of potato chips as she described the hedge row she was searching for. "I lost my science project in the hedge," Briley lied. "It's already past due. My dad will skin me if I don't get it turned in!" Wendell nodded, finishing off the potato chips, but Grace just eyed her crossways. Briley was reminded again that she wasn't very good at lying, but there was nothing to be done about it.

"OK, let's get going," Harrison called out. "It's getting late."

Grace, Briley, and Wendell all stood, putting water bottles and sandwich wrappers away. Before long, they were past the park and coming up on the second house. Luckily there was no fence bordering this one, and aside from Wendell chasing a toad through the owners' garden and getting stuck with some thorns, nothing exciting or dangerous happened. As they walked past the house, Briley looked up at the moon, which shone with such brightness it was like a giant eyeball glistening.

"Do you see that?" she said, pointing up at the night's sky.

Harrison peered up. "What?" he said.

"It looks like a ring around the moon. Do you see it? The moon doesn't have any rings, though." Briley pointed and they

29

all gathered around her, following her finger as she traced a circle in the sky.

"I think I see it," Grace said at last.

As Briley stared, the circle around the moon got a little bit brighter.

"I see it now!" said both of the boys.

"Ma says when there is a ring around the moon, trouble is brewing," Grace said. "But she also says that if a broom falls to expect company, and that never works."

"Maybe the ring is because of the dog?" Wendell offered.

"It's just a ring," Harrison stated, and started walking.

They all followed him as he led a ragged pace through the parks and homes, but Briley kept looking up at the moon and the strange ring that seemed to glow around it. It wasn't just her imagination. It was definitely getting brighter as the night grew darker. Before long, they arrived at the park next to the Yarrows' home with its hedge rows, and Briley instantly started scanning for her green man and the patch of hedge where she had gotten lost the first time.

The hedges were not arranged in a pattern that Briley could discern. They weren't connected to each other like in a hedge maze. The hedgerows grew haphazardly as far as Briley could tell. Nonetheless, they were all pristinely manicured. For the first time Briley realized that until the other night, she had never ventured into this particular park. She had grown up in Piedmont, and for eleven years she had explored the town, its woods and hills. How had she never discovered such a unique park? But there was no time for questioning. "It's around here somewhere!" she called out, and Briley began to feel along the hedge rows as she had the other night, tracing her hand along as she had before. "Keep your eyes and ears open!" she called out, laughing.

Briley ran with a huge smile. Behind her she heard Grace, Harrison, and Wendell all laughing as well. She wasn't sure what had come over her. Maybe just the fact they had gotten to the destination of their adventure without getting bitten by rabid dogs or caught by Mrs. Kerrington. They zipped throughout the hedgerows in different directions. Briley took turns between the hedge rows, tracing her fingers all the while, changing directions at random.

As she turned a corner, Briley saw a pair of eyes appear in the middle of the hedge. She stopped on the spot and smiled. She had found him, the green creature. "Found you!" she called out. But the eyes were not green, like the man's had been. These were a strange color of yellow, like the edge of the sun while it sets. The eyes just stared at her, unblinking, with pupils the color of vanilla ice cream. Slowly Briley advanced toward the eyes, pulling out her pocket knife just in case.

"Over here, guys!" Briley called out. "I'm over here!"

Briley felt something tickle the back of her neck and reached behind her, feeling along her hairline. "Harrison!" she called out "Harrison!" But Harrison didn't answer. "Grace!" she cried. "Wendell?" But she couldn't hear their giggling any more. In fact, her ears felt like they were stuffed full of cotton balls. "This isn't funny!" she cried out. If this was some prank, she was going to put burrs in her brother's underwear drawer.

There seemed to be a pine needle stuck in her neck, and Briley pulled it out. She brought it out before her eyes and stared at it. It wasn't a pine needle, but a tiny arrow, not even a quarter inch long. Her head felt fuzzy, like it was floating off her neck. Briley whirled around, crying out.

"Harrison! Grace! Wendell!" She felt tears welling on her cheeks. As Briley spun, she started getting really woozy and dizzy. She fell to the ground, and a little blue creature perched right on her nose. The creature was so small Briley had trouble picking out its details, especially since she was so dizzy. But she could make out tiny wings, and it was holding a bow so small, Briley wondered how it could shoot very far. The blue thing looked kind of like a little person, but it had tiny antlers growing out of its head. Its wings had a leopard print pattern. Briley tried to raise her hand to swat it away, but all of her strength was gone.

The blue creature stood on her nose, and Briley watched as the eyes she had seen earlier moved out from the hedge, closer and closer to her. Then she saw a pair of zebra decorated wings appear above one eye, and peacock wings over the other. There was no face attached to the eyes! She wanted to cry out. Then all of a sudden there were three of the blue creatures standing atop her, two of them carrying shields painted bright yellow to look like eyes. The creatures were motioning at Briley, and she could see their lips moving, but Briley couldn't hear anything at all. Then the one with the tiny bow smiled at her, and when it talked, Briley had no trouble hearing.

"Got you!" it said in a tiny voice.

"Ga…. Wha…? Shoo…. Harri…." Briley couldn't get her tongue to work properly either, and her eyes began to play tricks on her. Her head lulled back and she watched the stars above her spiraling. "Help!" she tried to cry out, but she couldn't even get her lips to move, and the next second, everything around her went black and silent.

***

As Briley opened her eyes, the world was bursting with color. The sky was like a donut filled with all the best flavors of cream. The sun was a bright orange she could almost taste in a sky streaked in the purples and pinks of sunrise. She was lying in

32

a bed of grass, and Briley stretched her arms out as high as they could go. It felt like a carpet made of velvet beneath her. She rolled onto her stomach and buried her face in the grass. It smelled like spring and rain, and was so fresh it made her cry. Finally Briley tore herself away from the grass and stood. She was no longer in the hedge row, but that hardly seemed to matter. As she gazed about her, she saw flowers so bright they almost hurt to look at them, and then she spotted Harrison, Grace, and Wendell in the distance. As she made her way toward them, she saw they were all sitting on a patchwork blanket set on the ground.

"Can you believe it?" she called out to them as she grew close enough for them to hear. "It's almost like a dream!"

Harrison turned toward her and smiled, waving her over. Now that Briley was closer to them, she saw they were all feasting on pastries and fresh fruit, and were being waited upon by the little blue creatures that had caught her earlier, but that memory seemed like a distant one. Years ago. They all had their wings folded, beautiful wings in animal prints, none of them the same. The way their wings folded was distinct as well, some wrapped about their tiny bodies like dresses or robes. Some of the creatures had antlers or horns growing from their tiny heads. Others had long vibrant hair growing down to the small of their backs.

Briley sat down on the blanket next to Harrison.

"You have to try the cream puffs, Sis!" he said around a mouthful of something delicious.

One of the blue creatures carried a small plate atop its head to Briley. Another balanced a glass of orange juice upon its head and placed it next to her. Before she had time to think, Briley's plate was being piled with the most sumptuous treats...cream puffs, fresh strawberries, turnovers baked a perfect golden brown with cream cheese and icing. Briley took a cream puff and brought it to her mouth. As she bit in, her mouth delighted in the cream that melted as soon as she tasted it. The flavor was magnificent but fleeting, and Briley couldn't help but take another bite, then another. Each time, the delicious morsels' flavor disappeared all too quickly. But they were so good! The orange juice was the same way. It tasted pure and bright, filled with sunlight and citrus.

"Now this is a proper adventure!" Wendell laughed between mouthfuls. "Even if it is just a dream!"

"Oh, but it's not a dream," one of the little blue creatures stated. Briley saw it was the one with leopard print wings. "This is but a small show of our appreciation. It's not often we have human visitors!"

"But if it's not a dream...," Grace began, "where are we?"

None of the creatures answered Grace's question. They went back to flitting back and forth and piling everyone's plate full of food.

Briley leaned over to her brother and whispered in his ear. "Let's get out of here. We can always come back. Let's see what else is near!"

Harrison nodded when she finished talking. He lumbered his pack from his shoulders and brought out a little bag from it. He started putting cookies and muffins and quite a few of the cream puffs into the bag.

"Good idea!" Wendell shouted, and then they were all shoving the fantastic foods into their packs. Briley took one last long pull on her orange juice and set it down with a sigh. When she stood, the creatures gathered around her feet, and the leopard one flew up to her eye level.

"Aren't you tired?" it asked her. "Maybe you should sit back down and gather your strength."

"No, we're fine," Briley assured the blue creature. She didn't want to admit that sitting back down and taking a nap sounded like a perfectly scrumptious idea.

"Besides, we'll be back!" Harrison assured the creature. Grace and Wendell nodded behind him.

The creature's leopard print wings beat at an eye blurring pace as it tried to keep up with Harrison's stride. "Take this then," the creature said. "It will call us, but it only works once." The creature handed Harrison a tiny flute that Briley couldn't imagine how you would blow on without breaking. She wasn't even sure how you would hold it without snapping it in half.

Harrison gingerly put the flute in a side pocket of his backpack.

"Thank you!" he said earnestly, stopping in his tracks and looking at the creature before him. "How does it work?"

"Why, you just hold it in the wind!" The creature laughed and then spun in circles. Between one second and the next, the creature was gone. Briley swore she could hear its laughter ringing around her still.

"What were those things?" Briley said aloud. No one answered her, so she gazed about taking in the landscape. The blanket and the blue things had all disappeared. The hill they were on seemed lonely without their presence.

"Pixie bites," Wendell said aloud. "Those were actual pixies! With actual pixie bites!"

"Is that what those were?" Briley looked to Wendell.

"It's as good a guess as any!" Wendell laughed. "I'm just hoping I stay asleep long enough to enjoy the next part of the adventure." Grace and Harrison laughed at that and ran off ahead of Briley.

"But the pixie said it wasn't a dream," Briley began. "If it's not a dream, what is it?" she wondered aloud. Briley felt a little afraid. Mostly she was curious and excited, but under all of that, Briley wondered just what was waiting over the next hill, and whether it was a good idea or not to find out.

She watched as Harrison, Wendell, and Grace all launched themselves down the hillside, rolling and laughing as over bright flowers burst into clouds of petals around them. "Hey, wait for me!" Briley called out. And all fear forgotten, Briley dove down the hill, spinning and laughing with the bright fresh grass filling her senses until she got so dizzy she couldn't stop laughing.

At the bottom of the hill they all chased each other, pelting one another with handfuls of grass. "Look!" Harrison announced. "A trail!" Briley trounced him with a particularly large wad of flowers and grass before looking where he was pointing. There among the grass were small cobblestones all in a neat row, leading through the valleys surrounding them. Briley could have sworn they weren't there before.

"Where did it come from?" Grace wondered aloud. But Wendell was already heading down the trail. He was carrying a large stick and swinging it like a sword.

"Avast!" he cried out before beheading a particularly large tulip.

"Wendell!" Grace called out. "Get back here!" But it was no use. Wendell was pillaging all the flowers along the path.

"I don't think he's coming back," Briley said.

"He's going to get us in trouble!" Harrison stated, heading down the path after Wendell.

"Boys," Grace said in a frustrated tone. But Briley noticed that she began skipping along the trail, her blonde pigtails bouncing around her head.

Briley smiled, watching the three of them. She was about to follow as well, but there was a hand on her shoulder, holding her back. Briley spun around and saw the green man from before standing there, smiling at her. Briley's heart swelled and she wrapped her arms around him. He even felt like a plant, lush and springy. He chuckled and returned her hug.

"You came back!" he said to her.

"What is this place?" Briley asked. "Is it magic?"

"You and your friends have ventured beyond the Hedge. Allow me to introduce myself. I'm Argon." He smiled so wide, his teeth looked like leaves in a mouth of vines.

"Beyond the...," Briley began, but then a small creature flitted from Argon's shoulder and hovered before her eyes.

"And I am Celeste!" She looked like a tiny, beautifully painted toy. She glowed, even in the glistening sun. She sparkled, her skin a bright yellow, her wings iridescent.

Briley curtsied even though she was wearing jeans and a button down shirt. "My name is Briley!" she announced. "So very pleased to see you again!"

Argon and Celeste both laughed at that, but then Argon grew serious.

"We don't have much time, Miss Briley," he said. "Things are changing beyond the Hedge, and not for the better. Your friends need to be wary of the dangers here."

"What dangers?" Briley asked.

"The paths that lead deeper beyond the Hedge are easy to find and follow," Argon said. "But it is much harder to find the ways back again. It has been so long since humans have visited us. Some, like myself, are overjoyed at your presence, but there are others who will want you removed."

"Are you sure she's not the one we're looking for?" Celeste interjected. She was sitting with her legs crossed in midair, a finger to the side of her mouth.

"Hush, Celeste," Argon said seriously. Already Briley noticed that the green of his skin and eyes had started to fade from bright green to a darker shade.

"Is she a faerie?" Briley couldn't help but wonder aloud.

"Phah!" Celeste stuck out her tongue. "I am a sprite!" She hovered, hands on hips, her little glowing wings beating at a remarkable place. It was probably about as close as she could come to being intimidating.

"Both of you listen!" Argon interjected. "Find your friends and lead them back! Follow the oaks! The oaks will always mark the trail back to your land. It is not safe here. Not now."

"But it is so wonderful here...," Briley began

"Ah, if only I had time to explain." Argon frowned at her and Celeste returned to his shoulder. Argon knelt down and pointed down the trail where Harrison, Grace, and Wendell had ventured. "Look," he whispered. "Watch."

And as Briley watched her friends cavorting along the trail, she saw what Argon was talking about. Two creatures with brownish green skin, dressed in long black coats and heavy pants, were darting from tree to tree, following her friends. As they moved, Briley noticed they had swords in scabbards hanging at their waists. Their pants had splits in the back for tiny tasseled tails. They wore no shoes or boots, and their feet were angular. They only had three toes, but at the end of each toe was a long wicked claw. Then Briley watched as the two creatures were joined by three others, seemingly out of nowhere. They moved silently behind Harrison, Grace, and Wendell.

Briley gasped, suddenly afraid. "What are those?" she asked.

Argon didn't answer her. When she turned around, he had disappeared. So had Celeste. Briley didn't waste any time looking for them. She hurried down the path, running as fast as she could to warn her brother and her friends. She had to get to them before those things decided to attack. She just had to.

Briley hurried up the cobble path with her pack bouncing. As she came up, she saw the creatures following Harrison and the others scatter. They made no sound as they moved, and even though she had her eyes trained right on one of them, she couldn't follow it as it disappeared into the trees surrounding the path. When she finally caught up to Grace, she was out of breath. The landscape had changed over the short distance she had run, from lolling hills to a light forest. Beyond, the path seemed to be swallowed by dense foliage, thick with trees and who knew what laying in wait.

"Hold up!" Briley gasped.

"Oh, there you are!" Grace smiled at her in a carefree manner. "We were just about to turn around to come find you!"

Harrison came to stand beside Grace, but Wendell was still in full pirate mode. Neither Harrison nor Grace seemed to care that he was wandering the path alone.

"We need to stop him!" Briley said forcefully. "We need to head back."

"Head back?" Grace laughed. "Are you kidding? This is the most fun I've had all year!"

"Yeah, no way!" Harrison agreed. "I'm taking this dream for all its worth!"

"But it's not a dream!" Briley screamed. Out of the corner of her eye, she saw the black clothed figures had gathered again. This time there were more of them, and they were following Wendell. "Argon said it's dangerous out here! LOOK!"

She pointed down the path toward Wendell. Harrison and Grace both turned to look. Now that there were several of the creatures and only one Wendell, they weren't bothering to hide.

Instead, they walked openly on the path in a solid line. One of them readied a net. Grace screamed out as she watched the creatures ensnare Wendell in their net. They all turned to look back as Wendell struggled. Their faces were ugly and misshapen, with long hooked noses and pointed ears that grew from the tops of their heads. One of them met Briley's gaze and she shuddered. Its eyes were like a cat's, angular and slitted. When it smiled, she noticed its teeth were like hundreds of tiny pointed rocks in its mouth. Its grin was a misshapen mess of colors and angles. Briley could only think of one word to put to the things…goblins.

Grace started to charge the goblins, but Harrison tackled her from behind. She punched him in the gut, but he held her. "We'll get him back, Grace, I promise, but we can't fight those things here."

The goblins made quick work, and in only a few seconds they had bound and gagged Wendell. They were small creatures, less than two feet tall, but they were much stronger than they looked. One of them slung Wendell over its shoulders. Briley watched as Wendell struggled against the goblin until another one struck him in the head with the handle of a sword. Then Wendell was still, and the creatures vanished into the dense forest beyond without a trace.

Grace was still struggling against Harrison, and Briley felt her heart sink deep down into her shoes. How would she feel if someone had stolen Harrison from her? She would be ready for murder. No doubt Grace felt the same way.

"You let them take my brother!" Grace screamed at Harrison. "How could you?" Her face was flushed. In school, Grace was one of the most ladylike girls Briley knew, but she certainly didn't fight like a girl. Grace punched Harrison square in the jaw, and the blow took Harrison by surprise. He went down like a toppled glass and Grace straddled him, punching him in the ribs. Harrison was quick to recover though, and he fought back hard. Soon they were rolling along the path.

"STOP IT!" Briley shouted, "This isn't helping anything!" But it was too late. Grace was too angry to think straight, and Harrison too proud to let her win. They fought each other, landing blows and kicks. Briley sighed to herself, wishing she was back home even if her father would ground her forever. As she tried to think of her house though, it was fuzzy, as if she hadn't seen it in years. The more she tried to remember the particulars of her home, her mother, and her school, the more distant they all became.

Harrison and Grace finally stopped fighting. They sat not far from Briley. Harrison had a bloodied lip, and Grace sported a bruised nose and eye.

"Sorry," Harrison muttered.

"Me too," Grace said sheepishly.

"If you are quite done fighting, let's rescue Wendell and get home," Briley said matter of factly. She was now more scared than ever of this world beyond the Hedge.

Grace stood and helped Harrison to his feet. "Yeah," Grace said. "Where should we look first?"

Briley noticed both Grace and Harrison staring at her as if she knew the way. Briley was younger than both of them, but somehow she had become leader. She wasn't sure how she felt about that.

"Well...." Briley was trying to think of a pattern to the events. There were the pixies with their welcoming feast, then the pathway and the meeting with Argon, and then the goblins had stolen Wendell. There wasn't any order she could think of at all. "We need to get up high," Briley announced. "Above the trees!"

41

A. Henry Moen

Harrison and Grace were both looking at her like she was crazy, but she figured nothing else seemed to make any sense here either. There had to be a way to get a bird's eye view...there just had to! "Come on!" she yelled, laughing as she ran off the path, into the thick of the forest. "Last one to thump a goblin is a rotten egg!"

Chapter Three:
Darrel the Brave

Briley thundered through the brush, followed closely by Harrison and Grace. "Wendell!" one of them would call out from time to time, but they never got an answer. Briley wasn't sure what they would do even if they did encounter the goblins and Wendell. The three of them were certainly no match for a pack of the strange creatures.

Briley leapt over a log and then ducked beneath a low hanging vine, and then sidestepped past a very thorny looking patch of flowers. "Wait up!" Grace called from behind her, but Briley didn't stop. She was trying to think as she ran how exactly they were going to get Grace's little brother back, and so far her best idea had been her first one — to somehow get way up high — and she had no idea how she was going to do that.

Briley's cheeks were hot as ovens as she ran puffing through the forest. Her legs churned, and as she skirted past a large tree, the forest suddenly stopped, opening up instead to an open field much like the one where they had their pixie bites. Only this field wasn't sloped and hilly, it was flat, and Briley felt like she could see for miles in all directions. Shortly Grace came barreling out of the forest about ten feet to her left. Grace immediately stopped running, and Briley caught her eyes as she caught her breath. Grace's bright blonde hair was filled with twigs and debris, and her cheeks were smudged with dirt. Briley guessed that she probably looked a mess as well.

"Where's Harrison?" Briley called over. Grace panted and shrugged. Briley looked behind her into the forest, but neither saw nor heard her brother in the trees. "Harrison!" Briley called out. "This isn't funny!" She knew her brother was likely hiding behind one of the massive trees just inside the forest, struggling to keep from laughing as Briley panicked about him getting abducted by goblins or worse.

Grace finally caught her breath and made her way over to Briley. The older girl put an arm around Briley's shoulders. "Just give him a minute. He probably tripped. I'm sure he's fine."

Briley nodded to herself. Grace was right, but it took all of Briley's resolve not to go running back into the forest and searching for her big brother. Grace plopped down into the grass next to Briley and rooted in her pack, pulling out some of the foodstuffs she had squirreled from the pixie feast. Briley took her water bottle out and drank thirstily. Briley was determined not to panic, but after two minutes passed, she couldn't wait any more.

"OK!" Briley said, not sure what she was going to say after that. "Harrison is a much faster runner than either of us, so what is taking him so long?"

As if to answer her question, Briley heard the boom of a drum in the distance. The drum beat was followed by another, and then another. Grace looked to Briley with fear in her eyes. Briley swallowed loudly. It was obvious the drumming was coming from somewhere out in the field before them, but squint as she might, Briley couldn't see anything. Grace and Briley backed slowly toward the trees of the forest, scanning about for any sign of danger, but all around the sky was a brilliant piercing blue, the field a calming sea of green.

Briley felt her back hit a tree and stopped momentarily as something fell onto her head. "Ouch!" she cried out, looking up. There, high in the branches, was Harrison, holding a finger to his mouth. He smiled down at her and uncoiled a rope. He fastened it to a branch and lowered it, and within a minute or two, the three of them were all perched high in the tree. If it weren't for the disturbing sound of the advancing drums, Briley would have cried out with glee.

"Watch!" Harrison whispered, and he pointed to the middle of the grass. Briley stared in wonder, and so did Grace. Nothing was happening.

"Watch what?" Briley wondered.

"Shhhh. Just watch," Harrison insisted. And then the grass where Harrison was pointing began to rustle and stir. Before long it seemed like almost all of the grass was shaking and moving, and then Briley saw a metal tube pop out of the grass.

"What's happening?" Grace asked in a whisper.

"I think I know where your brother is," Harrison said. "Just watch!" he insisted, still pointing. Briley felt her mouth hanging like a dead fish on a pole as it became more apparent what the metal tube was. It was a periscope!

The grass churned as more and more metal pieces became visible above the line of the grass, and out of the grass, a submarine appeared. Now that it was mostly above ground, Briley watched as goblins climbed atop it, undoing latches atop the submarine. They worked quickly and in concert. The goblins unclipped the metal, revealing a ship made of metal underneath. They then rushed to cranks and spun them wildly, and as they did, metal masts came up from the deck of the ship. They were made in sections, each smaller than the one below it, popping out of each other and ending in points. Then the goblins scurried up the masts, hoisting sails and casting ropes about. On each sail, there was a picture of a crown crossed with swords. The whole process only took a minute or so. The goblin submarine had transformed into a ship, and then they were sailing across the grass as if it were water. Briley was positive if she wasn't up so high she would have fainted on the spot. They watched the ship moving across the grass, none of them knowing what to do until Harrison spoke up.

"I took your advice, Briley, and climbed up high, and watched them bring Wendell onto that ship. Then I traveled from tree to tree since they were so close together. I'm not sure why they came back up, but I'm pretty sure that grass is a lot deeper than it looks." He hesitated. "If we are going to get Wendell back, we either need a flying machine or a boat."

Briley sighed. She felt guilty. The whole adventure had been her idea, and they seemed to be at a standstill. Not only that, but now Wendell was captured by goblins. "We can't just give up!" she said aloud, mostly for her own ears. "How many times have we gotten lost in the woods?" she asked, "But we always made it home all right! We just need to figure this out!" She looked into Grace's eyes as she finished. To Briley's astonishment, Grace smiled.

"You're right!" Grace said, "At least we know where he is now. Let's find a flying machine! Or a boat!"

"But where are we—?" Harrison began, but it was too late. Grace was already hopping to the next tree.

"The trees are all connected, just like you said!" Grace shouted. "We'll just stay at the edge and make our way around!"

Briley and Harrison shared a look and continued on after Grace. "Well," he said, "It beats sticking around here and crying about it!" Then Harrison took off, following Grace's lead. Briley set off too.

They traveled that way for perhaps an hour before Grace's efforts paid off. There in the distance, just on the edge of the forest, was a town with a harbor glimmering in the setting sun. The roof tops were all bronzed, and the setting sun set off an amazing display of reflected light. The only downside was the town had high walls all around three of its sides. The harbor jutted out into the grass sea with all shapes and manner of boats sitting atop the grass. There on the end, Briley noticed, were also tethered a number of hot air balloons. Grace had stopped and waited for Harrison and Briley to catch up to her. "It must be some sort of port," Grace said.

Briley watched as the sun set over the port town. They were too far away to make out the people inside of it. There didn't seem to be any roads or paths leading to the town. Apparently it was only accessible by boat or....

"What are those things called again?" Briley asked aloud, pointing at the hot air balloons. "Dirigibles," Harrison said with awe.

"I want to fly one!" Grace said aloud.

Briley found herself nodding and grinning, thinking of how wonderful it would be to soar through the air in one. She picked one out with a bright pink balloon floating above it. The basket below was huge, large enough to hold about ten people.

"Well, what are we waiting for?" Harrison chuckled, scampering down the tree. "Let's go!"

47

Once they were on the ground, Harrison suggested they stay in the trees until they got closer to the town, and everyone agreed that was a good idea. As they got closer, Briley's heart sank as she saw little flags flying above the town. Each of the little flags sported the same symbol as the ship had, the crown with the crossed swords.

They were about two hundred yards away when Grace squinted in the distance and whispered, "There are guards at the gates!" Briley couldn't see them, but she trusted Grace's eyes. Harrison often called her the hawk, because Grace could spot little things no one else could make out.

"Are they goblin guards?" Briley asked.

"No," Grace said. "They're a lot bigger than the goblins."

"Great!" Harrison sighed.

The three of them continued on, and as they got closer, Briley could make out the guards as well. Grace was right, the guards were huge! They looked like crocodiles in armor, with long spike tipped axes and shields like oaken doors. How were they ever going to get past them?

Finally, they had run out of forest to hide in. It was about sixty feet from the forest to the gates. The three of them stared at the gates and the giant guards for a few minutes, sipping water and taking a moment to rest and think. The guards never moved a muscle, and as far as Briley could tell, they didn't even blink. The giant crocodiles just sat there with their axes and shields, waiting for someone dumb enough to try and get in.

"OK," Briley finally said. "I think our only hope is a distraction."

"Like what?" Harrison asked.

Briley rooted in her pack and brought out her flashlight. She was trying to remember everything she had ever learned about crocodiles, which wasn't much besides not ever wanting to get near one. Crocodiles' bellies were soft, she remembered, which was why they never showed them, but these creatures were standing on two legs, and although they wore helmets, their massive bellies were exposed.

"Did you bring your pellet gun?" Briley asked Harrison.

"No," he said. "Sorry."

"I've got mine!" Grace said impishly, digging in her pack until she found it.

"Great!" Briley said, hoping she wasn't about to get herself killed. Or worse, eaten alive. "I'm going to climb that tree over there," she said, pointing. "When the crocs come for me, try and get into the town. Hopefully the gates aren't locked."

"No way, Sis!" Harrison argued. "I'll do it! Mom would kill me if you got eaten alive on my watch."

Briley was determined. "I'm smaller, Harrison. I can scamper among the trees quicker than you can." She grinned at him. "I'm going to use the flashlight and pellet gun to lead them deeper into the forest, and then I'll double back and meet you in the town."

Grace was nodding, but Briley could tell Harrison wasn't convinced. "I'm faster than you, Briley. I'll do it."

"Well, Mom would skin *me* alive if *you* got eaten!" Briley countered.

"Why are you two arguing over which one gets chased by crocodiles?" Grace asked, laughing. "I've got an idea. You two should draw straws."

It was settled, and Grace broke a stick in two. She held up the two halves for Briley and Harrison to see. "Whoever picks the longest stick gets chased by crocs!" She was giggling as she said it. Briley hoped the stress wasn't getting to Grace.

"Fine," muttered Harrison. "Let's do it."

Grace held out her hands, each one holding a stick. Briley and Harrison both grabbed one and held them up, comparing. Briley gulped, seeing that hers was the longest.

"Good luck," Grace said, handing over her pellet gun. "It sticks sometimes, but if you smack the side, it unjams."

"Thanks," Briley said.

"Be careful, Sis," Harrison said, but he couldn't meet Briley's eyes.

Briley threw her arms around him, hugging him hard, and whispered in her brother's ear. "I'll be careful, I promise. I love you, Harrison!" Then she kissed him on the cheek and began climbing before he could say anything idiotic to make her want to take her words back.

***

Once she was up the tree, Briley scampered from branch to branch until she had a good clear shot at the crocodile guards. She would have rather had Harrison's pellet gun, which had a rapid-fire option. She looked down and saw Grace and Harrison below. Her brother gave her a thumbs up. Briley gulped and took aim.

She fired two shots at the crocodile on the left and hit it square in the stomach both times. "Nice!" Briley said without thinking, and immediately slapped her hand over her mouth. The point was to lead the crocodiles away without being seen.

The croc guard immediately looked to where Briley was perched, and it smiled a big toothy menacing grin at her before moving toward her. Its companion followed suit. At least they weren't very fast. If she had to, Briley was certain she could outrun them easily. Briley alternated between flashing her flashlight into their eyes, firing the pellet gun, and then crawling to a new tree branch, but the guards didn't move into the forest.

They growled at her and shook their spears, but they would not enter the tree line. Briley moved in to a closer branch where they couldn't help but see her, took aim, and fired a pellet right at one of the crocodile's snouts. It roared in anger and tried to move forward, but couldn't. That's when Briley noticed the long thick chains connecting them to the walls surrounding the city. The chains were connected to metal rings on the back of the crocs' helmets.

"Great!" Briley muttered. "Now what!?"

She peered down and saw that Grace and Harrison were sneaking across the grass toward the gates, moving as quietly as whispers. If the gates were locked or if the guards noticed them, the crocs would surely turn on them once they noticed. Briley just had to make sure that didn't happen. She loaded and shot the pellet gun, and managed to lodge a pellet right inside one of the crocodile's nostrils. It was quivering with anger, croaking in some language that was nowhere near English. The other crocodile was shouting too. Briley flashed the light right in the second one's eyes, and then climbed closer to the ground.

Grace beat Harrison to the gate and began to pull it open. Briley was overjoyed that the gate swung easily for her, but the crocs were bound to turn once they heard the gate opening. Briley dropped to the ground and started making whooping noises, acting like a crazy person, waving her flashlight about and shooting the guards with the pellet gun. Harrison helped pull open the gate, and Briley watched them sneak inside the city once there was a wide enough opening. Now all Briley had to do was figure out a way to race across the field without getting eaten, skewered, or thumped unconscious. She was on the ground now, and Briley was having a flashback to the vicious dog that had chased Harrison. There was little to do but chance it. She just had

51

to pick her moment and run as if her life depended on it. Briley gulped. Her life really did depend on it! The chains on the back of the crocodile's heads rattled each time they surged forward, and that gave Briley an idea. She hooted and hollered and capered back and forth.

"Loony brains!" she taunted. "Big dumb green monsters!" She couldn't think of anything more creative at the moment, but Briley was pretty sure the crocodiles couldn't understand her anyway, just like she couldn't understand them. The crocodiles were seething at the mouth, they were so worked up, and Briley chose her moment.

All at once, she threw the flashlight at one of the crocodiles, held Grace's pellet gun tight to her chest, and ran to the right. The crocodiles paced after her. They weren't fast, but it would still be tricky getting between them and the gate without getting mauled. Briley zigged left and then doubled back and raced to the right. The crocodiles were slow to change direction, and as she had hoped, their chains overlapped one another. Then Briley changed direction again, each time getting closer and closer to the forest edge. By the time she reached it, the chains had overlapped at least three times.

When Briley finally decided to run for the gates, the crocodile guards were so confused that at first they thought she was simply running in a different direction. She was getting tired and out of breath, but it was only a couple of hundred feet. Her legs churned faster than they ever had before, and as Briley burst out of the tree line, the crocodiles lowered their axes, which had deadly points on the ends, and charged toward her. Briley ran, eyes on the opening in the gate. Thank goodness Harrison and Grace hadn't closed it.

She heard the crocodiles growling in their strange guttural

language and heard the creaking of the metal chains, but she didn't dare look back. The gate appeared before her all too quickly, and Briley vaulted inside the city walls and pulled the gate shut tightly behind her. Harrison was standing wide eyed at the opening, but Grace was on the ground laughing hysterically. Once the gate was closed, Harrison gave Briley the biggest hug he had ever given her, lifting her in the air and twirling about. Briley smiled. It wasn't often her brother showed that kind of affection.

"Good job, Sis!" he kept saying. "I can't believe you did it!"

"I can't believe I did it either!" Briley exclaimed. "What's wrong with Grace?"

Harrison stopped spinning her around and set Briley down on the ground. "Well...." Harrison chuckled himself. "Those guards never even got close to you on your mad dash here. They are all tangled up in those chains. They probably will be for quite a while!"

Briley laughed aloud, picturing the crocs writhing on the ground getting more and more tangled in their chains as they tried to chase after her. But Briley didn't waste too much time on the mental image, no matter how hilarious. "Let's find a boat and get Wendell. I'm ready to go home."

Harrison hugged her again. "Yeah," he said. "Me too."

***

Just inside the gates there was a large stone square where Briley imagined they must hold festivals during holidays. In the center of the square was a massive well made of stone. Briley, Harrison, and Grace refilled their water bottles and stuck close to each other as they wandered down the narrow streets. The city was huge! Briley goggled the tall buildings. They all seemed jammed together so closely there was no room in between them.

A. Henry Moen

As she looked up she saw bridges strung from building to building held together with ropes. Her mind reeled at how high the buildings went. She literally could not see the tops of most of them. On the street level, it looked like there had been alleys at once point in time, but those too had been built over with odd shaped houses and shops built more out of necessity than desire. As packed together as the buildings were, Briley couldn't figure out why there weren't more people milling about.

Every building had little lamps, glowing in different colors. As Briley stepped beneath one of the lamps, she looked up and noticed the light was coming from a small round ball, about the size of a raspberry. From time to time they would pass someone, but thankfully they did not run into any more crocodiles. But they didn't run into any other humans either. They passed a strange hunched over creature that looked part fox, part cat. Briley started to wave to the creature, but Harrison quickly pulled her hand down.

"Sheesh!" Harrison whispered. "Let's get to the docks without drawing attention to ourselves, OK?"

Briley nodded, and they moved past the half fox half cat. More than once they had to pull Grace away from the windows of the shops. She was becoming less and less focused and would simply stop walking, staring at some trinket she saw that she liked. "Is Grace going to be OK?" Briley whispered as they pulled her away from a jewelry shop window. Grace had been staring at a row of rings on display.

"I don't know," Harrison said. Briley looked at Grace and blinked. Was it just her imagination or were Grace's ears becoming pointier?

Some of the buildings jutted out into the street that ran through the center of town, and the road narrowed in those places. When they got to their first fork in the road, Briley looked first left and then right. Aside from the colors of the buildings being different, she couldn't see any difference between them. "Which way should we go?" she asked her brother.

"What I wouldn't give for a map!" Harrison said.

Briley nodded her agreement. Then she dug in her pack for a coin to flip. When she noticed a coiled rope she had brought, Briley had an idea. Briley and Harrison tied the rope around Grace's waist. Harrison tied the other end of the rope around his waist while Briley cinched up her backpack. Grace's ears were definitely pointier. Was it some sort of fairyland disease? She decided not to bring it up to Harrison. They couldn't do anything to fix it right then anyway. They needed a boat and a doctor and a way home, and Briley wasn't even sure which order those came in just then. Briley flipped her coin, and she and Harrison dragged Grace on a left hand turn past more oddly shaped houses. She had read somewhere that you could beat any maze if you always made left turns, but had never tested it out.

As twilight turned to darkness and the light fell from the sky, the city transformed. The lights outside the buildings burned brighter and brighter, windows lit up, and as the minutes passed, more and more people began appearing on the street. Shop doors opened, and creatures of countless description bustled from shop to shop. Feet clattered above as creatures of all kinds strode across the hanging bridges. People bustled and shopped, smiled and shouted. Some of the creatures had little carts or wagons with them that they loaded goods onto as they went along. Harrison and Briley tried to stay out of everyone's way, but it was almost impossible to make any real progress through the streets without pushing past someone.

Ladders were lowered from doors and people used them to

climb from their homes, which were stacked atop one another, to the stones below. Pixies and faeries flitted about as well, zipping in multicolored clothes past the people as they milled in the streets of the city. The three of them got knocked aside more than once, and Briley used her hands to stabilize herself on the walls of the buildings. In a matter of minutes, the city changed from nearly isolated to a bursting hive of peddlers and shoppers and people running errands. As the throng increased, Briley, Harrison, and Grace got pushed to the side of the street.

"We're not making any headway!" Briley fumed. "And we don't even know where we're going!"

Grace had returned to her normal self for the moment. The three of them shared a look of frustration. "It's like the whole city woke up at once!" Grace exclaimed.

"Yeah," Harrison agreed, crossing his arms. "So what do we do?" He leaned up against the wall behind him, and Briley gasped in astonishment as he fell through the wall.

"Harrison!" Briley cried out. She stretched out her hand, and it too passed through the wall where Harrison had leaned.

"Look!" Grace said, pointing to a tiny hand printed sign above the spot. Briley withdrew her hand and read the sign. It read, Hole in the Wall. Always Open in tiny bright red letters.

"This place keeps getting stranger by the second!" Briley said.

A second later, the rope around Grace's waist became taut. Grace let out a little shriek, and then she was sucked into the hole in the wall. There was nothing for Briley to do but follow. She ran her fingers through her hair and took a deep breath. Then Briley walked through what looked like solid brick. The instant her body passed through the wall, Briley felt her feet slipping across the ground as if it were oiled. She thrust out her arms to either side, but there was nothing to grab onto. Then she felt her body tilt forward and she fell.

It was pitch black inside, and Briley felt her body twisting down some sort of tunnel. It was smooth at least, but she couldn't see where she was going. Briley fought back a yelp of panic as she plummeted downward. After a minute or so of twists and turns through the tunnel, Briley saw a light appear in the distance. She came nearer and nearer to the light, but couldn't see beyond the opening. Then all of a sudden she passed through the light and landed flat on her back.

Her head was still spinning from all the twists and turns. Loud music blared in the distance, and voices chanted a song Briley didn't know the words to.

> *Muck out the stables or the innkeeper will get you!*
> *Mind your manners or Momma will beat you!*
> *Show up on time or the mayor will imprison you!*
> *I'd do all those things*
> *Oh, Oh, Oh, Before....*
> *Taking my chances with the Peacock Queen!*

Was this some sort of rebel outpost? Briley wondered. She realized she was in a giant cavern. The Hole in the Wall seemed to be a gathering place for people to sing songs and gossip and share a meal or a drink. Tables were arranged in a haphazard fashion with mismatched chairs and mismatchier people. There was a long bar that ran through the center of the cavern. Little lights like the ones she had seen on the buildings outside hovered midair, their colors mixing and colliding. Briley stood from the ground. The fall to the ground hadn't hurt at all.

"Briley!" someone called out. "There you are!"

Briley turned and smiled as she joined Harrison and Grace at a tiny table. In the center of the table was a platter heaped high with roast chicken and vegetables atop a mound of squared potatoes. The smell of the food reminded Briley how hungry she was, and she sat atop a stool. The three of them feasted on the dish until it was picked clean. Briley never thought to question how Harrison and Grace had paid for the food. They shared a smile as they licked their fingers clean. The atmosphere in the Hole in the Wall was contagious. Everyone was smiling, feasting, and talking rapidly.

"I found us a boat!" Harrison shouted after they had finished eating. He pointed to his left and Briley followed his finger. She locked eyes with a creature who sat at the head of a long table. He looked almost human, but his eyes were bright amber and when the man smiled, Briley saw he had several rows of teeth. Fine fur covered his face, but the man she was looking at could never be a cat. A lion, perhaps. That's when it occurred to her. The man Harrison was pointing at looked like a lion trying to live in the skin of a man.

His chest was wide as a barrel and he wore a three cornered cap. He stood, raising a glass to the others seated at his table, who all ate and drank with a will. It was a captain and crew if ever she saw one. The crew was dressed in heavy jackets and leather boots with swords at their waists.

"He said he hates goblins with a passion," Harrison continued. "They sail at first light. He even bought our dinner!"

"He looks dangerous!" Briley said. "Can we trust him?" She thought it sounded almost too good to be true.

"His name is Darrel the Brave," Grace said dreamily. "He captains the S. S. Arr Arr."

Briley looked over to the table where Darrel and his crew

gathered, and Darrel raised his glass high. "To plunderin' goblins!" he roared above the din of the crowd. "And rescuin' little brothers!" His voice boomed like a cannon, and Briley had to admit that he certainly seemed confident.

"When did all of this happen?" Briley asked. She hadn't been that far behind Harrison and Grace.

"We've been here for over an hour!" Harrison exclaimed. "When we told Darrel we were worried about you, he said you'd be along soon enough, and now here you are."

"An hour?" Briley gasped.

"Aye!" Darrel grinned at her. "The slide likes to play tricks sometimes."

"We have rooms on the ship as well," Grace added. "Compliments of the captain. Just think…tomorrow we will be sailing!" She paused for effect. "On grass!" Then Grace burst into one of her giggling fits, and Briley tried to fight back a yawn. With everything that had happened today, it was no wonder she was exhausted. She had a bad feeling in the pit of her stomach about Darrel the Brave and his crew, but she kept her thoughts to herself. If Harrison trusted him, she would have to trust him as well.

"All right," Briley finally said. Then she stood up and hopped on top of the table. She raised her fist high and shouted as loud as she could. "To plunderin' goblins!"

Darrel the Brave and his crew all roared and swallowed big mouthfuls of their drinks. "And rescuin' little brothers!" She met Darrel the Brave's eyes as he slammed his mug on the table.

"And to Darrel the Brave!" she screamed out. Darrel glowed as his men stood and applauded him. Harrison and Grace were on their feet, clapping as well. Then Darrel winked at her and shouted out.

"To Briley the Braverest!" he called out, and everyone applauded louder. Then Darrel set off marching from the Hole in the Wall, chanting. Darrel was followed by his crew, Harrison, Grace, and Briley in the rear. When they reached the streets of the city, people were still bustling about, but the crowds all parted before Darrel the Brave. In almost no time at all they were boarding the S. S. Arr Arr, and once they were shown to their rooms, Briley slumped into a hammock and fell asleep instantly.

Chapter Four:
The Peacock Queen

Briley awoke to the pitching of the ship about her. Her hammock was tucked high into a corner of the room, and it swayed first one way, then the next. She supposed it was a feeling you were supposed to get used to, but every time the boat lurched, she had to fight the urge to grab onto something. There was a little handle bolted into the wall, and as the ship swayed, Briley grabbed onto it and used the handle to pull herself out of the hammock, and she flopped to the floor. Luckily she landed on her feet. The grass whooshed by outside like a million whispers. She had no idea that traveling through grass would be so noisy. The sound seemed to fill up all of the space around her. Nonetheless, Briley smiled as she rummaged in her pack for a change of clothes. It was very exciting.

Once Briley found her extra clothes, she visited her toilet. There was a small basin for washing, and she had to use a hand pump for the water, but it was better than nothing. Briley cleaned up as best she could and changed into a pair of rugged jeans and a button down shirt. She decided to tie her hair into a tight braid since the ship swayed so much. The sound of several voices singing made her smile, and Briley packed her bag tightly and hurried out of her tiny room onto the deck of the ship.

She thrust open her door and watched as the crew ran between the railings, all in bare feet. They seemed to move with the pitch of the ship, but instead of finding railings, they just leaned back and forth as they walked. Men and women tossed lines to each other, climbed rigging, and adjusted wooden poles that Briley had no idea what they were for. Still, the crew all seemed to know what they were doing, and there at the helm, Darrel the Brave smiled so wide that his amber eyes glowed like drops of fire. He led his crew in a raucous song they all knew the words to. Some even sung in harmony or counterpoint, and as a whole, the crew would find convenient moments to bang their fists on the deck of the ship or bang a piece of metal on a pulley. Sailing, Briley immediately decided, was definitely something she liked very much, and she found herself joining in singing the song.

Oh the fire in my belly
Won't be put out
No it won't go out
You can clap me in irons
Or clap me in chains
But the fire in my belly
Won't be put out
No it won't be put out
You can make me drink poison
Or swallow my pride
But the fire in my belly
Won't be put out

Briley Van Campton

No it won't be put out
You can tar me
Feather me
Strangle me
Murder me
But the fire in my belly
Won't be put out
No it won't!
No it won't!

The song repeated itself, but the words changed with each singing of it. Briley smiled wide, running toward the rail to see how far out into the sea they had gone. She caught herself on the rail and used it to stabilize herself. For as far as her eyes could see there was luscious green grass whistling past. It was almost deafening as it rustled against the side of the boat. Briley had no idea how the ship "floated" on the grass, and she didn't want to know. The mystery of it was exciting too, and for what seemed a long time, Briley simply sang along with the crew of the ship, banging her fist in counterpoint to the melody. She found that after a time she would somehow know what words to sing next. She wondered what her mother would think if she saw her singing raucously with this wily crew, sailing on a sea of green, but she had trouble picturing her mother's face at all. In the back of her mind, Briley wondered if that should bother her more than it did.

More than once she had to back away from the railing as one of the crew would zip past her, hauling a rope. Briley took those moments to gaze up at the sails of the ship, which billowed out magnificently. The sails, like the rest of the ship, were painted in different shades of green, much like the grass around her.

There were no insignias on the flags, and Briley wondered if it was some sort of attempt to camouflage the ship. Briley spotted Harrison and Grace at a different spot on the railing and made her way over to them, trying to get a feel for the pitch and roll of the ship as it sped along.

"Steady now!" Darrel the Brave thundered. "Bring her in a bit deeper!"

The crew dropped weights, shifted ropes, and adjusted the sails, and some of them twisted large metal cranks set into the hull of the ship. Briley's heart shuddered, but immediately leapt as she watched the grass around them reaching higher up the side of the ship. The roar of the grass against the hull became even louder.

"Did you see that?" Briley asked her brother excitedly.

Harrisons face was glued to the crew of the ship and its sails. "Yeah." Harrison let out a long sigh. "I want to be a sailor!"

"How fast do you think we are going?" Grace goggled, leaning over the side of the railing. One of the crew grabbed her by the back of her shirt and pulled her back.

"Mind the railin', miss. We're getting ready for the undergrass!" Then that same crewman leapt up into the rigging and started climbing. Was this a submarine ship just like the goblins had? Briley wondered.

"Two points to starboard!" Darrel called out. "Ready the zingers!"

Briley watched as Darrel moved the wheel slightly. His eyes were locked on the green waves before the ship. As the ship turned, she felt it dip slightly downward, and she gulped as she realized they were definitely going INTO the grass. She wondered how deep it went and what kind of creatures might live below the surface. The crew tried hard not to bump into her and Harrison and Grace, but Briley couldn't help but feel in the way. Still, she didn't want to miss a second of the action. She didn't know what a zinger was, but at Darrel's order, some of the crew rushed below deck.

"Up the shanks! Look lively!" Darrel ordered.

"Zingers are ready!" one of the crew called out.

"Good!" Darrel called out. "Three points larboard!"

The boat shifted again and the three of them held fast to each other as it dipped further into the grass. The crew became a blur of activity. Some of them climbed the masts of the ship, unhooking the sails while others manned cranks at the base of the ship. Others rushed to the sides and began pulling at different points on the railings. The sound of the grass against the ship became almost deafening, and Briley watched with awe as the masts of the ship lowered and the sides of the ship started getting taller and taller. Then she heard several sharp snaps and the boat shuddered.

"Ready to drop!" Darrel called out.

"Aye, Captain!" the crew replied as one.

It all happened in a matter of seconds. The sides of the ship sprang up as the masts lowered. There was glass between the slats of the railing, and Briley both watched and felt as the ship sank lower and lower below the grass. It was marvelous! The sky disappeared from view and all about her, Briley saw the green of the grass. She looked to Darrel, whose jaw was set in a determined grin. He would shift the wheel slightly from time to time. "Heave!" he called out. The ship slowed significantly, but it lasted only moments before Darrel the Brave called out again, "Ho!" and the ship began picking up speed again.

"Heave! Ho! Heave Ho!" he called out. "Mortimer, call out the pace!"

"Aye, Captain!" one of the crew replied, and Briley noticed one of the big men finished tying a knot in a rope and then ran to a giant drum, which sat just behind the captain's wheel. Mortimer picked up two giant mallets, which were tied to strings on the drum, and began beating in a steady rhythm.

"I want to see what a zinger is!" Harrison called out, rushing through one of the doors that led below deck. Grace stood beside Briley, both of them transfixed by the passing grass around them and the activity of the crew. Some of them wore hats or had bandanas upon their heads, but for the most part, they kept their hair tied in tight braids with jewels or coins wound into them. They were all built like Darrel, broad chested, looking almost human with the exception of the fine fur which covered them. And their brightly colored eyes and their extra rows of teeth.

"What kind of creatures are they?" Briley wondered aloud before she could stop herself.

"Aren't they amazing?" Grace swooned.

"Jenkins!" Darrel called out. "Take the wheel, and for blunders sake, don't do anything stupid!"

Briley watched as a crewman stepped in front of the wheel, grabbing onto it tightly as Darrel stepped away from it. Then he surveyed his crew, making sure that each was doing their job. He walked toward Briley and Grace, occasionally stopping to help a crewman with a rope or a winch. Then he was standing before them, smiling, his face sweaty from exertion. "The lot of you were too tired last night for a proper tour of my ship," he said. "But what say I show you the S. S. Arr Arr in person, and then we grab some grub. I'm famished!"

Briley was nodding so fiercely she thought her head was about to pop off.

"That would be wonderful!" Grace said. Briley noticed Grace

was blushing.

Darrel the Brave held out his arm and Grace immediately looped her arm through his. Briley groaned inwardly, but followed as the captain showed them some of the different devices on the ship. "Entering the green is the most dangerous part," Darrel said. "Never know what's waiting for ya below the first blades!" He grinned at them and then led them below deck.

Briley hated to admit it, but she was starting to like Darrel the Brave. After all, he couldn't help the fact that he had so many sharp teeth. She just wished Harrison hadn't run off, and that Grace didn't keep tittering at every little thing Darrel said.

"Thank you so much for all of your hospitality!" Grace said as Darrel led them through a corridor below.

"But of course, m'lady!" Darrel the Brave replied. Briley groaned and followed along. There were three doors about the ship that led below decks. Darrel the Brave escorted Briley and Grace to one and opened it. "The S. S. Arr Arr was built with space in mind," he said proudly. As he opened the door, Briley saw what he meant. The corridor they were about to step into was very narrow. Grace let go of Darrel's arm with a sigh and Darrel led the way. His shoulders nearly touched the walls as they walked through, and from time to time, Briley noticed little metal rings at about shoulder height in the corridor. She was about to ask what they were for, but then the ship shuddered slightly, and Darrel grabbed hold of one of the rings, continuing to walk as if nothing had happened.

The wood of the ship was manicured and smooth. Even the insides were painted in shades of green. They passed doors that Briley assumed were crew quarters, and Darrel led them through a series of sharp turns she would have been hard put to remember. Finally, he opened up a doorway and led them into a room. Briley's heart immediately leapt.

"Harrison!" she cried out, running to her brother. Harrison was helping some of the other crew with winches in the room. There were several portholes and Briley looked outside one. All about them was the deep green grass they were traveling through, and intertwined in them were what she could only describe as hooked and bladed oars moving back and forth with the movement of the winches.

"Those...," Darrel bellowed, "Are the zingers!"

"Yeah!" Harrison said. "I've been helping out...uh, sir...uh, Captain."

"Just call me Darrel, boy," the captain said. "Darrel will do." He laughed then.

Briley watched through one of the port holes as the oars moved back and forth, both gripping onto and cutting into the grass. There were at least a dozen of the zingers she could see moving back and forth. It didn't look like they were moving, but she could feel the ship tilting back and forth as the zingers did their work. "It's amazing!" she said aloud.

Darrel grinned at her, obviously proud of his ship. "There's more to see! Come with me," he said. "Look lively and keep up. I want you to know this ship like the backs of your own eyelids."

***

Later, they all sat gathered around a table in a long narrow room Darrel called "the mess." Briley, Harrison, and Grace were each awed by different parts of the ship. Darrel had explained that the zingers didn't cut through the grass. They latched onto the grass and moved through it kind of like a caterpillar. Harrison was obsessed with the zingers. He wanted to know how fast the ship could go and how well it could maneuver. Grace was obsessed with the way the ship had been designed with so many rooms. As for Briley, she had finally asked the question that had been bugging her since they stepped foot aboard the S. S. Arr Arr.

"How are we ever going to find Wendell in all of this grass, Darrel?" she blurted out.

"Well...," Darrel began as he stuck his fork into a meat pie. "Goblins don't have much imagination. They onlys head downward, see. So we're heading straight down. We'll go into the belly of their caverns if we have to. Goblins only come up when they needs something from the queen."

"The queen?" Briley asked. The plate in front of her was filled to the edges with meat pie and steamed squash, and it was all smothered in gravy. Her stomach rumbled at the smell of the food, and she tried to remember her manners as she devoured her meal.

"The Peacock Queen," Darrel smiled. "She rules the lands beyond the Hedge. But no one I know has seen her in ages. She's got herself all cooped up in her castle, she does." He filled some goblets with something blue from a pitcher and passed them out to the three children. "Which is just fine by me. The less we sees of her, the better!"

"You mean she's not a good queen?" Grace asked.

"She's been a scourge since the day she drew breath!" Darrel's eyes flashed dangerously. "This land used to be beautiful," he mourned. "There were towns, villages. The fair folk frolicked. Nowadays if you needs something, you got to come abegging for it from her. Like as not, she'll turn you away without ever hearing your plea."

"Why do you put up with it?" Harrison asked.

Juice from the meat pie ran down Briley's chin, and she wiped it with a napkin.

"Well, that's a good question." Darrel smiled as he drank

from his goblet. "But not one I've got the answer to." He sighed. "The truth is, boy, that me and my crew are the last of our kind, and we prefer to stay as far from the Peacock Queen's armies as we can." He swallowed. "But mostly I would guess it's because of her dragons."

"You mean, real dragons?" Briley blurted out before she could stop herself.

"Aye, lass," Darrel said. "Her castle is high on a mountain, and the mountain is home to her dragons. If anyone were to ever rise up against her...." He grimaced. "Well, her pretty pets would make short work of them."

"What do you mean you're the last of your kind?" Grace asked.

"Once my people held control of an island, before the queen turned the seas into grass," Darrel said. "It was a safe port for travelers to come and visit. We are natural sailors. But one by one, us Horgles were hired on as crew for one ship or another. Which was fine until the people who hired us wouldn't let us return to the island when the contract was over. It was darker times then. The Peacock Queen was securing the lands with her armies. Most of us were just trying to survive, and in truth we Horgles are a peace loving folk."

Briley swore there were tears starting to form in Darrel's eyes. She put her hand on his arm. "Go on," she urged him.

"To put a long story into a short span, our homeland became overran with travelers. More and more of us were put into crews, or captured in cages by goblins, or worse. I myself was captured and put to work on a crew." He smiled. "I wouldn't be here today except for one day there was a terrible grastichurn."

"What is a grastichurn?" Briley asked, wide eyed.

"A storm that bellows up from the roots of the green." Darrel's eyes were fierce. "The blades of the grass all twist together. They've been known to break ships apart. The ship I was on was a mining ship. Most vessels don't go down that deep, but ours was near the bottom when the grastichurn hit. The rest of the crew panicked and like idiots, they abandoned ship. I was all alone with the grass, watching my shipmates get torn to pieces. So there I was all alone on the ship, but I refused to abandon her. Somehow I managed to get it past the worst of the storm, and here we stand."

"That was this ship?" Briley asked.

Darrel nodded. "When I got out of the storm there wasn't much left. I got lucky and was able to dock her at an under-green port. I fixed her up, and it was then I decided I was going to search out the other Horgles. One by one, I rescued or freed them. Our island is now controlled by the Peacock Queen, but I figure this ship," he patted one of the beams nearby, "this is all the island we need."

"Is that why they call you Darrel the Brave?" Grace asked, eyes wide.

"Well, it's a much better name than Darrel the desperate!" he laughed.

Just then the whole ship lurched to the side. Their plates went skittering down the table, and even Darrel had a look of alarm on his face.

"What's going on?" Harrison asked.

"Dunno," Darrel said.

Then one of the women of the crew burst into the mess. "Captain!" she cried. "It's goblins! We're being boarded!"

"You lot stay put," Darrel commanded, standing. "I'm coming, Mila. Get to the harpoons and make sure they are loaded!"

With that, Darrel burst from the mess like an egg from a skillet.

Briley shared a look with Harrison and Grace, and she knew they all had the same thought. If this was the same goblin ship that had Wendell, there was no way the three of them were going to just sit there.

Grace stood up. "Well, what are we waiting for?" she said. "Let's go get my brother!"

Briley exited the mess, following Harrison with Grace in the lead. Briley sincerely hoped that Grace knew which way she was going. Grace dashed through the narrow hallways, making turns without hesitation. Briley lost track after the third turn. More than once they had to throw themselves against the walls to avoid a Horgle running this way or that, more common than not with a sword in their hand.

"To the churners!" they shouted. "To arms! To arms!"

The three of them did their best to stay out of the way, but they soon got swept into the current of Horgles rushing toward the decks. The ship rocked all about them. Grace threw her weight against a door and the three of them all piled into the open door after her. "Wendell!" she cried out. "Wendell, I'm coming!"

The doorway Grace had barged through was another hallway, but this one was empty. After three doors, Grace opened another door and Briley gasped as she watched Grace run over to one of the many racks in the room. All about them were swords, maces, shields, bows, and arrows. Apparently Grace had dashed straight for the armory. Much of the armory had been picked clean, but there were still plenty of weapons to choose from. Grace heaved a sword to Harrison, who caught it deftly in his left hand. Then Briley snatched a short handled mace out of the air and a round metal shield from a nearby wall. She had never swung a mace before, and hopefully she wouldn't have to actually hurt anyone, but she had to admit holding the weapon did make her feel a lot stronger and less vulnerable.

Grace suited herself with two short swords and a helmet. Harrison's sword was in the style of a rapier, but he grabbed a short knife with his other hand. The three of them looked at each other for a moment. "This isn't some game," Briley blurted out. "Not like in the woods where we chased each other with rocks and sticks. Maybe this is all just a dream, but I've never had a dream this real."

"It's definitely not a dream," Harrison spoke up. "My imagination isn't this good."

"Right," Grace said. "So we stick together, the three of us, no matter what."

"We avoid fighting at all costs," Briley continued. "Running, dodging, and hiding are better for us in the long run."

"Agreed," Harrison smiled. "But if we have to, we fight!" He raised his rapier high in the air. Briley thrust up her mace, and Grace shoved both of her swords between their weapons.

"For Wendell!" Grace shouted.

"For Wendell!" Harrison and Briley both echoed.

"OK." Grace nodded to each of them. "Let's be quiet and quick, like cats in a field. Follow me. For some reason, I know exactly how to find my way around this ship. It's almost like I've been here before."

With that curious statement looming, the three of them crept out into the corridor and followed Grace's lead. She led them safely through the passages. From time to time they would hear footsteps or shouting and would duck behind one of the doors. But in almost no time at all, Grace had led them to one of the three passageways leading above decks.

"So far so good," Grace whispered. "Now comes the tricky part."

Briley gulped. Harrison stamped his feet and Grace opened the door. On the deck of the S. S. Arr Arr, madness held court between the goblins and the Horgles. The Horgles were much better trained fighters, but there were just so many goblins. Briley looked up and saw several small holes drilled in the wood above with ropes hanging down. The ropes were oiled slick, and the goblins slid down the ropes like sickening green spiders. Darrel's crew fought like frenzied ants, small in number, but hardy and determined.

The Horgles were on the defensive, simply trying to survive the attack of the goblins. Then Briley noticed that the goblins all wore purple gloves that looked like they had suction cups on the ends.

"Are those—?" she began

"Octopus gloves!" Darrel's strong voice bellowed over the crowd as he surged through a mass of goblins. "I told you lot to stay below!" he roared, but there was little he could do about their presence on the deck. Even as strong as he was, Darrel was hard pressed to do anything other than push back the goblins.

"But octopuses are sea creatures," Briley said. The instant it was out of her mouth, she felt silly. Why would anything here make any sense at all? Just because octopuses were sea creatures in her world, didn't mean that they couldn't exist in the grass beyond the Hedge.

The goblins were all of a height with Grace, Harrison, and Briley, so for the most part, the three children were ignored during the battle. "Harrison!" Briley said. "Let's get some gloves and climb the walls. With this many goblins attacking, their ship is bound to be next to empty."

"One step ahead of you, Sis!" Harrison called out. As Briley glanced back, she saw that both he and Grace were donning octopus gloves from fallen goblins. Briley bent over and took the gloves from the hands of a wounded goblin. She thought it was a he goblin, but had no idea how to tell the difference. Briley saw that Grace and Harrison were both finding ways to keep their weapons in the straps of their backpacks. Briley simply pushed the shield farther up her arm and let the mace go. She knew she was never going to use it, anyway. Even with as nasty as the goblins seemed, they were still living breathing things, and she knew she couldn't hurt them even if she wanted to.

They began climbing the walls of the ship using the octopus gloves. She didn't even have to grip...the gloves cinched onto her hands so snugly it was as if she had always worn them. With a thought she was able to grab onto and let go of anything she wanted. Soon the three of them were aboard the goblin ship, watching as lines of the creatures made their way for the ropes.

"Which way to the dungeons, do you think?" Briley whispered to Harrison once she had cleared the goblin deck.

"On ships it's a brig," Harrison answered.

"This way!" Grace called out, leading them onward. Briley and Harrison shrugged at each other and followed Grace, hoping that she continued to lead them in the right direction.

They were running full tilt through the ship. Grace had her swords out, and from time to time they would cross paths with a goblin charging toward them. Each time Grace would shout out and swing one of her swords, and the goblins ducked or weaved or tumbled out of her path and kept running. Once Briley watched as the goblin didn't react fast enough and Grace sliced his arm open. The goblin howled, but Grace didn't even seem to notice. It was like she was in some other world, her eyes locked on her goal.

The smell in the ship steadily got worse as they advanced, and the lighting steadily got darker. The goblin ship was all made of metal with wide hallways. Each time there was a choice of directions, Grace headed lower. Briley wondered how Darrel's battle was going. She felt like she had abandoned him, but also knew she wouldn't have been of any help at all in a battle.

They rounded a turn and another goblin appeared down the hallway from them. Grace let out one of her fierce roars. She readied her sword and charged, but the goblin standing there only smiled at her as she ran toward it. They were a mere five feet away from the goblin when Briley realized it wasn't a real goblin, but a reflection in the burnished metal of the ship.

"Grace!" she cried out. "Wait!"

Grace either didn't hear her or wasn't listening, because she barreled right into the side of the ship full force, with Harrison right behind her. Briley watched as they crumpled like a heap, and then she felt something pointy jabbing her in her back. "Theys all saids I couldn't catch you, but I proved them wrong!" a wickedly familiar voice said from behind her.

Briley turned around and screamed. "Wendell?!" she cried out.

Grace's smaller brother stood there, but he looked very little like the Wendell she knew. His skin had started to turn green in spots, and his ears were pointier.

"In the flesh!" he said, and smiled. Briley noticed that his smile even looked like a goblin's, and he wore the heavy coat and had a scabbard strapped to his hip. "But you can call me Wendell the Wiley!" Wendell put his now elongated fingers to his lips and whistled. Within seconds, goblins had amassed around Briley and her friends. Harrison and Grace were out cold.

"We came to rescue you!" Briley shouted at him.

"I tolds them you would. There is a heavy ransom on your heads!" Wiley Wendell hissed at her. His words were hard to understand. Briley assumed he must still be getting used to his new mouth. "Oho and lucky of luckys! You brought Darrel the Barnacle to us too!" Wiley Wendell smiled, and Briley blanched as the goblins forced her back and clamped heavy iron rings about her wrists.

"You can't do this!" Briley shouted.

Wendell didn't answer, only laughed instead. "When we take you to the Peacock Queen, I will be able to do whatever I wants!"

And then Briley was escorted out of the hallway and into a long chamber filled with barred cells. Grace had indeed been leading them to the ship's brig, but instead of rescuing Wendell, they were becoming prisoners of the goblins. Briley was shoved into a cell and then the iron door slammed shut. She heard other doors closing in the distance. It was so dark in the brig, Briley had no idea how the goblins could see at all. There was just enough light to make out vague shapes. To make matters worse, the three of them weren't even locked up together. In all her imaginings, Briley had never guessed that Wendell could have turned so sour. What could the goblins have done to him to turn him against them? That thought scared her even more than the darkness all around her, and she began to cry.

After the goblins left the dungeons were silent, and Briley listened as her tears hit the floor of her cell. This adventure of hers had turned all wrong. She had seen amazing sights and met amazing magical creatures, but Wendell had betrayed them, and she only hoped that Darrel the Brave could come to her rescue. She sobbed and sniffled in the dark. Slowly about her, the floor began to glow in a light green, and Briley immediately stopped crying.

"Argon!?" she cried into the darkness. "Argon, is that you?"

The green glow became more vibrant and brighter, and she watched as the green became the shape of the green man who had met her at the hedge. She ran to him and hugged him hard. "Oh Argon, you can help us, can't you!?" She stifled a sob. "I don't know what's going on."

Argon's green arms wrapped around her and she felt the warmth of his hug filling her with joy. It was as if happiness burst from his arms and straight into her heart. Her sobs turned to laughter, and Briley hugged him and hugged him for what felt like hours. Candice was there too, and she perched on Briley's head, running her tiny fingers through her hair.

"So brave," was all Argon said. "You will need to be very brave, Briley."

She backed away and looked up at him, the feeling of joy diminishing as she retreated. "But you can help us out of here, can't you?" She looked to him pleadingly. To her dismay, Argon simply shook his big green face with sadness in his eyes.

"It is hard to explain," he said. "I have very little power left, and even less time." He paused. "Candice and I have been looking for someone like you for a very long time."

"Ages and ages!" Candice announced from atop Briley's head.

"For me?" Briley asked. "But I am just a girl. What can I do?"

"In our world," Argon said, "a human girl can accomplish very much if she is brave enough and strong enough to stand up to the Peacock Queen."

"Was she ever a good queen?" Briley asked.

"Here, let me show you," Argon said, and he held out a small crystal ball in his outstretched hand. "Take hold of the crystal and see for yourself." Briley reached out a shaking hand, covering the crystal globe with her hand, and sensations rushed through her like flashes of lightning.

"Oh my," was all Briley had time to say before the crystal began spinning rapidly in Argon's palm. Briley felt herself whisked into the globe as if it had swallowed her.

***

Briley looked down upon a vast vibrant field. The land became more and more real around her, and Briley felt more than watched the land become smaller before her eyes. There were cities in the distance, and roads which ran between them. On the roads, people carted their goods or walked at a leisurely pace, joking with one another. Some of the people, Briley noticed, looked just like Argon, their skin a mass of green leaves and vines, and everywhere they stepped, flowers grew. Briley soared above them, laughing as she watched a juggler tossing pixies from hand to hand in little glass balls. The pixies were laughing as well, emitting different colored lights as they bounced against the glass. There was music and laughter in the air, and creatures beyond description frolicked in the woodlands beyond the cities.

Briley sped at an impossible speed toward one of the cities, which held a magnificent castle. Outside the castle was a marketplace where people sold trinkets and chocolates and jewelry and clothes. She zipped past the marketplace through an open window in the castle, and into a room. An aging woman laying upon the bed was surrounded by servants, and in her arms she cradled a tiny baby, smaller than it would seem possible for a baby to be. But even though it was small the baby was indescribably beautiful with perfect features, and the brightest crystal eyes Briley had ever seen. It couldn't have been more than a few months old, but still the baby had lustrous raven black hair that curled around its body.

"That," she heard Argon's voice say through the vision, "is the Peacock Queen. The woman who holds her just turned twenty last week. Even as a babe, the Peacock Queen took the life from the things around her."

"How long ago was that?" Briley tried to ask, but she found she couldn't speak. Nonetheless, Argon answered her as if he'd heard her question.

"A VERY long time ago. We do not measure time the way you do in years, so it is hard to answer."

Then Briley's vision blurred away from the castle, and she sped upward through the stone and into the sky. She was so high up that she felt as if she could see the entire world below her, stretched out like a giant blanket of fields and woods, lakes and cities. The sun set and rose in rapid movements. The world beyond the Hedge had two moons. She watched the world fill with night and stars, and she sped downward toward that same castle, but it had changed dramatically. Outside of the castle, beasts and creatures worked hard, digging a moat under the trained eye of the large crocodile creatures Briley had seen before. The crocodiles all held long whips at their sides, and from time to time, one of them would lash out at one of the workers if they dropped something or were not moving quickly enough. As she moved into the courtyard, she noticed the market place was filled now with people selling much less extravagant goods. The food for sale looked old, mushy, or moldy. At every intersection stood a band of the crocodiles, scowling at the crowd, and then Briley zoomed through into the castle, this time directly into the throne room.

The throne room was empty except for two people who sat

on massive chairs, a man and a woman. The man was perhaps the most beautiful creature Briley had ever seen. Briley noticed he had pointed ears and his hands were covered in a soft golden fur. She also glimpsed a furry tail which lay across his lap. Nonetheless, he was handsome to behold, his hair and fur both matching a beautiful shade of dark orange. His eyes glistened brightly with a hidden joke behind them, and he held hands with the woman next to him. She too was beautiful to behold, and Briley knew immediately that this was the Peacock Queen, only older. She looked to be a few years older than Briley. There was no denying those pure crystal eyes and dark raven hair. She was dressed in a fine silk gown with swirling colors that dazzled the eye.

The man held the Peacock Queen's hand in his and turned to her with a dazzling smile. "My father has seen to it that you will want for nothing once we are wed." His voice was rich and lustrous.

"Is that so?" The Peacock Queen arched one of her eyebrows, barely turning to look at him as she spoke. "But I already want for nothing, darling." She looked at him then and smiled, but the smile did not truly reach her eyes. "And I have yet to accept your proposal."

The man sprang from the chair and knelt before the Peacock Queen. "Ah. What must it take to win your heart?" he said romantically. "I have given you men, lands. Why, I'm even building a moat for you. Just say the word and it will be yours!"

"How about a drink?" the Peacock Queen said in an amused tone. "At the moment, I am parched. After I have cured my thirst perhaps I will feel more myself."

"Aha! But that is easy," the man cried aloud. "Drinks!" he called out. "A drink for the queen and her betrothed."

Moments later a servant entered the room carrying a tray with a pitcher of some orange liquid and two glasses, along with sandwiches and fresh fruit. The man took the glasses and filled them, offering one to the Peacock Queen. He raised his glass to her and made as if to drink.

The Peacock Queen raised a slim finger. "Not so fast, my love." Then she smiled and Briley gasped as the queen stood and transformed. The gown she wore seemed to melt away, revealing thick layers of feathers which glittered and glowed in purples, blues, and red. The Peacock Queen stepped toward the man who, just like Briley, was struck senseless by the beauty of the Peacock Queen's feathers. One by one the feathers spread from each other, each a different shade from the one next to it. The man stood speechless with his drink extended to her, and the queen took the glass from his outstretched hand. She lifted the glass to her mouth and drank deeply, but the man was so transfixed he couldn't move. The Peacock Queen drained her glass and then put it on the tray. "Poor thing," the Peacock Queen said. "A shame really."

The queen clapped her hands and servants entered. Briley noticed they all kept their eyes to the ground. "Take him away, please. I'm afraid the prince has fallen ill," she said as she walked back to her throne. As she sat back down, her feathers disappeared and were replaced again by a gown. Briley shuddered at the look of pleasure on the Peacock Queen's face as the servants escorted the man away. They had to help him walk, and Briley noticed that he looked considerably older. His orange fur and tail had turned to slate grey, and there was no life at all in his eyes.

"She was born on a night when there was no moon in the sky." Briley heard Argon's voice in her vision. "There is no other creature like her beyond the Hedge."

Briley Van Campton

Is she evil? Briley thought the question. *What did she do to that man?*

"I only have strength enough to show you one more vision," Argon said. "And not enough time to answer all of your questions. Even now, I feel myself pulling away from this place." Briley's vision spun once more, up up up into the night sky, nearly amongst the stars, while the world shifted and changed below her. "What you do not see happening," Argon's voice said through the spiraling landscape, "is the people rising up against her and banishing her from the land. You do not see the Peacock Queen living with the low creatures, making alliances with the dark ones who dwell only in midnight. You do not see what she did to the goblin king to make him her servant. You won't see how she planted the first seeds of the green sea to separate the fair folk from each other, or the war she caused in the free cities. Some say the Peacock Queen is ageless, but we know this is wrong, for we saw her as a babe. But the Peacock Queen is ancient, and perhaps very close to timeless. My people, Briley, are the chronicle keepers of this land. We are librarians of a kind, taking down the history and the stories and the knowledge that we witness. We are sworn to peace, Briley, and thus have always been revered among the Fair Folk. We travel, asking for nothing, giving stories in turn, taking notes and most of all, keeping track. This is my personal memory of her."

And with that, Briley shot straight down toward the earth. She landed knee deep in mud, and immediately felt it sink into her boots. She could tell this was Argon's memory because it was so much clearer than the other two. She could smell the scent of fire in the air, and hear the crisping and popping of a fire nearby. It was raining, but only slightly, misting and near dark. Briley looked to her left and right and saw several of the green men and women standing beside her in the muck. Briley looked on and saw a column of knights encircling a burning building. The knights wore armor painted every bright color of the spectrum. They had long plumes from atop their helmets and carried no swords, only shields which were decorated elaborately, each with a wildly different design. The one thing the shields all had in common was, they each had the head of a peacock fashioned at the top.

Briley almost lost her balance when one of the peacock shields blinked at her. "Quit yer gawkin!" the small peacock said, and Briley's mouth fell open. "Bring more wood!" The shield shifted slightly so that one of its corners was facing off into the distance, and Briley understood immediately that it was pointing. She looked behind her and the shield was pointing toward a wooded area behind her. Briley felt like snapping the little head off the shield, but this wasn't her memory. She wasn't in control here, she was just a passenger of Argon's, and so Briley felt and watched through Argon's eyes as he turned and headed for the wood.

Briley could sense the urgency in Argon's movements. There were bandits approaching, and they needed to build a fire to keep the town lit. As she watched through Argon's eyes, she could also sense the immense amount of strength he possessed. If he wished it, he could rip a tree from the ground with his bare hands.

"We are the lore keepers," Argon whispered through the vision. "We are a peace keeping folk. Ours is the duty of making sure the knowledge of the Fair Folk remains intact."

But you are so strong, Briley thought back at him. *Are none of you warriors?*

"There are some," Argon whispered back, but with the thought, she had a distinct sense of disappointment and sorrow in his voice. "We call them Blackroots." And with that, she knew he would talk no further of the Blackroots. "The Peacock Queen is about to make her entrance," he said instead. "Watch closely."

Briley returned to the center of the village with a massive armload of gathered wood for the fire. She watched/felt as Argon and his kind threw pile after pile of wood onto the fire. It was a raging bonfire now, far too hot to stand close to, and even though she was well past ten feet away, she could still feel the blaze against her skin...sweat gathered on her brow. And then from above in the dark night sky she heard a shriek which made her blood quiver. She looked up into the night, and from the distance the Peacock Queen approached, sitting upon the back of a....

Briley gulped. *Is that a dragon?!* she thought.

"Yes. Watch. Time is short," Argon replied.

The dragon that the Peacock Queen sat astride was massive, easily the size of her home in Piedmont. It was also bright yellow, scaled with wings that spread out, dwarfing everything beneath them. As she approached, the soldiers formed a ring with their shields out, the peacock heads atop them all daring someone to try and break through the ring. Briley looked on with the fire blazing in the distance as the Peacock Queen landed with her dragon in the center of the ring of knights. As the creature's claws touched the earth, the fire popped and Briley glanced at it. As she returned her gaze to the Peacock Queen, she stopped as she recognized the face of one of the knights.

"Is that...," Briley gulped, "her fiancé?"

"Ah, yes," Argon said. "Now you see the fate of those she takes with her power. Keep watching."

Briley watched as the Peacock Queen slid from the back of her dragon and her feet hit the ground in beautiful boots. She did not wear a gown tonight; instead, she wore black breeches and a black shirt. She also wore a long, heavy cloak of black. If not for the fire raging in the distance, the Peacock Queen would have been perfectly disguised against the night. Briley watched as the queen walked over to the fire, far closer than she herself would have ever dared get to the blaze. Then the queen reached into the fire with a dark gloved hand and a beautiful smile on her face. Several of the people watching gasped, but no one moved to stop her.

What is she doing? Briley wondered.

"Shhh. Watch," was Argon's curt reply.

Then the queen walked INTO the blazing inferno, and Briley would have screamed if she could. Nothing happened for seconds. Briley was sure that the Peacock Queen must have been consumed by the fire, but then the fire began to take shape as if molded by hands. It quivered, formed into strands of moving, seemingly living fire, and the strands wove into ropes of flame. The ropes twirled against the night sky, weaving together, shaping together, and then all of a sudden, Briley watched as a giant rope of fire lashed itself apart from the flame and wrapped around the closest oak tree.

"NOOO!" All about her Argon's people cried out in horror, but it was too late. The ropes lashed around the oak trees, turning them to ash in seconds. Argon's people began rushing toward the flames. Some of them fell over midstride.

"Each of us," Argon said, "Is linked to one of the ancient oaks. Its life is ours to guard, and if it dies, we perish."

The people of the village were screaming now as well, because the fire was spreading from the oak grove to the houses close by. Argon wanted to rush forward, but another, stronger of Argon's kind lifted him and hauled him away. All he could do was watch as the village and the oak grove was consumed by fire. The Peacock Knights were soon flying into action to confront the amassed people. Briley watched as the knights wrapped their hands around the necks of the peacocks and pulled them from the shields. The peacock heads were actually the hilts to the most amazing and colorful swords Briley had ever seen. She watched as the village burned, the trees going with it.

The Peacock Queen emerged from the fire, her black outfit entirely changed to one of crimson and yellow entwined about her. Her cloak seemed to be made of living flame, and the queen laughed as she watched the outraged people try to fend off her knights. One of Argon's elders ripped a shield away from one of the Peacock Knights and threw it into the glowing flames. Immediately the knight's eyes came into focus, and he looked around as if he had no idea where he was.

"The shields," Briley gasped.

"Yes," Argon said to her. "That is one part I wanted you to see."

And though she hadn't noticed the transition, Briley found that she was no longer inside of Argon's memories, but back in the cell aboard the goblin ship.

"She IS Evil!" Briley spat out. "Why do people put up with her?"

"Many have tried to unseat her," Argon said. "There is one who can, beyond the Hedge. My job...." He paused. "I have vowed to find her."

"You mean...a human?" Briley asked.

"Yes, one of your kind. A girl."

"Grace?" Briley gasped aloud. "You said it's not me. It must be Grace!"

"That...,"Argon stated, "I cannot see. Your friends are blocked to me. My power is not what it once was."

Briley suddenly felt so sorry and sad for Argon that she

launched herself at him, wrapping her arms around him and embracing him. "You are so brave to take this chance," she said in his ear. She felt Argon return the embrace, but his presence faded and soon, she was all alone in her cell. "I will find the girl," Briley decided. "I will help stop the Peacock Queen," she said aloud. "No matter what!"

There was a tiny sound of laughter behind her and Briley spun. Candice was hovering in a corner, clapping her hands and spinning in midair.

"That's the spirit!" she said. "Argon couldn't stay, obviously. He won't tell you why, but between us girls, his oak is little more than a stump." Candice winked. "But I'm going to help you, Briley, because I like you!" The tiny fairy spun about the cell. "Even if you aren't the chosen one, you are still my favorite human!" She winked. "Of course, I've only ever met one, but still, definitely my favorite!" Candice laughed and spun again, and perched upon Briley's shoulder. "We'll figure out how to spring you as soon as we do something about this hair of yours!" Briley could not help but laugh at Candice's priorities. The fairy began twirling fast about Briley's head, giggling and clapping and twirling in the darkness of the cell.

Chapter Five:
Four Wishes

Briley had lost count of the hours. After Candice had fixed Briley's hair and magicked up some new clothes for her, Candice had left the cell to "scout." At some point Briley fell asleep, woke back up, and then fell asleep again. It was hard to get any real rest, though. Her stomach was in knots. The ship she was in pitched fitfully, so unlike Darrel's smooth running S. S. Arr Arr. Either the goblins didn't know how to navigate their ship as well as Darrel, or it wasn't as well built. Either way, Briley had to hold her hands against the walls to keep from spilling over. It was dark in the cells, but not pitch black, and Briley couldn't see what Candice had done to her hair, but she smiled down at the clothes she wore. Briley wore a beautiful gown of light blues and purples, with sparkles that spiraled across it. Candice had also changed Briley's boots into light slippers that were ever so much more comfortable, and she had even spun a delicate necklace about Briley's neck. It definitely was not proper adventuring gear, but Briley couldn't help but smile at the change.

"Harrison?" Briley called out for the hundredth time. "Grace?"

"Quiet you!" growled a harsh but high pitched voice further down the hallway. "No talking! Talking's against the rules!"

From time to time a trio of goblin guards would walk up and down the hall between the cells. Whenever they passed her cell, they would rattle their swords between the bars on her cell and chuckle with each other. "Pretty little pigeon Wendell caught for us!" they would say. "Can't wait to see what the queen gives us for this little bird!" The goblins thought their bird jokes were so funny that the last time they had passed, they had left her a plate piled high with birdseed. "Eat up, pretty canary! But no singing! Singing's against the rules!"

Briley sat on the little cot with her head between her knees. She was trying really hard not to cry when she heard a faint sound. Tap tap, then a pause. Tap tap tap. Briley hugged her knees closer to herself and then the sound repeated. Her eyes lit up...it was her and Harrison's secret code! She couldn't tell where the tapping was coming from, but it didn't matter. Harrison was OK. And if he was OK, then chances were that Grace was OK too. Tap tap...tap tap tap.

Where are you? the tapping asked. Briley looked about her cell for something to tap with. She got up from the cot, dumped the seeds from the plate onto the floor, then hurried back to her cot and tapped out her message, banging the plate against the floor. She hoped Harrison could hear her. She didn't dare bang too loudly or the guards were sure to come back around and take away the plate. Their secret code didn't have quite the right words, but Briley hoped Harrison would understand her meaning. Tap...tap...tap...tap...tap tap.

Grounded, hungry, angry, her message said.

Same here, Sis. Grace next door, Harrison replied.

Briley pondered how to send her next message without confusing Harrison. At some point they needed to figure out how to do more words, but their code was already pretty complicated. Several words had the same number of taps. You had to pay attention to the rhythm and the other words being tapped out.

Friends helping. One big, one small. Where are we going? It was the best she could think of.

Friends are good. Wendell stopped by. He's crazy, Harrison tapped out.

What happened?

Too much to explain. We need to get out of here.

Yes, definitely; any ideas?

Not yet. Grace is crying a lot. She's not much help.

Briley heard footsteps approaching, along with the loud and raucous voices of the goblin guards. "What's that noise, pigeon? Picking at your seeds are ya?" one of them grunted.

Got to go, Briley tapped out quickly, then tucked the plate underneath her flimsy mattress. She wished she was back in her jeans and button down shirt. She could have easily hidden the plate in her pockets if she had any. Then the craziest thing happened. She felt her dress change slightly, and she ran her hands down the silky fabric. Low and behold, two pockets had appeared in the dress, neatly hidden by folds in the fabric so they were hidden from plain sight. Briley sucked in a breath and quickly switched the plate to a pocket just as the goblins came up to her cell and flung open the door. The guards stood aside as Wendell walked in, and Briley sucked back a gasp at how much he had changed. His skin was visibly darker...not quite green like the rest of the goblins, but it was heading in that direction. He wore a wide brimmed black hat with a red sash tied around it.

His ears had wandered higher on his head, and Briley winced as she noticed several round hoops which pierced his left ear.

"Well, well, well," Wendell said. "I hope you're getting along comfortably."

Briley tried to stare him in the eyes, but those too had changed. Wendell's eyes had become elongated with bright orange irises blazing above a malevolent grin. She wasn't sure what else to do right then and there, so Briley stood and curtsied for him without speaking. As she did, she saw Wendell's eyes flicker back and forth in confusion.

"What a pretty dress," Wendell said sarcastically, then he advanced on her with venom glistening in his eyes. "Where did you get it?" he snarled. Spittle from his mouth sprayed over her, and Briley wiped her face with her hand, staring at Wendell's snarling mouth, which was now filled with rows of sharp and dangerous looking teeth.

It took all of her self-control not to break down in front of him, but she refused to let Wendell intimidate her. No matter how vicious he looked, he was still just a little boy, younger even than she was. Briley sucked up enough courage to finally respond. "Do you like it? I got so tired of wearing those other clothes."

Wendell hissed at her, drawing his sword in a smooth motion. He seemed much more coordinated now that he was half goblin. He pressed the point of the sword against her cheek and grinned at her. Briley's insides twisted uncontrollably, and she backed away from him until her back was against the cold metal of her cell. Wendell advanced, keeping the constant pressure of the sword against her cheek. "Whooooo...," he growled, "gave you thisssss dresssss?"

"A fairy visited me," Briley squeaked out.

"Fairies! Phah!" he spat. "Useless, vain, ugly little monsters! It is of no matter...fairies can't help you here. I only came to find out how much you knew about that Darrell character you were sailing with." Wendell was snarling at her.

Briley's knees quivered. She felt a drop of blood making its way down her cheek, and tried to think of Wendell as a young boy, crying because he couldn't figure out how to get his baseball cards to make the thwacking noise in his bicycle wheels. But she couldn't. No matter how hard she tried, all Briley saw was a vicious, mean, snarling half goblin with murder in his eyes. But then something occurred to her, and she blurted it out without thinking.

"You weren't able to capture him!" she said triumphantly "You're scared Darrel the Brave will come for me!"

"Scarrreddd?" Wendell roared at her. "Wendell the Wiley Wun is not scared!" He was snarling, his eyes darting all over.

Briley winced as the sword pressed further, biting into her cheek. Her stomach was doing backflips and her knees were turning into melted butter, but the thought of Darrel out there searching for her gave her hope. She thought of how Darrel's ship was painted in shades of green. He could be out there, right now. Wendell had gone mad in his goblin transformation, but Briley was determined to be brave, just like Darrel. After all, this was HER adventure! A huge bubble of courage burst out from within. It started somewhere in her pinky toes and spread upward. It oozed to her knees and then up along her back. Finally the bubble of courage reached her heart. Briley's fear left her and she curled her fingers into a ball. She could no longer feel the pain of the sword against her cheek, or her queasy tummy.

"When did you become such a bully?!" Briley yelled at him, looking into his strangely shaded orange eyes. Wendell's eyes darted back and forth.

Briley took in a deep breath and punched Wendell as hard as she could right in the eye. Wendell dropped his sword, putting both hands to his injured eye, and screamed out in pain. Briley wasn't thinking very clearly, but she knew this was her chance. She picked up the sword he had dropped and charged up to the two goblins and swung the sword around wildly. "Give me the dungeon keys!" she commanded. The one on the left reached into his belt loop and took out a keyring and handed it to her. "And your swords!" she shouted at them. The goblin's eyes were wide with fear, and they unbuckled their belts and dropped their swords to the ground. "Now get in the cell with Wendell!" she yelled, chancing a look in Wendell's direction. He was just starting to stand up. The goblins hesitated.

"I SAID MOVE!" Briley commanded in a voice she didn't recognize, and she swung the sword around. The goblins' fear won out and they hurried into the cell just in time for Briley to slam it shut and lock it. Wendell had recovered himself and was furious.

"This isn't fun and games, Briley!" Wendell roared. "Give me the keys!"

Briley didn't stick around to have a conversation with him. She had friends to save. She gathered the two swords and ran down the corridor, plucking a torch from the wall as she did. It was an awkward bundle, but Briley managed to balance it all and keep a steady pace. Now she just needed to find Harrison and Grace before another goblin found Wendell and set him free. She could hear him in the corridor, yelling at the top of his lungs.

"Get the girl! Let us out! But get the girl, she's escaped!" Wendell's yells were accompanied by the rattling of his cell door. She definitely needed to hurry.

Briley Van Campion

Briley ran as fast as she could. The torchlight flickered oddly against the walls, and Briley was still wearing the fine slippers that Celeste had magicked up for her. She wished she was wearing more comfortable shoes. The entire ship was made of metal, and it was hard to keep her footing. Suddenly from one step to the next, Briley felt a difference and had to stop to look down.

"I can't believe it!" she whispered, looking at her familiar sturdy hiking boots. Then she remembered the pocket that had magically appeared as well. "Are these wishing clothes?" she wondered aloud.

"Briley!" a voice called out. "Is that you?!" Briley looked to the sound of the voice and saw Harrison in a cell, his face pressed eagerly against the bars of a cell.

"Harrison!" Briley ran to him, pulling the ring of keys out and jamming the biggest heaviest one into the lock. "Where's Grace?" she asked, looking around. "I thought she was with you." Briley found the right key on the third attempt and opened Harrison's cell. He came out and wrapped her into a big hug.

"I wasn't sure we would see each other again!" he laughed, and picked her up, spinning her in circles. Briley hugged her brother back just as fiercely. As she held him something felt weird, but for the moment she just enjoyed her brother's hug. It was so good to see him again.

Finally Harrison put her down and grinned at her, and that's when it struck her. Harrison's ears had changed. Not to a goblins, but to furry pointed ones. But that wasn't all…. "Harrison, you have a tail!" Briley said, pointing at his orange and white tail that had sprouted out the back of his jeans. "When did that happen? And where is Grace?"

"I've been trying to hide it from you for a while, Sis." Harrison said, stroking his tail. "But when we were in the cell, I started growing ears too. I think I'm becoming a fox!" He was grinning so widely that Briley couldn't help but grin too. So what if her brother was turning into a fox? At least they were back together.

"But where is Grace?" she asked a third time. "I thought you two were together."

Harrison's eyes lowered and he pointed across from where they were standing. Briley looked over and saw Grace laying on the floor of the cell across from them. Briley ran over to the door, opening it with the key, and ran to Grace. She put her hand on Grace's forehead and her eyes grew wide. "Harrison, she is as cold as ice! What happened?"

Harrison was standing behind her. Briley hadn't even heard him move. His fox transformation was affecting a lot more than just his ears and a tail. He even moved differently. "She collapsed shortly after Wendell came to visit us. I think he might have poisoned her."

"Why would he do something like that?" Briley demanded. "She's his sister!"

"Wendell is crazy!" Harrison said. "He calls himself the Wiley Wun now."

"I know," Briley said. "What do we do, Harrison? We have to get out of here. I brought swords and everything." And then Briley remembered her wishing clothes and decided to test its limits. "Oh, I wish I had an antidote in my pocket!" she cried aloud. Then Briley reached into her pocket and found a tiny vial there. Could it be? She pulled the vial out of her pocket and looked at it. The liquid inside was a bright purple. She pulled the stopper off and put the vial to Grace's lips. "Come on," Briley whispered. "Please be OK, Grace."

Briley stroked Grace's hair, watching. Slowly, color returned to Grace's pale face and Briley could feel the warmth returning to Grace's skin.

"Wow," Harrison said behind her. "That was amazing."

"Yeah," Briley said. "Celeste gave me a wishing dress. I just don't know how many more wishes are left in it."

"Maybe you could wish us all back home," Harrison said. Now why hadn't she thought of that? Grace's eyes fluttered open and Grace smiled up at Briley.

"Are you all right?" Briley asked her.

"Yeah." Grace's voice was a whisper. "Thanks. I feel better now. Wendell poisoned me or something. We need to stop him."

"I know," Briley said, helping Grace up to her feet. "I don't have a plan yet. But I brought swords and a torch, and Celeste is getting help, I hope. I don't know where she went off to."

"Who is Celeste?" Grace asked as Briley handed her a sword.

"She's a sprite, but there's no time to explain. First let's get out of here," Briley said.

They all agreed, each of them holding a sword. Harrison took the lead, holding the torch, and Briley watched him pad silently through the halls. Somehow the fox ears and tail suited him, and Briley wondered how long it would be before she too started to change.

"Take a left up ahead," Grace said to Harrison. "It isn't far now."

Briley wondered how Grace knew the ship so well, but she didn't bother asking. As long as none of them started changing into goblins, Briley felt she could at least trust Harrison and Grace. As they walked through the halls, though, Briley couldn't help but wonder where all the goblins were. Aside from the sound of the ship moving through the Green Sea, there was hardly any noise at all.

"Just through that door," Grace said, pointing. Briley had a really bad feeling in the pit of her stomach, and as Harrison opened the door to the bridge, her dread was confirmed. The bridge of the metal ship was swarming with goblins, all of them waving their nasty swords. At the very back Briley spotted Wendell, who was armed as well. He caught her eye and grinned at her, his mouth filled with countless uneven and yellowed teeth.

"Oh, Wendell," Briley said aloud. "What have you become?" The next thing she knew, they were swarmed by the goblins. Harrison and Grace swung their swords, standing shoulder to shoulder in the doorway, blocking it, which was a distinct advantage. Eventually the goblins would figure out that if they all attacked at once, they would overcome the three of them. Briley backed away from the doorway, wishing as hard as she could for Darrel the Brave to come to their rescue.

"That's the last wish in the dress," Celeste said, appearing suddenly in front of her. "Harrison was right. You could have wished yourself home. But I get the feeling you don't want to go back for some reason."

"Where have you been off to?" Briley demanded of the fairy. "And why didn't you tell me these were wishing clothes? I never would have wasted a wish on SHOES!" Briley shouted over the ruckus of goblins behind her.

"Tsk tsk," Celeste said. "How about a thank you?" the little fairy said, hands on hips. Just then the whole ship thumped as if it had hit a giant wall. "There comes Darrel and his crew now," Celeste said with a smile. "Good luck!" Briley goggled as Celeste spun out of sight. Then Briley saw Darrel charging down the hallway, with his crew roaring behind him.

"Glad to see you're alive!" Darrel called as he charged forward.

"You too!" Briley called out, stepping out of the way.

She watched as Darrel and his crew joined Harrison and Grace, battling with the goblins in the doorway, and wondered to herself how right Celeste might be. She had had the perfect chance to wish herself home, and instead, she had wished for Darrel to rescue them. It was then and there that Briley realized something. She liked it here in the land beyond the Hedge a million trillion times better than she liked being at home in Piedmont with her crooked yellow house. "In fact," Briley said aloud, "I hope we never have to leave!"

All at once the excitement bubbled up inside of her, and suddenly the idea of hurting goblins didn't really bother her at all. She took her sword out with a mighty cry and waved it above her head wildly, shouting out, "For Darrel the Brave! For the Green Sea!" She charged headlong into the battle. She caught Darrel's eye as they battled into the room, and he grinned at her so wide his face nearly split.

"For Briley the Braverest!" Darrel called out. "To pillaging goblins! And rescuing little brothers!"

The bridge of the goblin ship was a madhouse. Briley couldn't keep track of where anyone was or how the battle was faring. She focused on staying close to Darrel, and she swung her sword more in defensive moves than anything else. One of the goblins had managed to cut her arm with one of his wicked swords, and Briley began to feel a little woozy. She wondered if the goblin swords were poisoned similarly to what Wendell had done to his sister. His own sister! At the thought Briley's wooziness went away, and she focused on keeping the small area around her clear of goblins. She drew an invisible circle in her mind about six inches around her. Anyone that got inside that six inch area, she swung at and cleared them out. The tight little space around her became her world. She forgot about everything else. There was no time, there was no sound, only the position of her sword and the six inches of space it guarded.

The battle swelled, and although the bridge was large, it was overwhelmed with bodies. Briley swung her sword at a leg that had come inside her little circle, and almost too late, she had to check her swing. "Harrison!" she called out. "I almost cut your leg off!" She glanced at his face and he smiled at her. He was practically dancing among the goblins, so graceful now that he was half fox.

"I've got your back, Sis!" he called back. "It's almost over!"

Briley didn't have time to retort, for just then three goblins advanced toward them. Briley crouched beneath the sword swing of one of the goblins, and then dodged to her left as another swung. She pivoted, turning her sword midair to block a blow from the third, and then returned with a blow of her own on the shoulder of the goblin in the middle. He fell down, dropping his sword, but there was no time to feel guilty about hurting the goblin. Harrison danced through the hole she had made, rolling across the fallen goblin's body. When he came up standing, Briley saw that Harrison was now holding two swords and was swishing them through the air at a blinding speed. But he didn't see Wendell coming up behind him. He was too focused on the goblins in front of him.

"Harrison! Watch out!" Briley cried, charging forward recklessly.

But it was too late. Between one heartbeat and the next, Wendell had swatted Harrison aside as if he were a bug. Briley winced as Harrison crunched to the ground. When had Wendell become so strong? Suddenly Briley realized that she had charged right into the middle of the two goblins and Wendell. She cast her eyes about, dodging a swing from one of the goblin swords.

Sweat coated her body from head to toe, and in the background, Darrel's crew cried out in triumph. They were definitely on the winning side of the battle, but none of that would matter if Wendell cut her down.

Briley dodged another swing, but only too late she noticed Wendell's sword coming straight for her chest. There was nowhere to dodge, and she couldn't raise her sword in time to block the attack. Everything seemed to slow down around her, and Briley could hear her heart beating in her ears. She struggled to make her arms move fast enough to block Wendell's sword, but she knew she wouldn't be quick enough. At the last instant Briley closed her eyes, readying herself for the blow, but the blow never came. Instead, she heard the sharp TING! of metal against metal.

Briley opened her eyes. Wendell's sword hovered just above Briley's chest, and it took her a minute to figure out what had stopped Wendell's attack. Then Wendell swung again and again. Each time his blade was stopped in midair.

"Celeste!" Briley called out. "You are a life saver!" Briley couldn't help but laugh as Celeste flitted back and forth with the tiniest sword Briley could imagine. It definitely did not look large enough to block a life size sword, but Celeste flew back and forth, up and down, crisscrossing, zig zagging, and giggling as she countered all of Wendell's attacks.

All around the Horgles and goblins battled. Wendell was becoming visibly irritated, grunting and screaming at her. Celeste kept blocking his attacks, Wendell's sword being easily deflected by Celeste's tiny weapon. Briley was able to focus on defending herself from the other goblins. Then suddenly, it stopped.

Wendell stared at her out of half mad eyes, sword poised and ready to strike, but Darrel the Brave and three of his Horgle crew all stood with swords to his neck. Sweat rolled down Wendell's face, and he was breathing heavily as if exhausted. Briley's arms felt like wood. She looked around and saw that all the goblins were either fleeing, being taken prisoner, or lying unconscious on the ground.

Harrison ran up to her and wrapped his arms around her. "We did it!" he cried.

Briley was in a state of disbelief. "Yeah," she said. "But now what?"

The Horgles with Darrel drew out ropes to bind Wendell's hands together, but he winked at Briley. "Tut tut," Wendell said. "Not so fast." And quicker than anyone could react, Wendell drew a small sack out of his jacket pocket and threw it upon the floor. Fine white powder burst from the sack, coating everything in the room, and Briley's vision swam instantly out of focus. She felt queasy and couldn't see straight, and just like that she felt her body slump to the ground. She fell right across from Darrel, and she locked eyes with him before everything went black. She could have sworn the look in his eyes was anything but brave. In fact, if she didn't know better, she would have thought he was afraid.

Briley awoke coughing, still on the bridge of the goblin ship. Everyone around her was coughing as well. She saw Darrel stand and she tried to stand up as well, but her muscles were all wobbly and weren't working quite right.

"Dragon ash!" Darrel said aloud. "That settles it for sure. The goblins are in cahoots with the Peacock Queen!"

Harrison helped her to her feet, and they looked around the bridge of the metal ship. Wendell had taken most of the goblins with him, but there were still some laying on the bridge of the ship. Apparently the dragon ash didn't last long enough for him to take all of them with him.

Darrel was stomping around, rousing his crew members. "Get the goblins to their own brig!" he shouted. "That wiley little scourge took my ship!"

Briley and Harrison helped the Horgles round up the remaining goblins while Darrel took charge of getting the metal ship moving. "Find the bloody running kit and get it ship shape, Clanker!" he snapped at one of the Horgles.

Briley didn't stick around to hear the rest of the commands. She and Harrison had their hands full helping to get the goblins to the brig. Luckily none of them put up much resistance. They were all pretty beat up from the battle. After an hour or so, the Horgle crew had managed to get the metal ship running again, and all the goblins locked up down below. The ship didn't run nearly as smoothly as Darrel's green painted one, but not even Darrel complained about that. They all knew they were lucky to be alive. It was then, just as Briley came up to thank Darrel as he maneuvered the wheel to change course, that Briley realized something, or rather someone, was missing.

"Harrison!" she called. "He took Grace!" She smacked herself on her forehead. "Wendell's kidnapped his own sister!"

Chapter Six:
The Green Land

It didn't take long for Darrel the Brave and his crew to start making improvements on the goblin ship. They oiled rusted gears, cleaned out dirty passageways, and Briley was amazed at the amount of stuff she saw the crew pitching out the side of the ship. There were little portholes all over, and they would open them up, dumping boxes full of goblin junk into the Green Sea. Briley helped out too, cleaning out the lower decks of the ship. Briley wondered how long it had been since anyone had been down there. There were boxes and boxes of pilfered items and loot from their raids, and not all of it was useless. Briley uncovered more than one chest filled to bursting with silver coins. There were chests filled with moldy clothes, moldy food, and sometimes just a bunch of mold. The next box Briley opened was empty except for a single red glove. She reached in and took it out. The glove was made entirely of red scales and much heavier than it looked. She decided to keep it. It had to be valuable. Why else would it be in a box all by itself?

Celeste helped with the dust, zipping around, clapping her hands, and Briley watched as the dust all formed into a giant ball in the middle of the room. "That's amazing!" Briley called out as she shifted a box of rusty tools off a shelf in one of the rooms. Celeste giggled and snapped her fingers. One of the port holes opened, and the dust ball zipped outside like a flash.

They had been traveling for nearly three days now with no sign of Wendell the Wiley or Darrel's old ship. Darrel told her there wasn't any way to track them, that Wendell was likely headed to take Grace to the Peacock Queen. Every time Briley asked, he was very mysterious. He said he had a destination in mind, but wouldn't tell where they were headed. Harrison was spending all of his time with Darrel's crew. He was taking every spare second he could to learn how to use a sword and how to hand fight. Briley was learning a little too. She really wasn't that enthused about learning to hurt people, but some of Darrel's crew were teaching her how to use shields to block, and how to position herself in a fight. Briley had her own set of shields now, two that she carried in her hands and two smaller ones that strapped onto her arms. She was learning how to dodge and deflect, how to twist and bend, so that she could flit through multiple opponents.

After one of her training sessions Briley sat on a bench, wiping the sweat from her face and unstrapping her arm shields. Darrel sat next to her and patted her on the back. "You're doing great!" he exclaimed. "You're a natural, little Briley. Here, I got you something." Darrel handed her a belt with lots of little loops around it. "Try it on," he said, grinning. Briley wasn't sure what to make of the belt, but she stood up and put the belt around her waist, fitting it into place. She cinched it tight around her, and then Darrel started slipping little vials from his pockets into the loops around the belt. "My first officer had this great idea, since you don't want to practice with a weapon."

Briley looked down at all the vials. She took a practice spin and they all stood in place. "Now I just need to find out what they all do," she laughed.

"Well, they are all medicine of one kind or another," Darrel grinned. "I'm not too familiar with fixing up folks, but my guess is you can't mess up a person too much with medicine."

Briley bit her tongue. She knew some people had allergies, but Darrel was grinning so big she didn't argue with him.

"Oh!" she said of a sudden. "Do you know what this is?" Briley drew out the red scaled glove she had found and Darrel almost fell out of his seat.

"OHO!" he cried joyfully. "I most certainly do! A rare treasure!" he said. "Hold out your hand." Briley did. Immediately, Darrel slipped the glove over her fingers.

"What does the glove do?" Briley asked. She flexed her fingers. She could barely feel the fabric at all. It was almost as if it the glove wasn't there.

Darrel smiled at her. "Well, I'd tell you, but you wouldn't believe me. Hold up your hand," he said, and Briley did so. "Higher!" he commanded, and Briley reached her hand as high as she could. Then quick as a flash, Darrel unsheathed his sword and swung it as hard as he could onto her hand. Briley winced, squeezing her eyes shut. She tried to move her hand out of the way, but Darrel had swung so quickly and unexpectedly. When Briley opened her eyes, she couldn't believe them. Darrel's sword was caught firmly in her grip, and her hand didn't hurt at all. It was as if the sword was made of plastic, not sharpened steel.

"That's a dragon scale glove," Darrel said. "And mind, I've never seen another, so don't you ever lose it!" he said to her, his eyes boring into her.

From time to time, Briley felt just a little bit afraid of Darrel. She gulped. "I won't," she promised with a squeak.

"Good!" Darrel said, his grin back in full force. "Now as for the vials, I want you to start learning with one of our shipmates on how to use them. You're going to learn to be a field medic. You dodge hits, block hits, and heal wounds. You start tomorrow, early as the sun rises...not that we see it down here, mind!"

Briley felt herself nodding and then something struck her. "Wait," she said. "If this is dragon scale...how do you fight a dragon?" she asked timidly.

"Well, that's easy!" Darrel said, grinning at her. "You don't!" He laughed and everyone around him laughed just as heartily.

One of the crew came around, passing out flagons of drinks, and they all cheered. Briley drank from her flagon. The purple liquid burned in her throat, and she made her face into a smile. But she couldn't stop thinking that the Peacock Queen had dragons. If she had dragons with scales like the one her glove was made of, what was their tiny crew supposed to do against her? How were they ever going to get Grace back? Celeste chose that moment to zip straight into Briley's cup, and the purple liquid splashed out of it. Celeste came back up giggling, and sat on the rim of Briley's cup. She smiled, and then burped so loud that it echoed off the whole ship, nearly vibrating it with the force of her burp, and even Briley couldn't help laughing aloud at that.

With that, Darrel and his crew cleared out the tables and chairs. Some of them brought out instruments and others began pairing up to dance. Before long, the metal goblin ship was filled with the sounds of Horgles singing and clambering. The Horgles sang raucous tunes that made her feet itch to dance. Briley watched them dance and she did her best to sing along. She didn't know the words to most of the songs, but no one complained if she sang off key or sang the wrong words.

Celeste perched on her shoulder and Briley watched Harrison wend his way through the Horgles toward her. He sat down next to her, and Briley noted his tail was getting fuller. His cheeks had started to show some fox fur too. She couldn't help but reach out and touch his cheek. Harrison didn't flinch away; instead he smiled as she did so.

"We're all changing, Briley," he said. "Except for you."

"Maybe I was already too strange from the beginning," she guessed, laughing.

"Maybe." He shrugged.

"Do you feel any different?" Briley asked him.

Harrison shrugged his shoulders. "Actually, I feel great. I can move so fast now. And if I want to sneak up on someone, it's no problem at all."

"Do you miss our old home?" Briley asked him, gazing into his golden fox eyes.

Harrison didn't hesitate to answer. "No. I like it here. It's wild and scary, but it's hard to describe...." He took her hand and looked deeply into Briley's eyes. "I know this sounds crazy, but I feel like I've come home, and the place where we grew up was some kind of boarding house."

"Wow," Briley said, squeezing his hand. "That's exactly it. I've been trying to describe it, and that's exactly it!"

The music changed without warning and the sound of fiddles swarmed the room. "Do you want to dance?" Harrison asked her.

Briley launched to her feet, and Celeste let out a squeak as she toppled from her shoulder. Briley was pretty sure that Celeste had gotten drunk on whatever she was drinking, because Celeste sat on the table, rubbing her head before finding a napkin to curl up in.

"Yeah!" Briley said excitedly. "Let's dance!" They whirled and twirled to the music. Harrison's fox transformation made him ten times more graceful than he had ever been before.

They danced well into the night, stomping and spinning, drinking and joking. The Horgles were rampant partiers. They came and went in shifts, taking turns between dancing, cavorting, and running the goblin ship. When Briley finally made her way to her cabin, she didn't even bother washing or changing her clothes. She opened the door and flopped hard onto her mattress, the tunes still thrumming in her temples as she plummeted into dreamland.

***

The sound of cranking and grinding brought Briley out of her sleep, and she lifted her head from her mattress with a groan. The sounds of boots moving was all around. Shouts and cries rattled down the hallways, and Briley flopped out of her bed and opened her door to see the Horgles running frantic. "Get the jangles in place now, love!" one of the female Horgles shouted down the hallway. "Darrel wants us looking sharp when we hit the blue!"

Briley timed the traffic of the frantic crew and then fell into the hallway at a dash, rushing toward the steps to the top decks. As she cleared the top steps, she was amazed to see the sky up above. The sun glistened off the metal ship, reflecting in every direction, almost blindingly. Briley shielded her eyes, looking up at the sky, not realizing how shut in she had been feeling. "Out of the way, love!" the same Horgle from below shouted at her. "Well, get a move on!"

Briley shuffled out of the way, clutching to the railing as the ship bounded atop the thick grass of the green sea. Briley watched as the Horgles unrolled a giant piece of patchwork fabric across the deck of the ship, and her heart did a lurch. Briley didn't see Darrel anywhere around. Surely he was close at hand. Then she spotted him watching across the deck. He leaned against a railing with a lazy grin on his face. His clothes looked as disheveled as Briley felt, and the female Horgle was shouting out all the orders.

"That's good, lads! Very good! Keep it taut! On my mark!"

From time to time she would look to Darrel as if for confirmation, and he would just nod to her. Briley could only assume that he was training her. Perhaps she was second in command? Suddenly Briley felt very guilty, for she hadn't learned many of the Horgles' names aside from Darrel. He only really stood out because his clothes were so much finer than the rest of his crew. Truth be told, the Horgles all looked fairly alike to her, but Briley promised herself she would try and learn the names of the crew aboard the ship. After all, she owed them at least that much.

"Ready loves? Now blooowww!"

There was a great moment where all of the Horgles intook their breath in unison, then each of them set their mouths to the ends of the patchwork and started puffing. At the same moment there was a great grinding noise, and Briley watched as a pump was fastened to the base of the patchwork. The pump rattled and clanked, and the Horgles took breaths in unison. The pump was rusty and ancient, looking as if it were about to fall apart. Nonetheless, the three Horgles who handled the pump knew what they were doing, handling the device with care. The patchwork slowly took shape, filling up the entire deck, and then it began to float above the deck of the ship. Briley swallowed a gasp.

"READY THE RIGGING!" the Horgle bellowed over the

ruckus of the pump and the blows of the Horgles. "Grab your hooks! Ready on five!" She held up her hand, counting with her fingers. "One, two, three, four, NOWWW!" At once the Horgles let go of the patchwork balloon and grabbed tiny hooks from their belts. They twirled them around and then launched them over the top of the balloon. It all happened in a matter of seconds. The Horgles were obviously practiced, and Briley watched as the balloon took shape and lifted from the deck of the ship. As it rose the lines drew taut, and by the time it was lifting, the Horgles had all fastened their hooks to tiny holes all around the deck of the ship. There was a sudden lurching feeling and then they were off.

Briley ran to the rail of the ship and looked below as the green sea grew more and more distant from them. She laughed aloud as the cool breeze battled with the hot sun against her cheeks, and she couldn't hide the happiness inside of her. She closed her eyes and let out a whoop. She wasn't the only one to cry out either. All around her there were cries of triumph and Horgles laughing aloud.

"Good job, mates!" the female Horgle cried out. "Very well done!"

Briley ran up to her with a smile plastered to her face. "That was amazing!" Briley announced "My name's Briley. Do you know where we are headed?"

"Glad to know you, Briley. I'm Grindle, the first mate," the Horgle announced. "And as for where we are headed, it's all we have left of home."

"I would have been happy to help with the lift off," Briley announced eagerly. "You could have let us know."

"Ah, but we have to be careful, Briley," Grindle replied. "Times have changed, and as much as I hate to admit it, there are some amongst us who might betray us if they knew too much."

Briley looked around nervously. Luckily all the other Horgles were out of ear shot. They all seemed earnestly at work, moving the lines or moving along the deck at one task or another. "You mean...," Briley began, "That even your own crew might—"

"Hush now," Grindle interrupted. "Don't you worry about that. The Peacock Queen has spies everywhere. I'm not so much worried about one of our crew betraying us as there being others about that we don't know of."

Just then Darrel came up, grinning and swaggering. He clapped Grindle hard on the back and guffawed aloud. "Don't go scaring our guest now, Grindle," he announced. "Briley, are you feeling strong today?"

"Yes sir!" Briley replied immediately.

"Good, good. That's what I like to hear!" Then Darrel put his fingers to his mouth and let out a shrill blast of a whistle. Suddenly all hands on the deck of the ship stopped moving and looked up to where Darrel was standing.

"Lads and ladies!" Darrel announced in a strong voice. "Briley here says she's feeling strong today. Extra rations for the first three of ya to volunteer to help her and her brother train." The Horgles all clambered toward the front, and for the first time she didn't feel like an extra wheel aboard the ship. Instead, she felt like a welcome addition to the crew. Briley took a deep breath and took a chance along with it.

"I pick you, you, and you," she announced, selecting almost at random from the Horgles who had appeared before them. At her selection, Darrel and Grindle both let out boisterous laughs.

"The lady has chosen!" Darrel announced. "Now below decks until lunch with you. When she comes back up, I want to see her able to dodge and block with the best of them." He grinned at them, handing each of the three that Briley had appointed a little silver badge which she assumed was their extra rations token. "I needn't remind you that time is short," Darrel added grimly.

The three Horgles and Briley all exited, heading below decks. They found Harrison sitting next to a porthole, awestruck by the view. Briley ran up to her brother and hugged him hard, stroking his furry face. "Can you believe it?" she breathed. "We're flying!"

"I know, Sis!" Harrison grinned. "It's unbelievable!"

The Horgles caught up to the pair of them. "Come on, you lot!" the tallest one said. "Captain's orders."

"Come on, Harrison," Briley said, pulling her brother along with them. "We're going for some more battle training."

It didn't take long for the five of them to find a room large enough to train in. Briley donned her shields and her special glove, along with the belt of potions, which had all been gifted to her by the Horgles. She owed them so much. How was she ever going to repay them? Harrison took a stance with two small and thin swords. One was curved, the other straight like an arrow.

"You'll use that one," the tall Horgle said, pointing to the curved sword, "against enemies with no armor and to block attacks."

Harrison grinned, swinging the curved sword, and it swished wickedly through the air.

"The other is for wounding. Aim for knees, elbows, anywhere that isn't armored." The Horgle grinned at Harrison. "See, you slice and fend with the first one. The second one is for pinning your enemies in place. Use your speed to your advantage. Slow down your enemies, and keep your sister safe and close."

Harrison grinned, and Briley couldn't help but be proud of her brother as he began to practice with the other two Horgles. Harrison was a natural.

"He should have daggers," Briley observed as one of the

Horgles managed to knock Harrison's sword to the ground and then kicked it far out of reach.

"Hmm...." The tall Horgle stood next to her stoically, observing for now. "Yes. Just in case. Good idea!"

"What's your name?" Briley asked the tall Horgle. She watched Harrison yield, and then the three of them reset their practice stances. This time they arranged barrels and boxes haphazardly about the room.

"Begin!" the tall Horgle announced, and before Briley could blink, Harrison was darting between the barrels, kicking straw into his attackers' eyes. "My name is Dragus," the Horgle said to her.

Harrison got tripped by one of his attackers but rolled between two boxes, and then Briley laughed aloud as Harrison rolled into one. The attackers thought Harrison was as good as done then. They approached the box with their heavy swords raised, and Briley moved a hand to her mouth. She knew they wouldn't smash her brother, but they certainly looked intent on crushing the box.

Once they were both on top of the box, one of the Horgles lifted it from the ground, but Harrison wasn't inside the box. "What the...?" the Horgle said aloud. Briley was just as confused as he. She had watched her brother roll into that very box, but then he sprung out from behind a barrel, cartwheeling with his swords in hand, and landed atop the other Horgle, pinning him to the ground with both swords ready to strike.

"I yield!" the second Horgle said. Then the Horgle holding the box came for Harrison. He made short work of the taller opponent, catching him about the legs and tripping him in moments.

Briley laughed and applauded. "Good show!" she called.

114

"Apparently your brother is at a much better advantage when he's not in an open field," Dragus said. "I must be honest. I've never seen anything like it."

After a couple more bouts, Harrison and the Horgles were both tied in victories. Basically, if Harrison was given a little bit of space and time, he was able to trick the Horgles in one way or another and then launch a surprise attack. But if he was unable to get past their guard or unable to find a suitable distraction, he stood little chance against the larger and stronger opponents.

Dragus blew a ship whistle. "Water break," he called out. "And then it's your turn, Briley." Briley looked deep into his eyes, remembering what Grindel had said, that there might be those aligned with the Peacock Queen aboard this very ship. She gulped, but was determined not to show her fear. Something in Dragus's stare made Briley uneasy. She just couldn't say what.

Once they had all rested for a minute and gulped down some water, Dragus set about the training area with a paintbrush and a bucket of red paint. He marked some of the crates that were strewn about with a big red X. "The ones I'm marking, Briley, are your wounded partners." He finished putting an X on the side of a crate, and then hoisted his sword. "Your job is to not get hit, get to your wounded, and get one of your healing tonics to them." Then Dragus hoisted a big sword onto his shoulder, and the other two Horgles took up their swords as well. "Use your dragon skin to block. Try not to use your shields unless you have to. They're more liable to break or become dislodged after taking a blow."

Briley nodded, making sure the dragon skin glove was tight as it could be. Since she needed both hands for her job, Briley had buckled two shields on her forearms. A third, smaller shield was strapped to the back of her left hand. "I'm ready," she managed.

115

Briley looked over to Harrison, who smiled at her, and Briley tried to smile back, but she felt squishy inside. Before, when they were battling on the bridge of this ship, it had been easy not to think. And their previous training sessions had been haphazard at best. But she wasn't going to let Darrel the Brave or her brother down. They needed to rescue Grace, and if possible, Wendell as well. She knew that in order to do that, they would need to board the ship that the goblins had taken off in.

Before any more thoughts could creep in, Dragus blew his ship's whistle and the Horgles began advancing toward Briley. She ran for the nearest crate even though it wasn't marked with an X. One of the Horgles came around the side, sword raised, and Briley used her shorter height to its full advantage. She tucked into a ball and rolled away, then quickly stood and dashed past the Horgle just as the other was joining him. She got to the first crate and quickly plucked out one of her tonics, placing it atop the box.

When Briley cast her eyes about she saw Dragus barreling toward her, so Briley moved around the side of the crate and made for the next one, but Dragus had anticipated her movements. She only got two steps away from the crate before Dragus headed her off. He swung his sword toward her, and Briley raised her dragon skin in a fist. The blade met her fist and Dragus's sword rang out throughout the training area. Briley could see it vibrating as it repelled off her knuckles, and the impact jarred her as well. She smiled as she moved to the side. She made it to the next crate, placing another tonic atop it, and turned away quickly. Dragus and his two cohorts were flanking her now, and there was no easy escape. Her heart pounded in her ears, and Briley was unsure how to evade all three of them at once. Instead, Briley charged at the one to the left, crying out as she did so. She held her dragon skin slightly to the side, ready to swing. Once she was close to the Horgle, the Horgle swung his sword. Briley met the blow with her glove, smacking it against the sword, and then quickly turned away. But just as she had made it past, the other two Horgles appeared in front of her, swords raised. Briley couldn't see any escape routes, but she wasn't about to give up. She used her momentum and fell to the ground, rolling sideways as the Horgle swords swung down where she had been standing. She moved quickly, getting into a crouch and dodging the swinging swords. In the last battle she had been a part of, she had relied on the fighters around her to cover her, and of course Celeste had helped out as well.

"Celeste!" she called out. "Of course!" To Briley's dismay, though, the sprite did not appear to aid her. This time, she was all on her own. Briley managed to get two more tonics to wounded shoulders before she was outmaneuvered. Dragus used his forearm to block Briley's escape route, and the other two fell in on either side of her.

"GOOD!" Dragus roared as Briley's heart thudded in her chest. "Very good for a beginner." The Horgles all grinned at her, and she heard Harrison applauding in the background. "Again!" Dragus called out.

For the next hours they took turns practicing. Their shouts and clamoring must have drawn some attention, because groups of Horgles would come and go as their shifts ended. Some of them had even set up a table along the far wall, along with several chairs, and one of the younger Horgles was writing down orders and then running to the mess room to get them.

By the end of the session Briley was so sore, she just collapsed on the floor. Several Horgles laughed at that and carried her over to the table they had set up, shoving a plate of food and a full cup in her direction.

"Eat up, Sis!" Harrison said around a mouthful of turkey leg. Everything smelled so good, and Briley's stomach rumbled loud enough for everyone to hear. She devoured her own turkey leg, smashed potatoes drizzled in gravy, and heavy helpings of roasted squash and peppers, and she drank several cups of the blueish purple liquid they called sweet-juice.

"You're doing really well," Dragus said to her, sitting on the other side of the table from her and Harrison. Something about Dragus still made Briley feel uneasy, but he seemed genuine enough. Maybe he just wasn't a people person. Or a people Horgle, to be more precise.

"Thank you, Dragus, for all your hard work," Briley said, finishing her plate and pushing it to the middle of the table. Then she let out a gigantic burp...not quite as loud as the one Celeste had rang out earlier. Briley's burp didn't rattle the walls of the ship, but it was good enough to earn hearty laughter and jokes from everyone gathered around the table. After dinner, Briley barely had enough energy to make it to her bed before collapsing into a deep dreamless sleep.

The next few days became a blur of training and learning the ins and outs of taking care of a flying/submarine ship. She still couldn't believe everything that had happened to her on this adventure. From time to time she would pinch herself, and still not believing, she would have Harrison do it. He always grinned at her and offered to smack her in the belly instead.

"That way you'll know for sure that you're not dreaming, Sis!"

By the sixth day, when she awoke, every muscle Briley had felt like it had been twisted and bent and then shoved in a box. But it wasn't a bad feeling. It actually made her feel good about herself to know that she was learning how to fight and how to run the ship.

Briley was examining her muscles in her mirror while getting ready when the first mate called out in a huge voice. "All hands to the bridge! Green land ahoy! All hands, top decks!" Briley shuddered at the force of the woman's voice. Then the entire ship vibrated when the first mate called out, "NOWWW!"

Briley threw on a shirt and stuffed her legs into a pair of pants before running for the stairs.

**

Once she got into the hallways, the ship was a madhouse. Horgles were running every direction. They were all crying out, "The Green Land! The Green Land!" in excited tones. Briley tried her hardest to make her way through the rush toward the closest set of stairs. She kept getting bumped and jostled, and then out of nowhere Dragus scooped her up into his arms and lifted her as he ran.

"Got you!" he cried.

"Thank you!" Briley said, grinning. Maybe Dragus wasn't so bad after all.

Within minutes Dragus had carried her to the deck of the ship, where all hands were busy manning ropes that fastened the giant balloon to the top of the ship. Others were manning the pumps, and Dragus set her down gently next to the railing of the ship.

"Look!" he said, pointing beyond the ship. Briley couldn't help but smile as her eyes hit upon the Green Land.

"Oh my!" she gasped. Briley wasn't sure what she had been expecting, but what she saw was like nothing she could have ever dreamed up.

The ship was amid towering mountains. But one of the

mountains stopped halfway up as if it had been chopped in half. Sitting upon the carved mountain a city bloomed with multicolored buildings, as if thousands of flowers grew right out of the mountain top. Briley watched as the ship was steered carefully closer to the side of the mountain. All around the edge of the mountain, ships much like the one they flew were docked at giant platforms. Briley tried counting the ships, but there were so many.

"All hands ready for docking," Darrel's voice boomed. Everyone was moving excitedly. Briley just wished she was able to help out. She caught sight of Dragus manning one of the pumps as their ship moved closer and closer to a platform situated on the side of the mountain. There were several people at the platform holding hooks attached to the ends of ropes. "On my mark!" Darrel announced.

Just as Darrel was about to give his next command, there was a loud CRACK! One of the lines on the ship came loose, and a rope slithered across the deck of the ship. Attached to the end of the rope was a heavy metal wheel, and it caught Darrel square in the chest. Briley stared with her eyes bulging out of her head, and slapped a hand over her mouth to keep herself from screaming. Many, like her, couldn't move. Dragus ran after Darrel as he was carried across the deck of the ship. Darrel slammed against the rail of the ship and teetered there for a moment that seemed like a lifetime. Then Darrel disappeared over the side of the ship, and Briley screamed. The ship lurched to the side as the hooks from the docking station caught hold of the ship and started pulling it toward the mountain. Briley ran to the rail of the ship, looking over the edge. The rope was hanging far below the ship, and Darrel still clung to the wheel hanging far below.

Dragus was shimmying down the rope as the ship was pulled

closer and closer to the docking station. Briley let go of a breath she hadn't realized she was holding. At least Darrel was alive. All about her people moved to and fro, securing the ship against the dock. Darrel swung below, moving precariously close to the mountain like a pendulum. Dragus reached him and stabilized him as others began pulling the rope back aboard the ship. Briley felt hollow inside. She was overjoyed to finally be visiting the Green Land, but it wouldn't be the same without Darrel's fearless smile.

It seemed like hours before Darrel was hauled aboard the ship by his crew. Dragus and the other Horgles all saw to him, getting a litter and hauling Darrel off the ship. Briley just watched, and she was quite certain she wouldn't have ever moved again if Celeste had not flitted over to her just then.

Celeste kissed Briley on the cheek. "Cheer up now, you silly goat! Darrel was fortunate, and I've put a little healing magic into him. He will be just fine."

Briley sniffed, pulling her tears back in. "Really?" she said in a small quiet voice.

"Of course!" Celeste offered. "And Argon is here, Briley. He is looking forward to seeing you again."

Briley sniffed again and dried her eyes. "Argon is here?" she squeaked.

Celeste hovered about Briley's head, brushing her tiny wings against Briley's cheeks. "This is where Argon's stump is," Celeste said simply. "He can't wander far for long. This is as close to a home as Argon has."

Briley started feeling better. Having Celeste around always made her feel cheerful. And the prospect of seeing Argon again lifted her spirits more than she could say. The only thing that would make it all better was if Grace were there too. But Briley knew that they would have to rescue Grace and save Wendell if they could.

"You'll be able to meet a lot of special people here, Briley," Celeste said, perching on Briley's shoulder. "The Green Land is the last safe haven from the Peacock Queen. So come on, you stinky wart, and get your feet moving forward. Time is fleeting!"

Celeste zipped off at that and Briley went after her. She stepped off the deck of the ship onto a ramp that led to the Green Land. As her feet set foot upon the grass, she felt lighter. There was a bubbling energy to the Green Land. The earth almost trembled with magic. When her eyes hit upon the buildings and structures and people milling about, her heart quickened. So far this adventure had been a series of chases, escapes, and battles. But she could tell the Green Land was a place like no other. The ground and sky about her whispered that good things were to come.

Chapter Seven:
In Chains

Grace had gone in and out of consciousness more times than she could count. She had no idea how long she had been aboard the ship they now traveled in. The goblins had done something to the food they fed her, and it made the inside of her head feel like a bunch of wiggly worms. There were no cells aboard the ship, but the goblins had locked her inside one of the crew cabins and posted guards outside. From time to time a food bowl would be skittled into the room beneath the door, but ever since her first meal, Grace refused to eat. Wendell had not come to visit her. No one had come to save her. Grace hugged her knees to her chest, trying to figure out exactly how she had gotten herself into this mess. She counted the food bowls on the floor for the hundredth time that day, trying to get a sense of how much time had passed. There were eighteen bowls of food, but Grace had no idea how often they were sliding in the bowls. They seemed to come at random.

Then the door flew open and Wendell barged in, accompanied

by two of his goblin cronies. It happened so suddenly that Grace actually fell off her bed.

"Good morning, little treat!" Wendell howled with laughter as Grace tried to stand back up without looking foolish. "You've got a big day ahead of you!" he roared. Six or seven other goblins cluttered into the room behind Wendell.

Grace couldn't see any remnant of her brother. He was taller than the other goblins, but only just. He was also dressed better than the other goblins. The other goblins wore long black leather jackets, but beneath the jackets, most of the goblins had torn, stained, or ill-fitting clothes, often mismatched to the point of making Grace's eyes bug out of her head. It was as if the goblins took whatever clothes they saw first laying in a heap and threw them on in no particular order. But her brother was dressed in a well pressed grey tunic, with a sash of crimson across his chest. He had well-polished knee high boots, and Grace gulped as she saw that he had knives hidden in the sides of his boots. His pants were almost as black as his coat, and the buckle on the sword belt he wore was a miniature skull. Grace found herself wondering if the skull might be real. Possibly a fairy skull? Or a pixie? Upon Wendell's head, he had a broad hat with an upturned brim. Grace shuddered as she looked at Wendell's face.

"When did you lose your eye?" Grace asked, looking at the patch he had affixed across his face. There was another tiny skull sitting where Wendell's eye should have been.

"Ah. It's growing back," Wendell smirked at her. "I lost a bet." He laughed, putting his hands on his hips. "It's all fun and games until someone loses an eye!" He howled with laughter again. "Come on little girl, you've got a queen to meet. Chain her!"

Wendell and the other goblins chuckled together while two

of Wendell's cohorts clasped Grace into a pair of iron manacles. They each took an end of the chain and led her forward. It was the first time she had been out of this room in she didn't know how long. Grace noticed that the goblins holding her chains were both at least six inches shorter than Wendell, and they were less stocky than he was. She had never considered her brother tall or muscular, but compared to the other goblins, Wendell was massive. Was that why he was their chief? What did he call himself? Wiley Wun? What did that mean?

Apparently Grace was dawdling too much because the goblins pulled her forward, and then one came up behind her, jabbing her in the ribs with its sword. She stumbled forward, and then one of the goblins slapped a blindfold over her eyes.

"Keep her moving," she heard her brother say. "The queen is waiting!"

Grace lurched forward, trying to keep her balance without being able to see. From time to time, Wendell would call out for someone to make way. Grace could tell they had entered a city. There was commotion and hub bub all about. The air smelled cool and crisp, but no one commented on the goblins escorting a blindfolded girl through the crowd. Either nobody noticed, which was impossible, or nobody cared. That thought made her stomach do backflips. She couldn't help but think about how backward everything had gone ever since they started this adventure. It seemed like in a matter of hours, their lives had been twisted around and switched all backward. Granted, she and Wendell had fought at times, and sometimes they even said they hated each other. But it was as if Wendell was no more, and there was something else wicked inside of him. His skin was green and his eyes a sick shade of lemon yellow.

Suddenly they stopped walking and the goblins took her

blindfold off. Grace blinked away the light and saw they stood before a massive set of metal doors. Two guards with peacock colored shields opened the doors for them. "Make it quick!" the goblin to her left said, and jabbed her in the ribs. The gates opened into a grand castle filled with crystal furniture. Light spilled in all around, creating a cascade of colors she couldn't describe. Every inch of the castle seemed to be made of crystal, with the exception of the metal doors they had just passed through. Even the furniture, staircases, and floor were made of slightly colored crystals put together at eye bending joints.

A guard walked in front of them, leading them through a series of doors until they reached the main hall. At the far end of the hall, the Peacock Queen sat regally, her long dark midnight hair spilling all around her. People of all shapes and sizes were gathered at the edges of the hall, dressed in their finest, watching as Wendell led his group toward the throne.

When Wendell came to the steps leading up to the Peacock Queen's throne, he knelt down upon a knee and removed his hat, holding it to his heart. "My mistress," he said. "I bring an offering for thee."

The Peacock Queen's dress rustled as she rose and descended the steps. The luminescent fabric of her gown swirled about her, blending with the colors streaming through the crystal ceiling of the throne room. Grace trembled from head to foot as the Peacock Queen approached her and placed a hand upon her cheek. The queen's eyes were the purest blue Grace had ever seen. She could still not believe that her own brother had betrayed her this way, but there was nothing to be done for that.

"So pretty," the Peacock Queen said in a voice like crystal. "How old are you, child?" The queen stroked Grace's cheek with a lacquered fingernail, and Grace shuddered at her touch. Her

126

finger was so cold, it sucked the warmth from her skin. Grace tried to move away, but the goblins next to her held her still.

"Answer the question!" one of the goblins growled at her.

Grace took in a deep breath and looked around the hall. Several of the crocodile guards stood at the edge of the hall, and Grace wondered internally how many of the people gathered were here of their own free will, and how many had been forced to be witnesses.

"Thirteen years, my queen," Grace said.

The Peacock Queen stroked Grace's other cheek and stared deep into Grace's eyes. She dared not look away. She wasn't entirely sure why she was so highly prized, but she was not about to give the satisfaction of appearing meek. The queen strode round Grace. The onlookers had fallen into silence, watching.

"Yes. Thirteen. That sounds about right," the queen said, circling her. The goblins had all backed away as the queen examined Grace. Even Wendell had taken a step away to give her highness some room. Then the queen walked away from Grace, stepping back up to her throne. She turned and announced to everyone gathered, "Do you see this pathetic, dirty creature amongst you?" The queen's voice echoed off the walls of the chamber. "Why, she couldn't even escape from a handful of goblins," she cried out, laughing. "This is the human you have all been gossiping about. This…thing…is what you have all been fearing for so long!" The queen was laughing almost hysterically now. "I want you all to take a turn to take a good close look. Guards!" she called out. "Shackle her feet to the floor exactly where she stands!"

Two of the crocodile guards stepped forward, and fear flooded into Grace. She knew if she was going to do anything, anything at all, it would have to be right now. Once she was shackled, there would be no running, no fighting. Grace had no idea why the queen wanted her so badly, but she knew it couldn't be good. She was definitely not a warrior, but Grace was quick and agile, and she had survived a thousand adventures before. The chains at her wrists hung loosely, forgotten by the goblins. They were heavy, but maybe she could use that to her advantage. The crocodiles moved slowly, their big bodies not well suited to standing on their stocky hind legs. That would work for her as well. Grace looked around the throne room as the crocodiles advanced. When the guards were five feet away she took a deep breath, and then she moved.

She gripped one of the chains in her fist and lashed out with it like a whip at the goblin to her left. Grace caught him flat footed, and he toppled with the force of the chain. There was a gasp that escaped from the onlookers, and Grace rolled to the fallen goblin, taking his sword out of its sheath. All of the crocodiles were in motion now, but Grace wasn't about to fight them head on. One advanced toward her, and Grace skipped to the side as the crocodile swung a giant fist in her direction. When he missed, Grace gave the back of his kneecap a little kick and he fell down hard. To her disbelief, some in the gathered crowd applauded.

"Stop her!" the queen screamed out.

Grace ducked as another crocodile swung at her. Out of the corner of her eye she saw Wendell running for her as well. She had picked out her escape route, but it was at least a hundred yards to the doorway she had spotted. As Grace maneuvered around another crocodile, something wrapped itself around her ankles and Grace began to lose her balance. She swung out with her hand and was thankful her aim was true. The chain attached to her wrist flung outward, and wound around an ankle of one of the crocodile guards.

"Got you!" Wendell cried out triumphantly, and Grace chanced a look back. Her feet were wound in some kind of bolo, and Wendell was rushing forward with his sword drawn.

Grace took another deep breath, and then she pulled on the chain as hard as she could. She shot forward, sliding across the floor, wriggling her legs as she did so. The crocodile she had entangled just looked at her with a thoughtless expression as she rocketed through its legs. Grace used her other hand to change directions, passing between onlookers. One of the high ladies stood, tea cup in hand, with an enormous dress. When Grace went beneath the dress the high lady shrieked out, and that was the exact moment the chain on her wrist grew taut. She had no idea what was going on outside of the dress, but inside, Grace took a few moments to disentangle her legs. She withdrew the sword and pried the cuff off her wrist. The lady above her was dancing about and shrieking.

"Get it out! Get it out!" she cried.

Grace stifled a giggle as she dashed out the other side of the dress, rushing toward the door. When she reached the door, Grace looked back and saw the crocodiles had all created a pile atop the one she had toppled with her chain. She didn't see Wendell, but didn't dare stop to search for him.

Grace opened the door and hopped through like lightning. She slammed the door shut and threw the bolt into place. When Grace turned around, she saw she was in a tiny sitting room. The door behind her thumped with the force from someone on the other side, and Grace jumped away, watching as the bolt strained to keep out the giant crocodile guards. She had to think quickly. Grace fled for the only other door in the room, and found herself on a patio overlooking the mountains. She looked down and her breath caught. She was thousands of feet in the air! The bolt on the other door finally gave in, and three of the crocodile guards fell on top of each other. Grace chanced a look beyond the doorway and saw the throne room was filled with guards. Her eyes briefly met those of the Peacock Queen, who now sat regally upon her throne. If looks could murder, Grace would have died on the spot.

Grace threw first one leg over the edge of the rail, and then the other, contemplating her choices, and found she didn't have any choice at all. The only way to go was down. Grace had climbed before, but never at this height, and certainly never after going for so long without eating. Nonetheless, Grace edged downward, foothold by foothold. She used the chain about her wrist to her advantage, wrapping it around jutting stones to support her weight. Above her the crocodiles growled, filling the little patio, and Grace heard a creaking sound from the rocks above. As quickly as she could Grace edged to the side, handhold by handhold. Her hands were sweaty and her muscles felt weak, but Grace didn't dare give in. Then there was a loud CRACK, and Grace watched as one of the rocks supporting the patio gave way. Then another support broke, and another. The crocodiles were either too dumb or too slow to react, and the patio gave way, skidding down the mountainside like a giant sled with the crocodiles all growling and jostling atop it. One of the crocodiles swung an axe at her as he plummeted past. The blade came close enough for Grace to feel the wind of its passing, and she took a deep breath.

She looked around and saw another similar patio jutting out from the mountain not too far below her. Grace made her way for it, using the chain to support her weight and trying to take small careful steps. One or two more crocodiles fell from the doorway above her. Apparently they didn't realize the patio had become a roller coaster, and they had missed the ride. When Grace was directly above the patio, she climbed downward until she was about ten feet above it and let herself drop.

Grace landed and readied herself for the worst. She turned the handle on the door leading back into the castle and peeked inside. Thankfully the room was empty, and Grace edged inside. The room was large, with a four poster bed and a giant table with maps spread all over it. Curious, Grace made her way to the table, examining the maps. Whoever lived here was searching for something. There were tiny scribbles in a language Grace couldn't read all over the maps. The room had another, smaller table, with a sandwich on a plate sitting next to a pitcher of lemonade. Grace stifled a shriek when she saw an aged man sitting in a chair before the smaller table. She put a hand to her own mouth as she realized the old gentleman was snoozing away. Her stomach rumbled, and Grace moved almost without thinking toward the sandwich. She was so hungry she didn't know how to think about anything other than the food that was so close. Grace tiptoed over to the plate. She couldn't believe her own daring. She kept an eye on the snoozing man the entire time. He had a long graying beard, which fell down his chest like a waterfall. When she was close enough, she reached out and took the sandwich and began eating. It was possibly the tastiest sandwich she had ever had, with crisp tomato, roast beef, and cheddar cheese, smothered in some delicious tangy sauce that made her taste buds dance.

Grace contemplated the sleeping man as she ate. He was dressed rather haphazardly, with a checkered vest over a blue shirt that was buttoned the wrong way. He did wear a small dagger at his belt, but the man was so skinny, she figured it was probably for whittling wood and not for stabbing people. Grace polished off the sandwich, feeling much better, and thankful that the man didn't wake up. Did she dare to pour herself a glass of lemonade? Her hand was halfway to the pitcher when the door thumped open and Grace's heart leapt.

"Grandpa!" a young man shouted. "Grandpa! I think I found it!" Then his eyes fell on Grace and he rounded on her. "Who are you?!" he demanded. "And what have you done to my grandfather?" He had dark red hair, the color of a burning coal, and bright blue eyes.

"I didn't do anything," Grace said defensively.

The old man startled awake with all of the racket, and Grace backed away from the table as the young man rushed to him.

"Grandfather, are you OK?" the young man asked, steadying his grandfather as he rose.

"Oh yes, just fine," the old man said with a voice like sandpaper. "Who is this lovely young lady?" he asked. "Did you get yourself a girlfriend while I slept, Jaspar?"

"What, girlfriend? Ick! No! She was about to murder you, Grandfather!" Jaspar stuttered out.

"I was not!" Grace called out. "I was only eating his sandwich!" Grace clapped a hand over her mouth. She hadn't meant to blurt that out.

"Oho!" the old man chuckled. "Why, we have a sandwich thief in our midst, Jaspar! Should we cut off her hands?"

"What?" Grace cried out, pulling her hands to her chest. She noticed Jaspar was carrying a sword at his waist, and she gulped. "You wouldn't really cut off my hands, would you?"

Jaspar shared a look with his grandfather and rested a hand on the hilt of his sword. Grace noticed it was one of the long ones they called a rapier. "We need to figure out something to do with her, Grandfather. We can't have her running to the Peacock Queen and turning us in!"

"Oh well, that's not a problem," Grace said. "I just escaped from her guards. There is no way I'm going anywhere near that creepy old bird."

"Creepy!" the old man started chuckling. "Old...." He was doubled over, his face turning bright red. Grace noticed Jaspar was struggling to contain the laughter inside too. "Bird!" The man was rolling on the floor holding his middle, and Jaspar chuckled as well, locking eyes with her.

"What Grandfather means is that you can stay with us temporarily," Jaspar said.

"Oh, good!" Grace said, but Jaspar hadn't finished speaking. He held up a finger and Grace got very quiet.

"So long as you take a bath." Jaspar cracked a grin and Grace looked down at herself. She hadn't been allowed to change clothes since the day of her capture. Then she had gone climbing all over the outside of a stone castle, and she probably smelled worse than a wild dog. She blushed, nodding her head.

"You got yourself a deal, Jaspar," she said. "My name is Grace." Grace extended a hand outward and Jaspar shook it firmly. The old man had regained his composure enough to stand and smile at her.

"Well Grace, I was the advisor to the queen before this crazy old bird took over. I'm afraid I'm a bit useless now, but you can call me Horace."

Grace grinned. They all tried to talk at once.

"You can borrow some of my clothes after your bath, Grace," Jaspar said enthusiastically. Now that they knew they were all on the same side, he seemed much friendlier toward her.

"Thank you," Grace said. "By the way, what did you find?"

"Oh!" Jaspar smacked his forehead. "Grandfather! I found the secret passage you were talking about! It was just as you described. Obviously the queen doesn't know about it, or they would have destroyed it."

"Secret passage?" Grace asked, "Where does it lead?"

Horace chuckled and clucked at his grandson. "Now don't go spilling all of my secrets to your girlfriend!" Jaspar and Grace both blushed at that, but Horace continued on. "You go get cleaned up, young lady. I'm going to put together another meal, and then we are going to all go on a little adventure."

Grace felt for the first time since she had arrived in fairy land that she had finally found a like minded group. It was almost like family the way they teased and prodded each other. As Grace soaked in the tub, Jaspar and his grandfather made more sandwiches. She couldn't remember the last time she had a decent bath, and Grace took full advantage of the steaming hot water. She couldn't believe her luck at finding Jaspar and his grandfather, Horace. It seemed to her not very many people liked the Peacock Queen. "Someone needs to stop her," she stated aloud.

Chapter Eight:
Top and Bottom

Briley and Harrison walked between the buildings of The Green Land. "I still can't believe they built all of this atop a mountain," Briley said cheerily. "It's like magic!"

"I don't think it's *like* magic, Sis," Harrison countered. "I'm pretty sure this *is* magic!"

The buildings were plopped at haphazard places amongst the lush green grass that bloomed everywhere. Flower petals hovered midair, and as they walked, Briley would brush them aside. If she blew on one it would travel through the air until it landed on someone else's face or clothes. There were hundreds of little shops selling the most bizarre items. They passed by a two story building that leaned dangerously as if it were about to topple, and Briley pointed it out.

"Do you want a dashing cap for your new fox fur, Brother?" she said with a haughty accent.

Harrison laughed, looking at the hat shop. They both watched as someone else approached the shop and called up to the window. "A blue derby if you'd be so kind!" Briley only then noticed that although the building was dangerously slanted, the windows were all lined up with the ground as if the building had been done cockeyed on purpose. One of the windows opened and a green skinned chap popped out of the window and looked down. "Dy'a want a feather in it? Buttons? A sash? Perhaps a nice pin to adorn your new chapeau?"

"No, no," the person below called back up. "Just a regular blue derby will do."

Briley pointed and laughed as the green skinned man popped away for a few moments, and then a hat was flung out the window, floating through the air and landing perfectly on the patron's head.

"Pay the wife below, would ya?" the green skinned man called out.

Then Briley watched as the customer went to the door at the base of the building and handed over a few silver coins to a lady. "Shoes today, governor?" the lady asked, counting the coins. The customer just shook his head and walked off.

Harrison chuckled, pointing to the signs on the buildings. "Look!" he said. "Tippy's Tops and Betty's Bottoms!" He was laughing so hard Briley got swept up in the laughter as well. "What do you do if you need something for the middle parts?" Harrison held his stomach. "Look for one that's hovering?" They both snorted and laughed at that, and passed by the top and bottom shop.

Briley flit her hand through some flower petals that were clustered in front of her as they walked on. Everything seemed to be constantly growing. As they walked, the grass would reshape itself after they had passed, and flowers would bloom instantly with vibrant colors.

"This is amazing!" Harrison said.

Briley nodded her head, wondering if this had been what all of fairy land had once been like.

A small blue turtle wearing a bright green fedora crossed in front of them.

"Excuse me, sir," Briley said. "But do you know Argon?" She was anxious to talk with him.

The turtle stopped and took its time turning to them. "Is this a riddle?" the turtle croaked. "I absolutely love riddles!"

"No," Briley chuckled. "Argon is a friend of mine. I've been looking for him."

"Oh." The turtle sounded disappointed "Well, I don't know anyone named Argon. I met a girl named Aura once though. Very pretty, that one. She had a lovely shell."

"We need to be careful, Harrison," Briley whispered.

"Why?" he whispered back.

"I think someone cut the line that caught Darrel on purpose. One of the Horgles is working for the Peacock Queen."

"Wait."

Harrison stopped Briley midstride and held her shoulders firmly in his hands. Briley looked into his amber fox eyes, then at the hands that were holding her in place. They had once been human hands, but now they were covered in fur, equally suited to running like an animal, and yet he could still use them like human hands to hold and manipulate objects. He stared deep into her eyes, and Briley felt herself growing uncomfortable.

"I thought something was strange about what happened on the ship," he finally continued. "But now it makes more sense."

"What does?" Briley asked. She had rarely seen her brother more serious.

"When Darrel was giving the command to join up with the

docks," Harrison whispered in a voice so low she had to lean close to him to hear. "Everyone was working so hard to get the ship in line. At the time I didn't think anything of it, but now it makes so much more sense!"

"What does?" Briley strained her ears. She wished her brother would just spit it out.

"One of the crew," Harrison said. "He has a peacock feather pinned in his hat. When we were docking, I saw it glowing." Harrison was whispering in a hurried rush. "I think the Peacock Queen used it somehow to sabotage the ship."

"Wait!" Briley slapped a hand to her mouth. "If that's true, if she can see through that peacock quill, then she knows where the Green Land is!" Briley gulped. "What do we do?"

Out of the corner of her eye Briley saw some of the Horgles approaching, and Briley noted with dread that one of them had a peacock quill stuck jauntily in the corner of his cap.

"Well," Harrison said. "Something like this, I guess."

"Like wh—?" Briley started to ask, but then her brother had darted away with a crazy look in his amber fox eyes. She gasped as Harrison drew a slim sword and charged at the Horgles. The approaching group was all taken aback as well. There were six Horgles in all, and each of them took half a step back as Harrison bounded toward them, his fox tail bristling in the wind. As Harrison ran forward, flower petals swirled in circles as he passed through them. The next second, the Horgles had all drawn their swords as well and stood defensively.

Harrison weaved between them, and Briley gasped as one of the Horgle's swords whistled through the air where her brother had been standing just a moment ago. She marveled at his quickness, and so did the group of Horgles. Harrison spun between them, confusing the larger creatures until they were well out of formation. Then all of a sudden, it was as if Harrison had ceased to exist. Everyone, including Briley, was looking around for him, and it wasn't until one of the Horgles spun around in a circle that Briley saw her brother perched upon the Horgle's back. Then Harrison pounced toward the Horgle with the peacock quill, who never saw it coming. In one fell swoop, Harrison slashed his sword in the air at the Horgle.

Harrison landed upon his shoulders, grabbed his hat, and then leapt far from the group of Horgles, who all began chasing him. As they ran, chasing Harrison, the other Horgle began to shrink in size and turn to an ugly shade of green. His ears elongated, and his arms and legs changed shape. Harrison ran, hurdling over the turtle they had been talking to earlier.

"GOOBBLIIINN!" the turtle screamed.

Before Briley could blink everyone in the Green Land turned toward the goblin, and a ruckus like no other ensued. The Horgles all stopped mid-stride, grabbing the goblin next to them while Harrison disappeared into the Tops and Bottoms store. The goblin was soon being held fast by the Horgles, but suddenly other goblins started appearing from doorways with weapons drawn. Briley shrieked as one popped out of the ground next to her, waving its wicked sword through the air. Upon its head was a hat that looked exactly like a piece of the ground, complete with a couple of flowers sprouting out the top, and its sword was serrated, jagged, and rusty. The poor turtle could not move fast enough to get out of the way of the rushing goblins, and before Briley knew it, they were surrounded on all sides by goblins bearing weapons, each one uglier than the next. If there was ever a time she wished her brother was standing next to her, now was the time. Why had he gone into the shop anyway? And where was Argon? And would Darrel be alright? A thousand thoughts sizzled on her brain like bits of bacon.

Briley took in a deep breath and pulled out her dragon glove from her pocket, silently placing it upon her hand. She didn't have any weapons or any of her vials of medicine with her, but it was a lot better than finding a corner to cry in, which was about the only other thought that she had at the moment. Few of the Horgles were carrying weapons aside from small daggers, which were meant mainly for cutting ropes. The goblins formed a ring about them, snarling and growling, and they kept popping out of the strangest places. Some stepped from in front of buildings wearing clothes that matched the building exactly. "They must have been planning this a while," Briley said aloud to the Horgles next to her. She was relieved to see the one next to her was Dragus.

"Aye," Dragus agreed. "Foul faced good for nothings can't be trusted, not ever." Then he spat to finish the sentiment, and Briley grinned despite herself.

"What are they waiting for, an invitation?" Briley wondered aloud.

"Goblins are cowards, lass," Dragus said. "They're waiting for all their number to show up.

"Well...," Briley said. "Are we going to just let them accumulate?"

"Not sure what you have in mind, lass, but I like your vigor. What do you suggest?" he asked her.

"Catch them off guard," Briley said. "Stay in our group and attack. Get some goblin swords." The more she talked, the braver she felt. "Get Darrel out of the building and aboard the best air ship here. Get as many people aboard the ship as possible."

"And take the Green Land with us!" Dragus finished her thought for her. She looked to him and saw a wide grin spreading across his face. The other Horgles had all been listening, and were all nodding now. Briley didn't like the idea of fighting any creatures head on, but the more she dealt with goblins, the fewer options there seemed to be. The Horgles all gathered tightly together, as if waiting for the command.

Then there was a high pitched cry, and Briley watched as Harrison landed next to one of the goblins, seemingly sprouting from midair. "Yeeeehaaaa!" Harrison cried out, darting and slashing with his small swords. That was all the command any of them needed. Soon their small group was thrust into action, and Briley cried out as well as they all moved as one to where Harrison had landed. Harrison used his tail to trip one goblin, then spun low between the sword swings of two others, and Briley ran to him. She caught a sword in her dragon glove and plucked it from the goblin's grip. She handed the sword to Dragus, who grinned as he turned the blade around.

"That'll do, lass!" he cried. "That'll do just fine!"

Dragus became the center of their circle, and they moved together through the goblins, step by step. Briley dodged blows, blocked attacks, and tried to disarm the goblins. Harrison was their whip. He stood among them, defending, and then he would lash out at the surrounding goblins like the teeth of a tiger. All around people cried out, not believing that goblins could have found their secret hideout.

Soon their small group was closing in on the building where Darrel was, and Briley took the opportunity to leap into the building. The second she was through the door, Briley called out. "Darrel! Darrel, where are you?"

There were cots set up all inside the building, with people being attended to by little flitting fairies in white. One of the white outfitted fairies flew right up to Briley, and hovered in front of her with her little hands on her hips.

"Visiting hours don't begin until sundown, miss. I'm afraid you will have to leave."

Briley didn't have time to explain. She charged past the faerie nurse, calling out Darrel's name.

"Well I never!" the tiny fairy called after her. "Young lady, you need to learn your—"

Briley rounded on her, stopping the fairy's speech mid-sentence. "Look. The goblins are attacking outside, and I need to get Darrel the Brave onto a ship and we need to get out of here. You're all in danger here! The Peacock Queen knows where we are!" Briley wanted to say more, but just then the door to the building banged open and three goblins poured in, each swinging a nastier sword than the one next to it.

"Oh my!" was all the little fairy could get out before she fainted. Briley had never seen a fairy faint before and wasn't sure what to do, so she stuck out her hand. As the little fairy fell into it, Briley stuffed the fairy into her pocket and continued looking for Darrel. Harrison and one of the Horgles had followed the goblins into the hospital hut and were keeping them occupied.

Briley cast her eyes around and finally saw a large cot in the back of the room. Sitting beside the cot were the unmistakably pristinely shined boots that belonged to Darrel. She ran over and pulled the sheet off him and grabbed his shoulders. "Wake up!" Briley cried out.

Darrel was covered in bandages on his arms and legs. She wasn't sure how they were going to get him out of there if he couldn't move on his own.

"Wake up!" Briley called again, and finally Darrel's eyes opened, meeting hers, and he smiled so wide it melted all of her fears away.

"Briley, my girl," Darrel said hoarsely. "I met your Argon in a dream. He said he would wait for you to come to him another time."

"Darrel, can you move?" Briley asked him. She put her head to his chest and bit back a sob as Darrel shook his head side to side.

"No," Darrel said. "Not very much, anyway. What's going on?"

There wasn't any time to explain. The hospital was quickly becoming flooded with more and more goblins. Harrison and the Horgle he was with were doing their best to keep them occupied, but it wouldn't be long before they were overwhelmed. She couldn't let that happen.

"Darrel," she breathed "We need a way out of here. We need to get you aboard a ship and flee the Green Land. It isn't safe."

Darrel cast his eyes about the room, nodding. "Reach into my boot. The left one."

Briley reached into his boot and pulled out a small bottle filled with a pink liquid. "What do I do with it?" Briley asked.

Darrel smiled again. "For now just hold it tight and help me get my boots on. Whatever you do, don't uncork it until I give you the word."

Briley nodded, helping him sit up and helping him get his boots on. She buckled his sword belt around his waist and buttoned his shirt. He was at least starting to look like Darrel the Brave ought to, but it was plain he did not have much strength. She stood with him and turned to see the battle still going on around them. Two goblins turned toward them and charged, swords raised. Briley raised her gloved hand, ready to defend Darrel, but there was no need. Just as the goblins were closing in on her and Darrel, the fairy nurses whizzed through the air. There were many THWACKS as the goblins were struck in the sides of their heads, one by a frying pan, the other with the leg from a table. The goblins tumbled to the floor, and Briley laughed as she watched the fairy nurses whizzing through the air with makeshift weapons, dropping flower pots and bricks onto the goblins.

"Good shot!" Briley called out as one of the nurses flung a spoonful of hot soup into a goblin's eyes.

"How could this have happened?" Darrel asked, "The Green Land has been our haven for as long as I can remember."

"Somehow a goblin got into your crew." Briley blurted out "It probably happened when Wendell got us with that dragon ash."

"Why, that no good daughter of a feral mongoose!" Darrel clenched his fists.

"Curse her later, Captain! We have to get out of here!" Briley urged.

Darrell nodded and they walked forward into the fray. Briley mainly just guided Darrel as they moved closer and closer to the door. She looked for Harrison, but didn't see him inside the hospital. She hoped he was all right. Without the help of the nurses, she didn't think they would have ever escaped, but they managed to get out of the hospital, right into the group of Horgles outside the door. In the midst of them was Harrison. The Horgles cheered as Briley joined them, and Harrison smiled at her. Briley smiled right back. It was then that she noticed Harrison was sporting a bright red hat with a wide brim. He was also wearing fine boots, crimson in color, with little holes for the tips of his fox claws to stick out.

"Did you go shopping while we were dealing with the goblin mess?" Briley scolded.

"It was more like I was forced into shopping," Harrison

chuckled "Tippy and Betty pretty much assaulted me with finery in their shop!"

"I must say it suits you," Briley chuckled, half angry, but mostly impressed.

"OK," Darrel interrupted. "Good a time as any. Open the bottle, Briley, and spill the liquid onto the ground!"

Briley nodded, uncorking the bottle and tipping it upside down, but the liquid didn't spill out of the bottle. "Nothing's happening!" she called out.

Just then their little group was rushed by a group of goblins. Darrel was in no condition to fend them off, so everyone clustered around him. Briley stuck the bottle in her pocket, realizing as she did so the fairy nurse was still in her pocket as well. Arrows zipped through the air, striking the hut behind her, and Briley gasped as she watched an air ship loaded with goblin archers and reinforcements hovering above the Green Land in the distance. She didn't even know where most of the Horgle crew was.

"What are we going to do, Darrel?" Briley asked the exhausted captain.

More arrows streaked past her. Briley saw Harrison weaving between an advancing group of goblins. The air ship was close enough to the ground now that goblins were hopping over the side of the rail, landing upon the earth, grinning wickedly. She felt the fairy stirring in her pocket, and remembered how Celeste had helped her in the sword fight with Wendell. More than anything she wanted Argon to come to her just then and wave his hands and transform all of what she was seeing into something else, but she knew he had used most of his strength coming to her. He was here, somewhere, but his power had faded.

She reached into her pocket again, pulling out the bottle of pink liquid and the fairy nurse. Despite everything going on around her, Briley knelt in the lush grass with her hands open. In the palm of one hand the fairy nurse was just rousing. In her other was the pink bottle. Briley closed her eyes, thinking about all of the adventures they had been on. She did not want it to end here on the Green Land, surrounded by goblins. A feeling settled over Briley, a calm, a moment of perfect understanding. The magic in the bottle wasn't broken. It just needed a little bit of a jolt. She rose and slammed the bottle to the ground as hard as she could.

"Wake up!" she cried. Suddenly Briley wasn't talking to the magic in the bottle anymore. She was yelling at the people in fairy land who had been serving the Peacock Queen for so long. "Wake up!" she shouted. She was shouting for Darrel to wake up and be his brave old self again. "Wake up! Wake up! Wake up!" She was yelling at the world around her, the goblins for being so blind, the Peacock Queen for being so power hungry. "Wake up!" Most of all she wanted Argon to wake up and come to her. She felt safe when he was near. "Wake up!" she screamed as loud as she could. If she was dreaming, she wanted to wake up now before it was too late.

The pink stuff in the bottle must have heard her cry. Or perhaps it did just need a jolt, for it began to bubble and hiss upon the ground, spreading across the Green Land. A circle of pink goo covered the ground, and Darrel grinned at her as she looked to him with wide eyes.

"Hold onto something," Darrel chuckled. "I've never actually done this before."

"Done what?" Briley called out.

"Well, you just opened up my ship in a bottle." Darrel laughed aloud, grabbing the shoulders of the Horgle next to him. "I half expected it to be a dud. It's been sitting at the bottom of my boot for close on ten seasons now. I imagine it won't smell very fine!"

"Ship in a...." Briley watched, dumbfounded, as the pink ooze intermingled with the Green Land, creating a mast and a deck, all in the vibrant colors of the lush green grass and the bright pink of the liquid in the bottle. The hull formed out of the ground, including parts of the buildings around in its structure. Ropes formed out of the lush green grass. The Horgles pushed the goblins off the forming ship as it lifted into the air.

All around them creatures cheered as they clambered for the ship. Briley's jaw hung open as the buildings and ground around them swelled. Although Darrel was wounded and winded, he still held fast to the rails of the ship, delivering commands. "Mind your flanks, lads!" he called out. "Crop up your lines, Jonas!" The Horgles all hummed as the ship rose further and further into the air. They were coming even with the goblin vessel that had been firing arrows upon them. "Knives out!" Darrel's voice boomed across the ship, and the Horgles each drew knives from their boots or behind their sashes. "On my mark!" There was a tense moment when the ships lined up perfectly. If the goblins hadn't been so stunned by the ship forming out of the ground, Briley wondered if the outcome might have been different. Luckily though, the goblins aboard the other ship were just watching with open mouths. Many of them had dropped their bows from utter disbelief.

"Loose!" Darrel called out, and the Horgles launched their knives into the air, not at the other goblins, but at the balloon above it which was keeping the boat aloft. There was a sad sighing sound like putty getting squished as the goblin balloon deflated. Briley launched herself to the rail, watching as the goblin ship fell onto the earth of the Green Land, and she smiled. They were officially flying aboard either the ugliest or most beautiful boat she had ever seen. She couldn't decide which. Darrel wasn't finished giving out commands. "All right, lads and ladies!" he shouted above the roar of the wind. "Time to shape up our fleet! The Green Land is lost, but the day is won!"

The pink and green ship maneuvered between the different boats tethered to the docks of the Green Land, and they took the time to fasten the boats in a long chain. Darrel had rope ladders lowered to the ground so that the inhabitants of the Green Land could climb upward. It took a lot less time than Briley would have imagined maneuvering the ship around, but from what Briley could see, the goblin threat had ended. The goblins all huddled in the center of the clearing, trying to free their comrades from the broken ship. Much quicker than she could have thought possible, their pink and green ship was laboring through the sky with a literal army for a crew, and seven other ships all tethered behind it. The creatures and Horgles were swinging from ropes from ship to ship, making sure everything ran smoothly, and as the sun fell out of the sky, their ship crested through the clouds and Briley gasped at the billions upon trillions of stars shining over fairy land. Both fairy moons were full and shining. She turned to Harrison, who grinned at her wickedly.

"Let's do that again!" Harrison called out "Only next time without the attacking goblins and Darrel being hurt!" He launched onto the rail of the ship, holding out his hands to the side, and let out a yelp. Briley couldn't help but laugh. She hopped up onto the rail next to him and held his outstretched hand.

"Harrison, you're crazy!" she cried out, watching as the stars rushed by her. The wind whipped through her hair. "I'm never doing that again! I never wanted to do it the first time around!"

"Aww, come on, Sis!" he laughed "This is your adventure after all. You might as well enjoy it!"

Briley laughed at his words, but then she turned to him in all seriousness.

"Harrison, I think this stopped being my adventure a long time ago." She gulped. "I wish I could have at least spoken to Argon before we left the Green Land."

"You know what I think Argon would tell you right this second if he could?" her brother asked her.

Briley turned to him with her eyebrows raised. "What?"

"I think he'd tell you to relax a little bit, Sis, and enjoy the wonders around us." Harrison laughed aloud. "I mean, look at us...I'm half fox! Wendell's mostly goblin! We're sailing through the stars on a bright pink ship!"

Briley tried to smile, but her insides were twisted up like shoelaces. She looked behind her at the string of ships bobbing along atop the clouds. Maybe her brother had a point. Maybe she did need to relax more. She just wished she knew how to rescue Grace and Wendell, and turn her brother back into a human. All of those problems seemed so big by themselves. She found herself wishing she were small, like the fairy inside her pocket. Most of the time, Briley wished she was bigger, because being bigger usually meant you had more freedom, or more allowance, or both. But right then she would have traded a thousand allowances to be small and tiny like the fairy. There were a hundred billion stars out and Briley wished on them all, but try as she might, she didn't turn into a fairy. Instead, she held Harrison's hand, watching the stars dance by, twinkling wonders, each a little prettier than the next.

Chapter Nine:
Born to be Wild

"Sit still!" Horace groaned.

Grace cringed each time she heard the wisp of the scissors. He had a bowl placed atop her head, and was holding it down with the force of a giant.

"Is this really necessary?" Grace asked as the scissors came at her again. All around her, her golden hair fell. She had borrowed some clothes from Jaspar. A finely woven green tunic, grey pants, and a pair of gloves.

"Only if you don't want to get caught by the queen's guards." Horace growled as Grace wiggled in the chair. Jaspar stood in the corner of the room holding a hand over his mouth.

"It's not funny!" Grace demanded, glaring at Jaspar. But that only caused him to laugh harder. The scissors kept going wisp wisp all about her, and Grace was scared to death Horace was going to cut off an ear. Finally, the pressure on her head eased up and the bowl was removed.

"There!" Horace cried out. "All finished! She will never

recognize you now! Go take a look."

Grace vaulted from the chair and stood in front of the mirror. She looked nothing like her old self. "I don't even look like a girl anymore!" Grace cried out.

"Exactly!" Horace agreed. "Now onto the food, and then for the adventure, young lady.... Er, young sir!"

Jaspar rushed to the table and pulled out a chair. "Please be our guest, young master!" Jaspar joked, and Grace couldn't help but laugh. She guessed in the grand scheme of things, a little bit of hair wasn't going to be the end of her. Horace busied himself at a side table preparing a platter of breads, meats, and cheeses, while Jaspar filled the glasses with a purple liquid he poured from an earthen jug.

"Small sips, mind," Jaspar said as Grace reached for it. "A little goes a long way."

"What is it?" Grace asked, taking a tiny sip from her cup. The instant she tasted it, Grace sighed. "Ohh, that's good!"

Then Horace placed the platter on the table. It was piled high with the makings for sandwiches. "Dig in!" Horace said, and immediately he began to build his own sandwich. Grace only hesitated a second longer than Jaspar before piling fresh meat, cheeses, and vegetables together. Grace hadn't felt this hungry in ages. Horace and Jaspar ate at a leisurely pace, while Grace tried not to eat everything in sight. She was so focused on the food in front of her that it didn't dawn on her for some time that Jaspar and Horace were deep in conversation.

"...and so we should time it between the patrol changes," Horace was saying. "That will give us the most time before we are noticed missing."

"Are all the preparations in order? Is there anything else we might need?" Jaspar asked. He glanced down at a little notepad he had pulled out.

"Oh, for fairy's sake, Jaspar, you can't plan for everything," Horace chuckled. "I think the arrival of your young girlfriend here is a sign the time is right. We've been planning for so long. Now that we know where the entrance to the passage is, let's seize the moment!"

Jaspar blushed and glanced sideways at Grace. As she met his eyes, Grace was suddenly very aware that her mouth was full of food. She tried to smile, but as her lips moved, little bits of bread started falling out of her mouth, and Grace brought her hand up to her mouth. Jaspar busted out laughing, filling the room with his rich mirth, and Grace blushed as she tried to chew without meeting anyone in the eyes. Finally, with an effort, she swallowed and dared to ask her question.

"Just what is this adventure you two are planning?"

"Why, a heist, of course!" Horace chortled.

"Grandfather!" Jaspar shouted.

"Well, it's the truth." Horace smiled at Grace's reaction. "No reason to be coy about it."

"What he means to say...," Jaspar looked Grace in the eyes, "is that we are liberating certain objects of value from the queen's treasure room."

"Exactly!" Horace said. "A heist!"

"What are you going to steal?" Grace asked. Her heart beat faster by the minute.

"Well, basically—" Jaspar began

"Whatever is in there!" Horace finished.

"You mean you don't know what her treasure room contains?" Grace asked.

Jaspar shook his head. "No. We've been tucked away in this corner of the palace, and any contact beyond our set boundaries is strictly forbidden."

"Oh Jaspar!" Horace stood as he spoke. "Stop talking like a nincompoop and say what you fairy well mean, for fairy's sake!" He looked Grace straight in the eye and stated in a quiet, serious tone, "We're prisoners here, lass, plain and simple."

Grace nodded. If this was the queen's version of a prison, she would have traded places with them any day. It was much, much better than being held in the goblin brig, being served poisoned meals without any changes of clothing.

"Political refugees," Jaspar interrupted her thoughts. "The queen thinks she still might have a few uses for us, so she keeps us here in comfort."

"Ahh," Grace said. "So you're more like presents she hasn't opened up yet."

Horace chuckled. "Oho, Jaspar, I like her. You've got good taste! When is the wedding?"

"Grandfather!" Jaspar jumped to his feet then. "Stop embarrassing us!"

"Nope!" Horace said simply. "Not today. Try again tomorrow, or maybe the day after yesterday."

Grace chuckled as Jaspar growled in frustration. They spent the next couple of hours packing backpacks and waiting for the switch of the guards. Jaspar even handed Grace a sword belt with a frog attached to hold a rapier. "I've only managed to snatch one sword," Jaspar said. "But maybe we'll find another along the way."

"All right," Grace said.

They heard the sound of heavy boots passing the door, and Grace ducked behind a tall freestanding mirror. The door opened briefly as one of the Peacock Queen's guards stuck his head in, but he didn't really look. Perhaps if he had, he might have noticed the sword at Jaspar's hip, or the old man coiling rope and putting it into a pack. If the guard took his job even just a little more seriously, he most likely would have noticed the map of the passages that lay sprawled out on the table, with little notations all over it. But luckily for Horace, Jaspar, and especially Grace, the guard wasn't really thinking about the likelihood of any of the prisoners actually doing anything. He was more worried about getting his job over with as fast as possible.

When the door closed, the three of them all glanced warily at each other until Horace let out a laugh like a river. "Hah!" he said. "And all this time we've been worried about secrecy. Probably could have gotten him to help us if we had asked politely enough."

Grace and Jaspar both laughed, and in less than an hour, the three of them were walking down the hallway. "Well." Grace said. "Here goes nothing."

"Oh no." Jaspar stopped her suddenly, turning and holding her by her shoulders and looking her fiercely in the eyes. "Here goes something very, very extraordinary."

The light filtered through the crystal of the palace, creating color schemes all throughout the hallway. It was strange, Grace thought, that light could get through and yet the walls were too thick to see through. Suddenly Horace stopped, and Jaspar and Grace almost bumped into him. Horace knocked three times in quick succession on one of the doors, which immediately opened. Two younger men hopped out of the door.

"Is it time, Horace?" the taller one asked.

Horace nodded, and without another word he kept on walking.

The two men who had popped out of the door walked behind Jaspar and Grace, who kept looking back at them questioningly.

"I'm Hamper," the taller one whispered.

"And you can call me Trick." The shorter one winked at her. Before long, Hamper and Trick were joined by several others in a growing assortment of creatures, all led by Horace. "If any guards happened by just now —," a blonde centaur woman said.

"Then, there would be an awful lot of explaining to do," Trick finished for her.

"Luckily," Jaspar whispered to them all, "Horace and I have watched the guards, and we know their schedule like the tops of our shoes."

"Exactly!" Trick said. "Otherwise we would never have agreed to your devilish plan."

"Oh, get off it," Hamper chided. "You would have been all in regardless. The queen needs to be taken down a peg."

"She needs to be fed to the sewer rats," a short round man with tiny horns puckering out of his forehead said.

"And then drawn...," the centaur woman said, "and quartered."

Finally Grace asked the question which had been exploding in her brain for a very long time. "How did she get to be so powerful? I mean, why did you let her have control if all of you hate her so much?"

But there was no time for anyone to answer. "Guards!" Horace cried over their heads. "Coming this way!"

Everyone froze and Grace looked to Jaspar, looking for some sign of what to do. Jaspar was hiding behind one of the stone pillars which ran from floor to ceiling. It seemed like everyone except for Grace and Horace had managed to find one hiding spot or another. Then Grace felt strong hands about her waist. She would have screamed, except Trick also put a hand over her mouth. She was lifted up in the air, and Trick rubbed his hand along the ceiling, creating a milky white substance on the crystal. Then he placed Grace against it. "Shhhh." Trick held a finger up to his lips, which Grace only then noticed were an odd shade of blue. "None of them ever bother to look up...or down, for that matter. Or sideways, or backward, or diagonally—"

"Trick, be quiet!" Hamper said.

Grace looked over and saw that Hamper was also held to the ceiling by the sticky white substance. Horace stood in the middle of the hallway, leaning on his cane. Four of the queen's guards came up to him, holding their Peacock Sheilds.

"Halt!" Horace cried out. "I demand to know what you are doing here!" Horace chuckled, and the guards all looked at each other before one of them stepped forward.

"Come along, old man. Back to your chamber," the guard said.

"Alas. That won't be happening today," Horace said. "You're under attack."

"What?" the guard said.

"I said." Horace chuckled "You are under attack!"

Hamper and Trick both dropped down, wrapping the guards quickly in their white web like material. The centaur woman kicked another guard in the chest with her hind legs, and he went crashing into a wall. An old lady with antlers growing out of her shoulders backhanded one of the guards, and in a matter of seconds, the four guards had been defeated.

"Grab their shields!" Horace said. "Quickly!"

Grace felt her jaw drop open, for when the others took the guards' shields, they transformed from tall, overbearing guards into quite normal looking fairy folk. "They're fakes!" she cried.

"Not fakes," Horace said, taking one of the guards by the legs. "Just enchanted. Now help us move them out of the hallway before any more guards come looking for them."

Hamper and Trick each took an unconscious guard and opened up the closest door. Grace watched up and down the hallways as everyone helped haul the guards into the empty room, and very soon they were continuing onward. Horace led them, muttering to himself, twisting and turning the map in different directions. Grace lost count of the number of turns they had gone down, until finally they came to a wide hall filled with statues.

"Is this the treasure room?" Grace gasped as they entered the hall. Many of the statues looked to be made of gold or silver. Some appeared to be cut from gems. Each one was a statue of the Peacock Queen.

"No, no, no," Horace said, "but the key to opening the treasure room is here."

"I'll do it," Jaspar said, stepping forward. "Everyone else keep watch. We only have a few minutes before the next guard detail is due."

Hamper and Trick each stepped near the entryway to the hall. Grace neared one of the statues. It looked to be carved from solid emerald. She looked up into the eyes of the carved Peacock Queen. "Why does she have so many?" she asked.

"The Peacock Queen is one of the most vain, self-loving folk I've ever known," the centaur lady spoke. "She holds a contest for the artist who can create the best likeness of her."

"Oh," Grace said. "Well, what do they win?"

But there was no time for the centaur to answer. There was a loud click in the room and Jaspar cried out, "Found it! Let's Hurry!"

Grace watched as the center of the floor opened up, revealing a circular stairwell. While the light from the crystal palace flittered all throughout, it looked very dark down in the stairwell.

"Guards on the way!" Hamper cried out.

"Hurry everyone!" Horace shouted.

Grace ran for the stairwell opening in the floor. Whatever switch Jaspar had pushed did not last very long. The floor opened up, but once the opening was at its maximum, it began closing again, and everyone scrambled to get down the stairs.

"Grab a torch!" Horace shouted, slinging a bag down the stairs. The bag landed and torches rattled out, bouncing down the stairs. Grace grabbed one and then Jaspar was beside her, holding his lit torch to hers. Grace looked up, watching through the closing tiles above her as Horace waved goodbye.

"Isn't he coming?" Grace asked Jaspar.

"No," Jaspar said coldly. "Someone had to stay behind to lock the door."

"But...," Grace began, feeling a tear forming in her eye like a storm-cloud over rocky seas. "He was so sweet."

"Shhhh," Trick scolded. "We aren't safe yet, loves."

"But—" Grace began.

Jaspar whispered into her ear. "Horace can take care of himself. He's been around longer than most, and he taught me everything I know."

Grace nodded, trying to fight back the hurricane in her eyes. She had only known Horace for a few hours, but already she had come to think of him as part of her family. She hated the thought of him all alone up there with the guards. "Wait!" she cried out, and her voice echoed off the walls around her. Wait...wait... wait...wait....

Immediately every one turned to her, and she motioned to the shield that Hamper was carrying. "Do we have any idea what is down here?" she asked.

Jaspar shook his head. Hamper and Trick both shrugged their shoulders.

"Then hand me a shield," Grace said, stepping to the front of the line. As she took a shield from Hamper and strode forward, she suddenly felt taller, as if she was growing by the second. Her back straightened and something inside of her broke. A tiny little piece of her which had been held together throughout the years snapped in half and fell into her belly. It might have been her fear. It might have been her insecurity. Grace couldn't tell what it was, but she felt totally different as she strode forward, shield at the ready. "Follow me!" she cried, stepping forward with a shield in one hand and a torch in the other. Amazingly, they all did.

***

Briley woke with a start. When her eyes popped open she was looking down, thousands of feet, through a break in the clouds. "Argon!" she yelled out. "Argon, can you hear me?" But there was no response from the ground below. She looked around and realized their fleet had gained some organization. There were still ropes connecting the ships, but each one was maneuvering all on its own. Briley waved at the people aboard another ship as it passed and some of them waved back. Darrel had split his crew, ensuring there were Horgles aboard each ship.

Dragus came up to her, grinning. "Beautiful sight, ain't it? Only wish Darrel was feeling better. He ain't half the Horgle he was."

Briley nodded, unsure how to respond.

"There's talk amongst the crew Darrel should give up the command," Dragus said. "But I say he's earned a few weeks of light duty, he has. Saw us through the thick of it. And the thin of it!" Dragus put his massive hands upon the rail, looking down at the ground below, and spat. "That's what I says to those who say Darrel ain't up to snuff."

Briley grinned and spat over the rail. "Me too!" she cried. "Where are we headed?"

"Darrel is charting for the heart of it all, though I'm a bloody fool if I know what we'll do when we get there."

"The heart of it all...." Briley gasped. "The palace?"

Dragus grinned and nodded to her.

"But isn't it guarded by dragons?" she asked.

Dragus nodded again.

"And guards?"

Dragus nodded.

"And magic?"

Dragus shrugged. "Dunno about the magic, but likely the queen has a few tricks in store for us when we get there."

Briley watched as the ships maneuvered together above the clouds. Their ranks had swelled with the addition of all of the people from the Green Land. Was Darrel planning an assault?

Just then something black appeared on the horizon, and Briley squinted against the sun, holding her hand above her eyes. "Do you see that, Dragus?"

He looked too, frowning, and after a couple of minutes, the black thing on the horizon resolved into hundreds of tiny black shapes coming toward them. Not only that, but in the background, she swore she could hear music. The sound was unmistakable, like a drum beat, and then one of the shapes zipped out from the pack, streaking over her head. Briley ducked out of reflex as the shape cackled wickedly. It moved so quick, Briley was having a hard time tracking it as it whipped between lines, rigging, and ships.

Darrel limped up behind them, laughing. "Ah, the witches

always do have to make an entrance."

"Witches?" Briley gasped.

More and more of the shapes came closer, whooshing between ships and cackling, all the while the music thrummed in the background. Then about twenty of them landed in a circle all around Darrel and Dragus and Briley. In unison, they sang out with the music, "Born to be willlld!" Once they were sitting still, it was a lot easier to make out their features, but if these were witches, Briley had a lot to learn about witches.

There were equal amounts of men and women. When they removed their black hats, Briley saw young grinning faces all around her. She watched as one of the male witches removed his black cloak and stuffed it into his hat. Then he placed the hat atop his broom, which stood perfectly still. Underneath the black clothes, he wore khaki pants and a torn button down shirt. Then another bunch of the witches landed in time with the music, and they all cried out, "Born to be willlld!"

Briley couldn't help laughing and applauding at their spectacular entrance. Then all at once the music ceased and a woman strode toward Darrel as she removed her hat and cloak. Underneath she wore a rather plain looking dress, and she had long blonde curly hair. Briley gasped. The woman looked just like the lady who ran the ice cream shop in Piedmont.

"Miss Johannsen?" Briley cried.

The witch woman turned to her and smiled. "Briley! What on earth are you doing here?"

Darrel limped up to Miss Johannsen and extended a furry paw. Even though he limped, he still carried himself like a king, and Briley tried to keep from glancing at all of the witches around her to see if she recognized anyone else.

"You can call me Isabel," the witch said to Darrel. All of the witches had wild looking hair, and beneath their black cloaks they wore vibrant colors.

Briley looked from witch to witch, and saw each one was wilder than the next. Many of them had tattoos, piercings, or wore chains. Some even had tattoos on their faces. Her eyes met with one of the younger witches, who had vibrant orange and purple striped hair.

"These aren't anything like the witches I've ever heard of," Briley said.

Dragus whispered in her ear. "The witches are one of the only creatures that can pass through the Hedge. They soar in gangs on our side. But to be honest, I've never met a witch before."

"Really?" Briley asked.

"They keep to themselves for the most part," Dragus said. "Occasionally they'll swoop in and steal someone away to join their gang."

Briley watched as Darrel shook his head at something Isabel was saying. Three of the witches now stood talking to Darrel, but a lot of conversations had sprouted up all around, and it was impossible to hear what Darrel and the witches were discussing.

"They steal people?" Briley finally asked once her eyes stopped doing backflips.

"Well, from everything I've heard," Dragus said. "There's only two ways to become a witch. First way is you can give up everything you own and seek them out. Second way is they pop into your room when the darkness is at its thickest, and they steal you away. I've never ever heard of anyone going about it the first way."

"Why not?" Briley asked, looking around at all the brooms standing aloft with the hats and cloaks. "They look like they have a lot of fun."

"Well," Dragus whispered, holding his hand to her ear and speaking even softer. "When I say the witches give up everything they own, it's not just physical stuff. They give up their names, their old faces, their memories. To become a witch, I've heard, is one of the most painful things you can go through."

"I wonder how they choose who they are going to recruit," Briley said.

Just then Harrison bounded up to Briley and Dragus, vaulting through the crowd that had gathered. "Did you see that?" Harrison's eyes were wide. "That was so cool!"

Briley laughed as Harrison mimicked being a witch on a broom.

"What's going on?" Harrison pointed to where Darrel the Brave and Isabel were talking.

"They're working on a deal," Dragus said. "Best to stay out of witch's affairs, I always say."

"But if they can help us at the castle," Briley urged, "It'd probably be worth it, don't you think?"

"Depends on the price," Dragus said flatly, with his arms crossed. "It always depends on the price."

Darrel spun away from the witches suddenly. Three witches waved their hands up, and Darrel hovered upward. His voice boomed out as he made his announcement. "The witches of the southern skies have offered a deal with us, and the terms are more than fair. They'll stay with us until the crystal castle falls." There was a cheer from the crowd, not just on their ship, but on all the ships. Somehow the witches were making it so his voice was heard across their floating armada.

"The price will be three volunteers from amongst our numbers to join these southern witches," Darrel said. "I'm not going to force anyone, but if we want their help, then the price must be paid."

"Why wouldn't the witches help us for free?" someone shouted. "Do they like the Peacock Queen sitting on the throne?"

All around her, people groaned and argued with each other. Briley tried to think about what it would be like to not remember anything about who she was. Becoming a witch was definitely not a decision to be made lightly.

"I'll do it." A young Horgle stepped forward. Briley tried to put a name to him...Gander, she thought.

Gander was immediately lifted into the air, so that he was hovering just as Darrel was.

"Two more and the deal will be sealed," Darrel cried out. "I wouldn't ask this of any of you individually, but for the group, for the cause I would." His voice started to gain in momentum. "If any amongst you have lived the hard life, if you've lost your home, your family, now is an opportunity to forget all of that. If you've ever wondered what it would be like to be freed from your current obligations and duties, to start out on a new path, now is your chance!"

"I'll do it!" a young girl cried, running forward away from her family, who looked like they were trying to hold her back. Briley saw her skin was covered with green boils all over, and she wondered if that was why the girl wanted to be a witch. She was lifted into the air, hovering next to Gander. Briley almost raised her hand, but just as she was about to move, she caught Harrison's eyes. Even though he was half fox, he was still her brother. And there was Wendell and Grace to think about. And maybe someday they would find a way home, and she did want to see her family again.

"Don't do it, Sis," Harrison pleaded with her, reading the look in her eyes. "I can't lose you too."

Briley ran to her brother and hugged him till he groaned with the effort. "Of course I won't, Harrison!"

Just then another hand shot up. "I will volunteer!" Briley and Harrison both gasped as the turtle they had talked to earlier was lifted above the crowd.

"Can a turtle ride a broom?" Briley asked.

"They'll change him," Dragus muttered solemnly. "He won't look anything like he does now. None of them will."

Briley thought about that. All around her, everyone cheered as Darrel was lowered and the witches all gathered around them. "Break out the good mead!" someone cried. Some of the witches were back on their brooms in their black hats and cloaks, and the music started in the background again. The three volunteers were soon lost in the tide of traffic as the music grew in volume.

Briley danced right along with everyone as drinks were poured into cups. The witches clapped their hands and tables appeared out of nowhere, already festooned with food piled high on silver platters.

"What just happened?" Briley asked. Between the music and the dancing she had found a way to make it to Isabel and Darrel the Brave, who were also dancing together. "Why has everyone suddenly gone crazy?"

"Because the Peacock Queen is about to get a very nasty surprise." Darrel grinned at her. "This party is the first of thousands of parties, and it only cost three of our number."

Isabel spun Darrel just then, who laughed, and Briley tried to keep asking questions, but just then witches zipped through the air trailing pink smoke behind their brooms. It also looked like the witches had mended Darrel. He was dancing with Isabel and laughing. The witches zig zagged over the ships, and people cheered as the witches created designs in the air. The smoke from their brooms created flowers and ships. They zipped through the air creating floating coins made of smoke. Then the coins fell onto the decks of their fleet, and Briley snagged one out of midair. It turned to solid silver in her hand.

"Now that's magic!" she grinned at Harrison.

"Told you, Sis!" he laughed.

Then some of the witches gathered around a huge cauldron that had appeared on the deck of the ship.

"When did that get there?" Briley asked Dragus.

But Dragus was no longer standing next to her. She looked around and saw him dancing furiously with one of the female Horgles. Then a cup was handed to Briley and she took a sniff of the liquid in the cup. It smelled like raspberries and fresh dew and birthday cake.

"Drink up!" a witch encouraged her, and Briley smiled as she drank deeply from her cup. When she swallowed it was like a bubble of excitement burst inside of her. The music was too good. The food was too good. Everything was just too good to resist. The witch grabbed Briley by the hand and spun her in circles. She laughed and twirled, getting dizzy watching his lime green hair change colors with each spin. She danced and sang, and they all celebrated until their feet fell off.

***

Grace squinted into the darkness of the cavern, trying to ignore the trembling in her stomach. They had all lost count of how many steps they had traveled, and they were down to their last torch. So far all they had seen were spiders, stairs, and each other. Grace was beginning to wonder if they had been duped by Horace. Had he led them to the wrong staircase and kept the treasure for himself?

Jaspar stood just behind Grace. Hamper and Trick had taken

to crawling along the ceiling. The rest of their band huddled together. Just as Grace was about to ask if the tunnel ever ended, she saw a giant wrought iron door looming at the bottom of the staircase.

"I'll check it out!" Hamper cried above her. Immediately he quickened his pace, crawling toward the door. At that exact moment, the torch in Grace's hands sputtered, guttered, and then went out with an audible hiss.

Grace heard more than saw Hamper banging on the door. Trick fell to the ground spreading his arms out, keeping the group from running forward. Behind her, everyone muttered.

"Just wait until he opens it," Grace called out in a commanding tone. She could hardly believe her own ears. The voice that was coming from her sounded far more confident than she felt. "We have to trust one another," she finished.

"Do you think it's safe?" Jaspar whispered so that only she could hear. All Grace could do was shake her head from side to side. She had no idea how to open the door or what lay on the other side. But she also knew there was nothing she could do about any of that at the moment.

"Hamper!" Grace called out "What's going on?"

"Uhhhh...." Hamper's reply was far less controlled than Grace might have liked. "I think it's a puzzle. There are handprints all over the door in different sizes. One of them has to be the key."

"Hold on," Grace said aloud. "I'm going to help you." She began walking, breaking past both Trick and Jaspar's grips on her arms. She could not see the handprints at all when she got to the door, but she felt along them. "Oh my. Hamper, I don't think this is a puzzle," she said with a gulp. "I think these hands are burned into the door."

"But...," Hamper asked. "What could burn handprints into

167

a door like this?"

"There's only one thing I know of," Grace said.

Hamper gulped and they said the word aloud. "Dragons."

Then there was a thunderous growl from above them, as if a thousand bears had all woken at once. "Come on!" Grace shouted out. "Everyone, we need to break through this door!"

And then the hallway was no longer dark at all. Far above them they saw the flames in the distance. Grace had no idea how many dragons were swooping down the steps. Her only comfort was knowing that the spiral staircase was not very wide. Horace must have betrayed them after all. Grace gulped and heaved against the door. In moments, they were all pushing against it. The door was huge and made of iron, but she swore she felt it budge slightly as they pushed. The centaur lady was kicking against it with her hind hooves. Hamper and Trick were crawling along it, feeling for levers. Grace pushed with all of her might.

"I don't want to die down here," Jaspar said aloud.

"Then try harder!" Grace commanded. "Everyone stop. On my mark, we push together! Hold!" she cried out. "Push!" she screamed. "Hold!" Everyone held off for a split second. "Push!"

As one they held and then pushed, and Grace could feel the door surrendering. They could feel the heat from the dragons' fires in the distance. And then all at once the door gave way, and everyone toppled into the room beyond. There was a massive underground river, and Grace didn't think twice about jumping in. She didn't even take the time to look about for treasures. She knew there was only one chance of surviving this, and that was to get away from the dragons. The river swept her away like a tidal wave. Immediately she felt chilled to the bone. It was possibly the coldest water she had ever been in. All Grace could do was try and keep her head afloat as she was swept away in the icy current.

Chapter Ten:
Patience

Briley woke in the middle of the night. They had all sung and danced themselves into exhaustion, and everyone slumbered on the decks of the ships. All around her, Horgles and witches snored. The giant cauldron still simmered on the deck of the ship, and Briley's head felt like spiders were crawling around inside of it. Her stomach didn't feel much better. She scanned the sleeping bodies and saw Harrison curled up just like a fox amidst some of the rowdier Horgles. Briley ran to the rail and looked out amongst the other ships. Not a soul stirred on any of the decks. If it weren't for the fact they were tethered together by sturdy ropes, the ships all would have likely wandered apart from each other.

As she gazed over the railing, a strange feeling settled over her — the one where you know someone is watching you — and she almost jumped out of her skin when she heard her name whispered as if through the breeze. "Briley...." Soft and sweet the whisper came again, as if echoed across the skies. "Briley...."

She spun on the spot, looking all about her, but everyone still slumbered. She spotted Darrel the Brave even curled around a barrel, clutching it in his sleep. She started walking toward him. As she walked, the ship around her transformed. It was like walking inside a dream. The wood beneath her feet tilted, and Briley had trouble keeping her balance. The colors around her all melted together. Reds were dripping into blues, and yellow splotches blossomed and spread all around her. Briley couldn't really tell her up from her down or her left from her right.

"What's happening?" she said aloud, and the words echoed about her.

Out of the mad colors, there was a solid splash of green, and then another. Slowly the green took form, and Briley ran forward when she realized Argon was the source of the green.

"Argon!" Briley called out. "Oh, I've missed you!" She threw her arms about him, but it was like hugging a cloud. "You're not really here, are you?" she asked, crestfallen.

Instead of responding, Argon swept his arms in a wide circle. "My grove," he whispered, "has become part of this ship."

Briley stared at him wide eyed. "Are you part of the ship now too?"

Argon nodded. "I tried to let you know I had to leave...," A tear formed in his eye, "In order to be with you." His eyes locked with hers and green tears began trickling down Argon's face. "Pain," he said. "So much pain. You need to wake up."

"But I am awake," Briley said. She put her arms around him again, trying to comfort him. "You'll be fine!" she said cheerily. But then it occurred to her how odd the colors were all around her, and how distant everything seemed, as if bobbing in water. "Oh, I'm only dreaming." Briley cut back a sob.

Argon nodded, wincing in pain, and Briley saw scratches

begin to appear across his left cheek. "I'm with you now. I always will be, in a way." Then he doubled over, clutching his stomach. Briley tried to hold him, but it was like clutching onto smoke. "You need to wake up now, Briley!" Argon cried out. Briley saw blood oozing out of the scars on his cheek. She didn't want to leave him, but the sight of it jarred her out of her dream. She sat bolt upright, looking all about her as Horgles and witches darted about. Then she smelled smoke. The ship was on fire!

Briley shot up like a lightning bolt. Smoke billowed everywhere, and she could barely see in front of her face. There were shouts of panic all around. Just the night before they had been celebrating...what had happened? Briley spun, coughing as smoke clouded her throat and eyes. She saw groups of goblins running back and forth, carrying torches or swords amongst the panicked Horgles and witches. All she could think of was the pain that Argon was in. Knowing he was somehow a part of the ship made her jump into action. She pulled on her dragon glove and ran into the fray.

"Darrel!" she cried out, running toward a goblin. "Dragus?" Briley slammed her gloved fist into the jaw of a goblin, sending him scattering across the deck like a hockey puck. She stomped on its torch and grabbed the sword he had dropped. "Harrison?" she cried as she swung the sword at another goblin. Briley hated fighting. She didn't want to hurt anyone. But she hated the thought of losing Argon even more, and seeing what the goblins had done to Wendell only sealed her fury. How had the goblins found them? They were so high above the clouds, she would have thought it impossible for the goblins to track them.

None of that mattered at the moment. Briley gritted her teeth as she caught a goblin blade in her gloved hand and pulled, bringing the poor goblin with it right into her knee. "Can't you leave anything in peace?" she cried, slamming the goblin to the ground. "Can't you appreciate anything that's beautiful?" She stomped on the small of the goblin's back and kept moving.

Something inside her had snapped. No longer was there any doubt or fear about hurting the goblins. Somehow between one moment and the next, Briley had turned into a dervish, striking and ducking, smashing and screaming. She slid across the deck to the railing. Briley took one second to glance across at their little fleet and her heart dropped. Goblin ships swarmed amongst their own, and the goblins had fastened ropes from their ships to those under Darrel's command. The goblins slid down the ropes in packs. Witches zoomed through the air, cutting the goblins' lines and casting water spells toward the ships. From time to time a whoosh of water would spray down where a fire brewed, but the goblins were thousands compared to the hundreds that manned Darrel's fleet. Her heart sank, but Briley reminded herself to focus on what was happening right in front of her. She had to save Argon no matter what. If their ship went down, she knew he would die along with it, and she was not going to let that happen.

From the pit of Briley's stomach came a cry so ferocious that everyone, including the goblins, stopped to stare at her.

"AARRGGOONN!" Briley shouted. "FOR THE GROVE!" Briley swung, striking three goblins at once, sending them all tumbling across the deck of the ship.

"For the grove!" she heard others cry out, following her example and laying into the assault with a new energy. She saw fairies zipping about with tiny strings, sweeping about the legs of goblins and tripping them in masses. Arrows landed on the deck just in front of her, but Briley did not stop, could not stop. She leapt and swung and shouted until she grew hoarse. And then she leapt and swung and shouted some more.

Witches flew past on their brooms, bringing great tides of water in their wake, dousing the fires and drenching the ship in a fine mist. Then three witches landed next to her. One of them was Isabel, who ran the ice cream shop in her hometown. Maybe the fact she had bought ice cream from a witch her whole life should have bothered her, but it didn't. Isabel held her broom in one hand and made motions in the air with her free hand, chanting in a strange language that sounded like chimes one second and growling the next. As Isabel's fingers moved, Briley watched shards of ice appear out of midair, striking the goblins in their arms and legs, causing them to trip, stumble, and drop their swords.

"Wow!" Briley shouted over the clamor all around them. "That's amazing!"

"It is," Isabel said through gritted teeth. "But it won't hold them off for long."

"I have an idea," Briley said quietly. "I have to get to Darrel."

"He's near the wheel," Isabel motioned.

Briley didn't spare a moment. She had no idea where the goblin force had come from, but it didn't matter. "For the Grove!" she cried out, springing into the fight. As she leapt out, she tried to remember everything she had learned during her lessons. Darrel had known that she and Harrison were going to need to fight. At the time Briley had done her best, but now as it was happening all around her, she had to rely on instinct. She wished she had studied harder. Her teacher had shown her how to react in chaotic situations, but lessons were definitely not the same as the real thing.

"The trick," Dragus had said, "is to slow everything down in your mind. When people are fighting, they often make mistakes. Don't let the one who messes up be you, Briley. Don't let it be you."

So in spite of everything around her, Briley shoved out all the distractions around her. She shoved out the smell of the smoke and the shouts, and even her thoughts of Argon. She focused on minimizing her movements and remembering to breathe. She was small and she used that to her advantage, sidestepping as the goblins swung. She saw Harrison in the distance, surrounded by a group of goblins. He had a sword in each hand and one in his tail, and it was like watching an amazing dancer. He spun and twisted, lashing out. The goblins were taking turns trying to take him on. Briley could see that if they all attacked in concert, Harrison would be in big trouble. And she knew it wouldn't be long before the goblins realized that as well. She made her way toward him, blocking blows with her dragon skin glove and only attacking when absolutely necessary. She knelt, sensing a blow toward her head, then rolled, sweeping her arm out and tripping goblins as she moved.

"I'm only eleven!" she cried as she dodged a sword. "I'm not cut out for this kind of stuff!"

After a few close calls, she made her way to the edge of the circle surrounding Harrison. He was still holding off the goblins, but she could see sweat matting the fine fur on his face. He was probably still woozy from last night. What she needed just then was a diversion. Briley dodged an oncoming attack, and then did the only thing she could think of. She began singing the song the Horgles had sung the first night they had sailed together.

"Oh the fire in my belly. Won't be put out!" Briley sang at the top of her lungs.

To her surprise, others picked up the song around her. "No it won't go out!" she heard some of the Horgles cry.

"You can clap me in irons! Or clap me in chains!" The witches were singing now too. "But the fire in my belly. Won't be put out!"

The goblins surrounding Harrison heard her singing too, and they all turned toward her. Briley gulped, her eyes going wide. The goblins began to rush at her, but apparently it was just the distraction that Harrison needed.

"You can make me drink poison!" Harrison cried out as he came forward. "Or swallow my pride!" Harrison used the shoulders of one of the goblins as a vault, and leapt high into the air, spinning like a thunderstorm, and his feet struck down right next to Briley.

They joined together in song. "But the fire in my belly. Won't be put out. No it won't be put out!"

"Hi, Sis," was all he said, grinning like a loon. Briley was quite one thousand percent sure she had never been so happy to see her brother's smile as in that moment.

"We need to get to Darrel," Briley said. "I have an idea." They both glanced up toward the wheel of the ship, where Darrel struggled to fend off the goblins. Luckily, he had some Horgles and witches with him, but the tide of goblins seemed endless.

"I say we just try your idea," Harrison said, grinning. "It's not like we need permission, and nothing else seems to be working."

Briley grinned at her brother. Sometimes he could make things sound so simple. But he was right. If they didn't do something drastic, they were going to be overwhelmed before long. "All right," she said. "But it's pretty crazy, so don't say I didn't warn you."

"I've got your back, Sis. Now come on and out with it before we all end up in goblin stew."

"Let's cut the ropes," Briley said. "All of them."

"But without the ropes to the balloon, the ship will just

fall...." Harrison's eyes got huge just then. "Into —"

"Exactly!" Briley said. "Right into the sea of grass!"

"What about the other ships, though?" Harrison said as they both dodged blows from either side.

"We'll tell the witches!" Briley said. "They can help spread the word."

"That's the part I don't get," Harrison said as he knocked a sword from a goblin's hand and tossed it to a nearby Horgle. "Where did all these goblins come from? Don't you think it's weird they showed up just after the witches?"

Briley ducked beneath a sword and punched a goblin square in the jaw with her dragon skin glove before answering. "Well, I'm glad they are here. We would have lost this battle a long time ago without them."

Harrison nodded, but she could tell from the look in his eyes he wasn't convinced. Just then some of the witches zoomed overhead on their brooms. Each of them was chanting with an ethereal look in their eyes. Briley watched as a mixture of wind and fire swept through the goblins. "They are on our side, Harrison!" Briley called out, but she wasn't sure if she was talking more to herself or to him. She charged forward, following the wake the witches created, and sang out, "You can tar me. Feather me. Strangle me. Murder me. But the fire in my belly. Won't be put out."

All around her the Horgles sang, "No it won't! No it won't! No it won't be put out!" Harrison was right next to her, but he wasn't singing. She knew her brother had changed in many ways since their journey into fairy land. She just hoped he didn't give up. This had to be the main force of the goblins. If they won here, there couldn't be much left to defend the crystal palace.

As if he heard her thoughts, Harrison started talking as

they fought. "And then there will be the crocodiles and the Peacock Knights, not to mention the dragons." His mouth turned downward. "Not to mention the Peacock Queen herself. Who knows what she is capable of?"

"Shut up and fight!" Briley said. "When did you become such a grump? The brother I grew up with always made the best of everything!"

"Humph," was Harrison's only reply.

Briley rolled between two goblins. They both swung for her, but had turned as she passed and knocked each other out. "Do you remember our camping trips when we were small, Brother?" Briley asked, catching a goblin sword in her glove and chucking it over the railing. "There was one trip we took where it rained on all of our firewood and squirrels got into our cooler. Our tent began leaking too, and it was so cold." Briley glanced at her brother. At least he was listening. "Mom and Dad and I were all ready to pack back up and head home, but it was you who kept us smiling during that trip." Briley chuckled, managing to trip three goblins at once. "You said 'let's go fishing' and Dad caught that giant trout." Briley couldn't help but smile as she remembered the look on their dad's face. "And you and I searched through the forest for dry wood and managed to get a fire going. Harrison, you didn't give up then, and I'm not going to let you give up now."

Lightning creased the sky as if to punctuate her words, and the bolt managed to strike one of the goblin ships. Briley watched as it veered in the sky, smoldering like a burnt twig. Then there was another blast of lightning and the wind gusted, pushing the falling ship into another of the goblin vessels. Cheers rose up from the Horgles. Briley cheered too. "For the Grove!" she called out. She glanced over at Harrison to see his reaction. Harrison wasn't cheering or smiling, but at least he was still fighting with the rest of them. Briley's heart burned with the need to see his playful smile again. When the world was darkest, Harrison was always able to see the bright side and make her laugh. She needed to see that side of him again.

Overhead the sky swirled with dangerous clouds. Thunder and lightning bloomed like blinding flowers, but the storm was entirely focused on the goblin ships. It had to be the work of the witches. There was no other explanation. Briley kept moving and the next thing she knew, she was closing in on the wheel where Darrel and a group of Horgles struggled against a swarm of goblins.

"Watch your left, Margus!" Darrel called, and then his eyes landed on Briley and they shared a smile. "Make a hole!" Darrel cried. "We've got reinforcements!"

Briley laughed aloud at the thought of herself being reinforcements, but the Horgles around Darrel began focusing on the center of the goblin swarm. Briley charged forward, dodging and twisting through the goblins. Soon she was standing beside Darrel. He had cuts on his face and arms, but he was grinning nonetheless.

"Good to see you, lass. Where's that foxy brother of yours?"

"I'm working on the fire in his belly," Briley smiled. "I won't let them put it out."

"Thatta girl," Darrel chuckled. "It's not the brightest times what define ya, but the darkest. Looks like the witches are proving their worth."

From their vantage point Briley could see out over the fleet of ships, and she saw what Darrel meant. Many of the goblin ships reeled through the sky, fires blazing on their decks. The wind was blowing them into one another, knocking each other off course.

"Their magic takes a little while to pick up," Darrel said. "But once it brews, there's not a thing can stop 'em."

"Not even the queen's dragons?" Briley asked.

"Well, we'll see about the dragons," Darrel said. "Might be just a story she's told everyone to keep 'em in check!"

Briley considered that for a second, but she wasn't sure how to respond. "I was thinking we should head for the grass," she said. "To keep us hidden from the goblins."

Darrel nodded. "Aye, lass, that be the plan, but first we need to clear our decks. We won't be able to use ropes to keep our ships together in the Green Sea."

Briley hadn't thought of that, and she was grateful she hadn't just gone around cutting ropes as she had originally planned. "Do you really think the dragons are just a myth?"

"Ah, who's to say?" Darrel said with a grin. "I've never seen a dragon, but I reckon there's a lot of things I haven't seen that exist." He took a breath. "Blast you, Sargen, mind your flank! You almost lost your head just then!"

Briley scanned the deck of the ship. Harrison was still in the thick of it, but he was being helped by the witches and Horgles. She watched as the witches' storm blew the goblin ships into one another and lightning bolts blasted out of the storm, striking goblin ships apart and setting fire to their decks.

"They're kind of scary," Briley said in awe.

"Aye," Darrel said with a grin. "Which is exactly why I wanted them on our side." Then he chuckled. "Get it…? Which…. Witch…."

"Keep to sailing ships," Briley chuckled. "Leave the comedy to someone else."

Instead of responding, Darrel just pointed out across the

deck to where Harrison battled. "I think it's time you go rescue your brother, little lass. He's growing tired."

"Well." Briley smiled as she leapt forward. "I've already saved his hide once today. I guess he can owe me his life twice over."

"To the fox, lads!" Darrel cried out, stepping forward as well. "Stay with us and move as one now! Don't lose your heads! The battle is nearly won!"

Together they moved forward into the battle, and Briley could see that Darrel was quite right. The goblin swarm had thinned considerably. Most of the goblin ships were careening away, limping off into the darkening sky. She wondered if Wendell was on one of those ships. He had somehow been promoted to a goblin general. No doubt Wendell was behind the attack. How had he known where they were? Was there another spy in their crew? But all of those questions would have to be answered at another time. Right now she had a brother to help and witches to thank, and after all of that, she would be in desperate need of a hot bath.

"For the Grove!" Briley cried out as they strode forward. All around her, cheers rang up. Horgles and witches sang and cried out. The goblins were trying to escape now. Some of them leapt off the side of the ship, hoping to land on one of their own ships below. Others ran for the few ropes that were still connected to the goblin ships, and clung on for dear life. Once she got to Harrison, Briley threw her arms around her brother. "You see, Bro? It's all right! We won! And all because of the witches!" Harrison hugged her back, but Briley could tell something had changed. "Come on, Harrison! Darrel said we are taking the ships down into the Green Sea! You can help!" Harrison shuffled after her. Briley just hoped he went back to his old self soon.

***

The water churned all around Grace. She was swept away by the current of the river. Above her, she could see the light of the fires as the dragons raged. She flung out her hands, trying to grasp onto a rock or someone nearby. Unfortunately, she was whirling at such a speed it was hard for her to tell her up from her down. The river was furious, and she kept getting jammed against rocks and other debris as she spun. Hamper clutched her hand in one of his and Grace clung on for dear life. She could hear the dragons above them, matching their speed, waiting for them to surface. The water rushed in her ears, and Grace could not keep track of which direction she was headed. Then the river tilted downward, and Grace took a gasp of air before getting plunged under water.

Suddenly the speed of the water became impossibly intense. It swept downward harder and harder. Then the bottom fell out of the river and Grace fell straight down. She plummeted with water rushing all around her. Grace tried to scream, but her mouth filled instantly. Then Hamper caught her hand in one of his and they fell together, eyes locked on one another. Although they were rocketing downward, there was no fear in Hamper's eyes. "I've faced worse than this," he said as they rushed downward.

Grace saw a giant lake below them and clenched her teeth. She was trying to imagine what might be worse than plummeting hundreds of feet after being chased by dragons and betrayed. Then she splashed into the lake. Luckily it was deep. The force of the fall sent her almost to the bottom. She had just enough strength left to struggle back to the surface and make her way to the edge of the lake. Grace looked around, feeling woozy and out of sorts.

The base of the mountain had been hollowed out either by

magic or by the dragons. There were stone walkways spanning here and there from opening to opening, but the belly of the mountain was open air. Dragons flew from cavern to cavern inside the mountain. Most of the dragons were small, impish things. Children perhaps? But some were massively muscled and armored with scales as dark as dreams could conjure. Then Grace saw the glimmering of gold in the distance.

This had to be the treasure which the Peacock Queen held so dear. There were countless coins and jewels, emeralds the size of boulders, and diamonds cut to perfection, all glimmering in the distance. Jaspar flashed into the lake and Grace cried out to him, but of course he did not hear her. Soon, though, he emerged.

"I thought we were going to die!" Jaspar gasped next to her. Grace nodded numbly. Her body felt like it had been trampled by ogres. They swam to the edge of the water, hauling themselves up onto the shore. There was a small clearing around the edge of the water, less than a foot wide, where it was just plain rocks. Beyond the clearing, the dragons perched atop piles of gold, each one staring down at them as if daring them to try and take some of the treasure. Hamper and Trick hauled themselves up as well, and soon most of their party was standing before the treasure.

"Well, it looks like we found it—" Trick began.

"Yes, but now what?" Hamper finished.

Then a massive dragon landed atop one of the piles of gold. She didn't know if it was a boy or a girl, but it was by far the largest of the dragons. Its eyes were pools of dark water, almost impossible to pick out in its face, but they glittered strangely like the gold surrounding it. Grace had no idea what she was supposed to do, but it seemed only right to show her respect to the beast. It was so massive and regal, like a legend come alive. Grace got down on one knee and knelt her head to the dragon.

"Thank you for sparing us." Grace said. "We are at your mercy." She had no idea if the dragon could understand her speech.

Beside her, Jaspar knelt also, followed by the centaur and Hamper. Trick was the last to kneel, but he did, and they all repeated what Grace had said in their own words.

"I beg you to spare our lives," Jaspar said.

"Your glamour holds us all in its grasp," the centaur said.

"We are awed by your powers," Hamper said.

"I really like your scales," Trick said. Hamper snickered next to him, but the dragon's roar quieted all further comments.

The ground shook as the dragon swept its neck back and forth, roaring out. Grace put her hands to her ears. Once the dragon had stopped roaring, Grace unplugged her ears and looked up. The great black dragon opened its wings to their full spread, and Grace gasped. On its belly, amidst the black scales, was an outline, as if engraved in its stomach, shaped like a person. Grace stood watching as an aged woman stepped forth from the dragon's belly, leaning on a cane, her hair as white as winter.

"Step forth, child," the woman said. "The time has come."

She tried to walk with confidence, but her legs felt like they had melted into butter. The woman waited for her, leaning on her cane. She was dressed in plain grey robes. Her face was kind, but definitely not soft. The woman's eyes were vibrant and pure blue, sapphires that seemed to burn into Grace's soul. When she was within arm's reach of the woman, Grace stopped.

"Tell me your name, child," the woman commanded.

"G…ggg…Grace, my lady."

"Ah. Come, follow me," the woman said. "And you don't have to call me your lady. My name is Anatauna, but you can call me Ann for short." The woman began walking between the dragons with surprising agility, and Grace had the funny feeling she didn't really need the cane to walk with. "We have been waiting for you for a very long time, Grace," Ann said. "Soon, you will see."

Grace kept losing her footing on the coins. Each time she stepped, gems slid out beneath her feet. Ann seemed to have no trouble at all as she walked, and Grace struggled to keep up. The woman seemed familiar somehow, but in what way, Grace couldn't put her finger on.

"The goblins dug all of these tunnels," the woman said as they walked. "They hollowed out the entire mountain with their own hands."

"Were they searching for something?" Grace asked.

"Oh ho, yes they were, my dear, but they didn't find what they were looking for."

"Oh? What were they looking for?"

"I honestly don't know." Ann stopped mid stride, waiting for Grace to catch up to her. "That was before my time, I'm afraid." Ann paused and looked Grace deep in her eyes. "I'm about to show you what they found, my dear, and I don't want you to be alarmed."

"I promise I'll try not to be." Grace finally caught up to Ann. "Did the goblins build the palace as well?"

"No, the fairies built the palace and infused it with their magic. That is why the sunlight travels through the crystal, no matter how deep in the castle you are. Although, they built it for a different queen."

"You mean the queen before the Peacock Queen took over?" Grace asked.

"Oh ho, no no no no no!" Ann laughed at that "No, my dear, the castle was built ages and ages before her time. But of course she took it for her own."

185

"How do you know so much about her?" Grace pondered.

"I know many things."

Before Grace could press her further, Ann maneuvered past a statue of a strange looking feathered horse.

"Everything here is so upside down," Grace said. "I can't keep track of who anyone is or was or where they come from, or—"

"That's exactly the point of our land, my dear." Ann stopped Grace before she could get too exasperated. "In this land, you have to FEEL your way around. In yours, you have to THINK your way around. Stop thinking so much!" Ann laughed. "And do what feels right! Our world is the heart to your brain, Grace, and the world we live on is the body. The rivers are the veins and the mountains are its hands, reaching up, up, up. None of us could function without the other, which is why I don't want you to be upset when I show you what I'm about to show you."

Grace swallowed her questions and tried to think about how it all connected together, and between one step and the next, Grace realized it wasn't something she would ever be able to figure out, because Ann was right. Things didn't make sense here, not in the brain way. But maybe they made sense in the heart way.

Ann had just reached the mouth of a cave amidst the piles of gems and gold. "Come along, dear. And take a deep breath." Ann beckoned.

As Grace followed Ann into the cave, she did just as directed and swallowed a big gulp of air to steady herself. Grace had to remember that somehow, this aged old woman was part of the giant dragon. Or was the giant dragon. It was all so confusing, and her head swam. "Stop thinking so much," Grace admonished herself aloud.

Ann led her deeper into the cave. "It is normal for you to want to think, dear. But to see our world clearly, it is impossible to do so with your eyes open and cataloging all of the evidence." She paused, grabbing a torch and lighting it, then continued. "Your scientists could never make two and two add up to four here. Sometimes two and two is eleven, and sometimes two and two can't add up at all, because by the time you take note of them, they have changed."

"That's why Wendell became a goblin; he's been trying to prove he's stronger than me for ages!" Grace cried out suddenly, smacking herself in the forehead. "And why Harrison turned into a fox! This whole time I've been searching for the explanation, it's been right there in their hearts!"

Ann stopped, turned to Grace, and smiled. "Yes my dear. Because they followed their emotions and did not let their heads get in the way. You are the head strong one, yes?" Ann ventured as they walked deeper into the cave. "You are the one who keeps the rest of them from getting too deep into trouble. Am I correct?"

"Yes," Grace replied in a whisper. "How did you know?" Grace felt vulnerable all of a sudden. It was strange to talk about these kinds of feelings out loud, let alone with someone she had only just met. "How do you know so much about me?" Grace asked, trying not to sound afraid.

Instead of answering, Ann stopped walking. In the middle of the cave was a small wooden door, only just a little bit taller than Grace. There was no door knob or catch that she could see. The only feature on the door was an intricately carved silver ornament shaped like the head of a dragon. Its mouth was open, and every detail had been mastered so well that Grace would have sworn it was a living creature. Each tooth glistened in the open mouth, and even little rivulets of saliva had been carved onto the piece. Where the eyes would have rested, there were two small insets for keys.

Ann rummaged in her robes until she drew out a silver chain with several keys on it. She handed the chain to Grace with a hopeful look in her eye. "The right keys will open the door. The wrong ones will seal our doom."

"What?" Grace exclaimed. "How am I to know which is the right key?"

"With your heart, dear. Follow your heart."

Grace held out the silver chain, examining the keys. Her first instinct was to try and figure which ones looked like the right sizes and shapes to fit into the eye sockets of the dragon. But nothing in this alternate world was mapped out the way it was back.... "Huh," Grace said aloud. "It doesn't feel like home anymore."

"What doesn't, dear?" Ann asked.

"My house back in Piedmont. The town." Grace's heart skipped a beat. "It's been here, all along, hasn't it, Ann?"

"What's that, dear?" Ann asked.

"My rightful place. The one where I fit. None of these keys will work," Grace said, tossing the chain aside. From about her own neck, Grace took the cord that held her house keys in place. She drew them out and pushed the key to her front door into the right eye socket. Then she put the key that opened their garage in the left eye socket. There was a decisive click as they slid into place. Grace took a deep breath, twisted the keys at the same time, and the silver dragon head's mouth snapped closed.

For a split second nothing happened. Then the silver dragon head shuddered, and Grace stepped back as the head moved back and forth, the scales atop its head glistening as they shook from side to side. The keys Grace had put in sunk into the head, and eyes of emerald green grew in their place. A silver tongue flicked between the jaws of the dragon's head, licking its mouth. Grace's heart raced as the dragon head moved away from the door. The dragon's emerald eyes took everything in, blinking first at Grace and then at Ann, and then at its surroundings. The jaws opened again and the beast spoke. Its voice was like the wind crisscrossing on glass.

"Has the time finally come? I have waited for so long," it said in a musical voice.

Grace looked to Ann, but Ann only looked on, motioning for Grace to continue. "Yes," Grace said. "The time has come. We would like you to open the door."

The dragon head nodded, but instead of opening the door, the silver beast flowed forward from the door. Its head flowed onto the floor of the cavern and its body followed, coil upon coil of silver scales flowing from the door, glistening in the darkness. The head snaked around Grace's feet, winding up her legs. Its body followed, and there was nothing Grace could do to resist. The silver was surprisingly smooth against her skin, and she realized it wasn't metal at all, but flesh and blood that looked like molten silver. The beast snaked around and around her until its head was staring her in the eyes and Grace was covered from head to foot, unable to move or resist. She dared not let her fear show. Even if the silver beast ate her alive, Grace vowed on the spot that she would not quake and quiver in fear. Every inch of her brain told her to scream out in horror, but Grace's heart spoke louder in the depths of the cavern, urging Grace to be bold and brave and stand up to this being.

"What is your name?" she asked the head as it wavered back and forth in front of her. "You may call me Grace."

"Hmm...." The beast hesitated, tilting its head so that one of its eyes was level with both of hers. "An interesting question. A name. I do not believe I have been given one. What does a name do?"

Grace had to think about that for a second. It was indeed an interesting question. She had never really thought about what names *did*, they just were. It was what you called yourself, how you thought about yourself. "A name is a part of you that you can never lose," she finally said. "No matter what."

"Hmm...." The creature swiveled its head so that its other eye was now level with hers. Grace had the feeling it could only see out of the sides of its head. "Well, I have lost eons and eons of time, so time could not be my name."

"If you would like me to give you a name, I could," Grace offered.

"Ah," the creature said. "But if I lost the name you gave me, it could not be mine any longer." It hesitated. "No. I know there is one thing I have never and will never lose."

Grace tried to smile as the creature's coils tightened and loosened about her. It wasn't constricting her. Not yet anyway. The creature could crush her to bits with a thought, but it seemed more curious than anything. "What is that?" she finally worked up the nerve to ask after swallowing.

The creature's mouth opened and Grace could swear it was smiling at her, if that was possible. "You may call me Patience," the beast said. "And since you have waited so long for the answer, I know that your name is true as well." Its tongue flickered in and out of its mouth. Patience uncoiled its body from around her "You truly are full of Grace." Then the creature flicked its tail toward the door and it fell inward. "Now go," it commanded. "I will wait here for you, Grace." She was positive it really was smiling as it added, "Patiently...."

Grace shared a look with Ann before moving toward the

door. When they reached the doorway, Grace turned to the silver beast coiled on the cavern floor. "Thank you, Patience." She smiled. "For not crushing me to bits."

Patience opened its mouth, displaying several rows of razor sharp silver teeth. "Of course," it hissed at her. "And thank you for not making me."

Then Ann grabbed Grace's arm and pulled her though the doorway without another word.

"Good job!" Ann whispered to her as they passed through the doorway "I knew you could do it!"

Grace looked back at Patience, unsure whether to run or wave goodbye. "Thank you for warning me not to be alarmed," Grace said. "Otherwise I would have totally freaked out over that silver creature!"

"Oh ho!" Ann said. "Well, truth be told, that wasn't the part I was warning you about. It's still to come." Grace shuddered and followed Ann through the passageway.

Thankfully Ann still had her torch...otherwise the passageway would have been impossible to see inside. The cavern was low, and Grace had to duck in places so as not to hit her head on the uneven ceiling. Stalactites dripped down like teeth filling a mouth, but Ann weaved effortlessly through the cavern, pulling Grace along. It twisted and bended and at times split into separate tunnels. Ann seemed to know where she was heading though, because she never faltered or second guessed. She just kept moving with deceptive ease for an old woman.

Grace became aware of a rushing sound, which became louder and louder as they moved forward. The ground became slicker as well. "Are we headed towards a waterfall?" Grace asked.

"Yes," Ann said simply. "We're nearly there, I think."

A. Henry Moen

"Should I be scared?"

"Just be ready," Ann said.

"For what?"

"Well," Ann chuckled. "For anything, of course!"

"Wait!" Grace grabbed Ann by the shoulder and stopped her. "You know what we're headed toward. The least you can do is take the edge off my nerves by giving me some kind of clue!"

Ann turned to her, the little jewels on her necklace jingling as she did. "Young lady." Ann's eyes settled on Grace's with unsettling ferocity. "I am over two thousand years old, and I will not be spoken to in that manner."

"Well, I am over two thousand DAYS old!" Grace demanded back. "And I'm not taking another step unless you give me some kind of hint."

Ann stared at her, hands on hips. Grace stared right back. Grace was determined not to break first. They stood in the sputtering light of the torch with eyes glued to each other. Grace had often tried this tactic with her mother, but she always lost. But now she had been through too much. In the past hour she had escaped from dragons, fallen down a waterfall, discovered a secret treasure, and outsmarted a silver creature named Patience. Then Grace remembered. Patience had waited in that doorway forever for her to come along. Ann said she was over two thousand years old. It all started to form a picture for her that not only made sense, but also FELT right.

"You don't remember, do you?" she laughed aloud.

"Of course I don't!" Ann blushed, not meeting Grace's eyes.

"Finally!" Grace laughed. "I finally got a straight answer out of you!" She smiled at Ann and stepped toward her, yanking the torch from her. "Well then. I'm ready. Let's go!" Grace stepped on deeper into the cavern and Ann followed her.

"Well I never." Ann grumbled behind her as Grace trod toward the rushing of the waterfall. She could just see the mist beginning to form in the cavern as she walked.

"Well, maybe you should!" Grace laughed as she walked. For some reason, knowing that Ann didn't know what they were headed toward made her feel braver.

Chapter Eleven: Kraken

Briley ran across the deck, laughing as they untied the ships. The goblins had all either escaped or been captured. No one really wanted to keep the goblins as prisoners, but they hadn't had the heart to throw them overboard either. "Come on, Harrison!" Briley called as she bounded from a railing. "We need to be quick! The ships are already heading down!"

The witches were helping too, transporting people from ship to ship, making sure everyone knew what the plan was. Briley was looking forward to riding along with the witches on the brooms. Several of them had offered to take her whizzing through the air, but everyone knew the work had to get done first. Briley leapt onto a railing and pulled on one of the cranks to lower the ship's balloon. Then she vaulted from the railing and began running for the next rope. Above her a witch zoomed past, weaving between the lines and rigging.

"Tighten up the deck, lads!" Darrel cried "We're getting ready for a stunt such as I ain't never tried!"

Briley Van Campfon

The witch winked at Briley as she passed and dipped low to the deck, depositing a laughing Horgle onto the deck. The Horgle rolled and Briley bent over to help him up. She extended her hand, but the Horgle only laughed as he hopped straight to his feet. "Thanks to ya, miss!" the Horgle said. "But I'd be more likely to pull you down than you pull me up!"

Briley grinned as the Horgle ran across the deck, making straight for the sails. They were beginning to fold in. The Horgle leapt onto one of the sails, hoisted himself up onto a beam, and ran straight across the beam for the balloon holding the ship aloft. Whoever he was, Briley was glad he was on their ship. "Did you see that?" Briley shouted to her brother, but he only grunted in response.

She continued pulling the balloon lower and lower as others let the air out of it. Darrel had said the timing would be tricky. They needed to angle the ship just so before letting all the air out of the balloon, or it would be disaster. The deck of the ship sizzled with joy and activity, like fresh popped corn drizzled in butter. The only person who seemed to be dragging about was Harrison. Not once in her life had Briley ever had to cheer him up. It was always the other way around. He was always the one bringing laughter to her heart when she needed it. Briley cut through another rope and then cast her eyes about, looking for the next one. But she had cut through all of the connecting lines.

"Steady!" Darrel called out above them all. "On my mark!"

Briley stood on the railing watching the rigging and the balloons on all of the ships changing into their under-grass mode. The zingers popped out of the sides of the ships like legs on floating caterpillars. The ships were all uniquely painted and decorated. Some had strange designs painted on the outside.

"Look, Harrison!" Briley called out, pointing at one. "It looks like an octopus!"

The ship was painted all in different colors of purple on the outside, and the blades that extended out from the ship were curved to look like octopus arms. She turned to him, grinning and trying to make him smile, but Harrison had slumped against a barrel with a strange brooding look in his eyes. It was as if some poison had taken over. "Oh my gosh!" Briley cried out. "That's it! Why didn't I realize it before?" She ran to her brother as the sails on the ship finished folding up.

He wore his hat so that it covered his eyes, and he looked up as Briley ran toward him. "Go away," Harrison muttered. But Briley charged at him, gripping his hand in hers and lifting up the sleeve of his shirt. There on his arm was a long jagged scar, pink and puckery, like an ugly smile along his arm. The cut was oozing, and dried blood was matted all around it. "Leave me alone," Harrison said, trying to jerk his arm away.

Briley kissed her brother on the cheek. "Not a chance, bro!" She had to pull him forcibly to his feet. Normally she might not have had the strength, but Harrison wasn't at full strength. "No way I'm letting that goblin goo get to your heart. Come on! I know who can help!" Briley ran across the deck, calling for the nurse fairy she had brought aboard. "Zinky!" she called out. "Zinky! Please help!"

"Just leave me alone," Harrison grumbled at her, stumbling as she pulled him as fast as she could.

Behind her, Darrel cried out, "NOW, ladies and gentleman! The first ever, Darrel's Brave Plunge!"

Briley gripped Harrison's arm harder. "Come on, Harrison! We need to hurry!" She plunged through one of the doors leading below decks. Just as she and Harrison cleared the door, she felt the ship falling through the sky. "Hold on!" she cried out. "This could get very, very interesting!"

Briley held onto the railing as she felt the ship angle downward. Even below deck, she heard Darrel's voice booming out above. "Steady lads and lasses! Ready the gain anchors!" She had no idea what a gain anchor was. All she could think about was that Harrison's joy was slowly leaving him. She had to find the medic fairies to help get Harrison back to normal.

Just as she began to move, the ship began to plummet through the sky, falling like a comet toward the Green Sea. Briley clung to Harrison as they fell through the passageway. She braced herself for impact, knowing eventually that they would hit a wall or a door. She cringed, clutching Harrison by the arm.

The ship not only fell, but spun as it fell, whirling through the sky. She dared not close her eyes. Her stomach was doing backflips as they fell through the passage. There was a door just ahead, and Briley cried out, "Hold on, bro!" The door they were headed for was of heavy wood, likely oak, with a great metal hinge that jutted out dangerously. She knew if her head hit that hinge, she'd likely never wake again. "HOLD ON!" she screamed, trying not to panic. She was inches away from the door, daring not to blink when everything stopped.

"Hold on, Sis," Harrison whispered to her. She looked back and saw that Harrison had wrapped his tail around one of the brackets in the passage way. "Brace yourself!" he said as they swung toward the wall. His hand was wrapped tightly about her ankle, and she was amazed all over again at Harrison's wiry strength. Tears formed in her eyes. She didn't care if she broke every bone in her body, but she couldn't stand losing her brother, especially to some stupid goblin poison that made you not care about anything.

"I love you, Harrison," she said before smacking against the wall. As she collided, Harrison cried out in pain. Briley cried out as well.

"Love you too, Sis," he said as they jarred against the wall.

Then Harrison lost his grip with his tail and they fell onto the door below. Luckily it was a fall of less than a foot. Briley could feel blood coursing down her face, and her brother had bruises forming all over his. They huddled on the door for a second before Briley threw her arms around him. "Are you back, Bro?" she cried. "Really back?"

As they hugged, she felt Harrison nodding on her shoulder. The ship was still spinning fitfully through the air, but at least she had her brother back. "I'm going to get you to the fairies," Briley said. "I don't ever want to lose you, Harrison."

It was the first time in her life when Briley could understand how her mother felt when they went on their outings without warning her…that feeling of not knowing if her family was safe. She wondered for a split second what her mom and dad must be thinking right at that moment, but there was little time to dwell on things she couldn't control. The door opened below them, and Briley and Harrison fell through the open doorway, bowling into the Horgle who was clutching the other side. It was the same one they had seen scampering along the sails earlier. "Oops," was all he said before they tumbled midair all over again.

"This is either a really bad dream—" Briley said aloud.

"Or a really fun ride!" the Horgle chortled as they spun midair.

"You are both crazy," Harrison countered.

"Oh, aye," the Horgle laughed. "I might be crazy, but at least I brought my rope!"

As they fell, the Horgle twirled a loop of rope in his hands and cast it out, latching onto one of the brackets as they fell.

"Hold on now, kiddos!" he laughed. "I'll take good care of ye!"

Harrison and Briley clung to the mystery Horgle as he slowly let out his rope. They were able to descend through the hallway with minimal bumps and thumps as the ship spun through the sky. "Darrel's my brother," the Horgle said conversationally as he maneuvered his rope from one hand to the other. "I didn't know he was alive till three days ago." Briley listened intently, unsure why the Horgle was telling them all of this. "I was making armor in the Green Land, and then I got caught up in that green storm when the goblins came." He spat as he said that. "Nasty things. Whoever dreamed them up has some explaining to do." Briley nodded in agreement. "The name's Bracken," the Horgle said, using his legs to brace himself in the hallway. "Yeah. Then when the witches came, I saw ol' Darrel acting like he was in charge, and I thought to myself, well that's a curious thing! Now we're in a war all of a sudden, and Darrel's a'plannin' to storm a castle. Well, he won't do it without Bracken at his side, that you can say for sure!" They maneuvered through a few more passageways before Bracken swung them into a side room. "There ya are now, kiddos," Bracken said, saluting them. "The fairies have all gathered in here for now. Hopefully they can help you lot. For my part, I need to help my brother steer this ship. Dragons above know he doesn't know his port from his starboard, no matter how much he boasts!" With that, Bracken swung back out of the doorway.

Briley looked to her brother. His cheeks looked hollowed out and discolored. Then his eyes rolled upward into his skull and he passed out. "NO!" Briley screamed, clutching Harrison to her. She hoped she wasn't too late. "That may have been the strangest person I've ever met," Briley chuckled to herself. "But at least he was helpful." She looked about the room that Bracken had placed them in. Several crates and boxes had been lashed to the walls, but she didn't see any fairies lingering about. "Zinky!" Briley called out. "Zinky, I need your help!"

There was a sound in the room as of crystal glasses being clinked against one another, and then, one by one, the fairies appeared like stars in twilight, glittering before them, each more delicate than the next. "Of course," the fairies all said in unison. "Of course we can help you, Miss Briley. What do you require?"

"It's my brother," Briley said, trying not to cry. "He's hurt and poisoned, and I don't know what to do."

The fairies all flitted around her and Harrison, their wings glittering and twinkling as they examined both her and her brother.

"Ohhh," one of them said.

"Mmm-hmmm," another agreed.

"Open your brother's mouth," said a third.

Briley took her brother's jaws in her hands and two of the fairies flitted around the opening. They put their hands to their mouths and blew what looked like stardust down into his throat.

"Now you," said one of the fairies. Briley realized it was the medic fairy she had saved from the Green Land. "Open up!" she commanded. Briley opened her mouth and watched as the fairies gathered before her, blowing that same stardust into her. She swallowed and her body felt as if it were lifting off the ground. All of her hurts and cuts and worries went away like raindrops in the breeze.

"Oh...," Briley said as her eyes drooped heavily. "Oh, that feels much better...." She felt so light she might float away, and then she began to fall asleep, but it wasn't a forced slumber. Briley entered the land of dreams, the way one does on a warm summer day, without a care in the world and the sun upon their skin. She dreamt of music and light and laughter and ice cream and dancing and skipping through the woods.

As she dreamt, the fairies worked their magic. As she slept, Darrel and Bracken maneuvered their fleet safely into the Green Sea, plunging deeper and faster than anyone had ever dared before. As Briley slept, thousands of things happened all over the world, and in the fairy world as well. But she had not a care in the world as she dreamed. She was weightless and airy, a cloud in the sky. While the fairies worked their magic, she drifted to and fro through lightness and laughter.

***

Briley awoke feeling better than she had felt in years. A smile exploded on her face. She rubbed the sleep out of her eyes and looked around. It was as if all of the colors around her were brighter, better, and tastier. The world looked delicious, like a basket of fruit ready to be peeled. She hopped right out of the cot she had slept in.

"Good morning!" she called out to the room. "Merry awakenings!" she cried out, unsure where that turn of phrase came from, but not really caring either.

She looked around and saw Harrison still slumbering in another cot. He was breathing deep in the midst of dreams. Two fairies popped out of the woodwork and flitted up to her.

"Happy dreaming?" the one on the left asked.

"Did you have pleasant fancies while you slept?" the other asked.

Briley laughed out loud. "Oh, I feel so wonderful!" Briley said, spinning in circles. "Like a cloud ready to sing!"

The fairies giggled, spinning as well. "I don't know what that means!" one of them said.

"And neither does she!" chuckled the other.

They spun together and Briley heard a tiny ukulele begin to play. She glanced about and noticed more and more fairies appearing out of the hidden crevices in the room. There upon a wooden shelf, a group of the fairies struck up a lively tune. One was playing the ukulele, another fingered the tiniest zither. There was a fiddle player, drummers, and tambourines. They sang in and out of key and in and out of harmony. One plucked a dulcimer, and Briley could only laugh and she sang right along. They joined hands, dancing in a circle. She lost time as she twirled about the room with the fairies.

She likely would have danced forever, but there was a sudden THUMP! The ship lurched to one side, and Briley stumbled mid-step toward one of the walls. Then came another THUMP! This time the noise was accompanied by a low growl, which seemed to fill the whole ship.

"What was that?" Briley asked, standing back up to her feet. She looked over and saw Harrison had spilled out of his cot onto the floor, but he was still deep in his magical slumber.

"Dunno!" said one of the fairies.

"And neither does she!" said another.

There was another THUMP. This time it shook the whole ship from side to side, and Briley stumbled across the room again. Staying there and wondering wasn't doing any good, so Briley got to her feet and headed for the door. It was hard to make headway as the room kept tilting from side to side, but whatever was out there was obviously not going away.

"Thank you for your help!" she cried out as she got to the door. She looked back and saw the fairies all working together to lift Harrison back onto a cot. "And take care of my brother!" With that, she pulled herself out into the hallway to see what was going on.

"Why is it," she wondered aloud, "that every time I start to relax, the world goes haywire?"

The hallway outside was eerily quiet. No one was running around in a panic or rushing for the hatches. Briley didn't stop to question it. She ran toward the ladder leading above decks, climbing it as quick as she could. She grabbed hold of the handle, pushing it out, and climbed onto the deck. That's when she saw everyone running around like crazy, scrambling like mad people. She looked to the wheelhouse and there Darrel stood, obviously straining to keep control of the ship.

Just as she took another step forward, a bright purple tentacle shot straight across the deck. "Oh no!" Briley cried out, jumping to avoid it as it snaked across the deck. The tentacle grabbed hold of the first thing it found, a large chunk of wood which had become dislodged, and then with lightning speed, it left again, leaving a hole in the side of their ship. She looked about and saw several similar holes in the ship, and through them, she saw the deep green of the grass surrounding them.

"What was that thing?" Briley asked a nearby Horgle, charging forward and searching for anything that might serve as a weapon. There was debris all over the deck of the ship. Briley picked up a bent piece of metal and cast her eyes about.

"That," replied the Horgle, "is a kraken!"

"I thought krakens were just myths...and that they lived in the sea." Briley realized as she spoke how dumb she must sound.

"So did I!" the Horgle replied. "But I guess we were both wrong!"

The ship shook again, lilting to the side, and Briley stumbled but caught herself.

"Brace yourselves!" Darrel cried out, holding onto the wheel.

Then another of the tentacles crashed through the wood of the ship, shooting straight down. Many of the Horgles ran away from the tentacle as it grasped through midair. But Briley charged toward it, raising her bent piece of metal. "For the Grove!" she cried out. The tentacle hit the deck, squirming around. The deck shook below her feet, but Briley ran forward.

"Keep away from it!" one of the Horgles cried.

But Briley jammed her piece of metal into the very tip of the tentacle as hard as she could. The instant she did, the tentacle whipped into the air, taking her metal with it. Purple ooze fell in thick drops from the tentacle as it squirmed about the ship. Then another tentacle shot in on the side of the ship, heading right for her. Briley jumped, none too soon, as the second tentacle zoomed right where she had been standing. Horgles jumped out of the way as the thing whipped forward, but one of them drew his sword and charged, cutting the tip of the tentacle off in one swing.

"For the Grove!" he cried and Briley grinned at him.

Purple goo gushed out of the tip of the tentacle as it recoiled in pain. The ship shook more violently. The sound of creaking wood echoed all around. "Hold fast!" Darrel cried. He was putting all of his weight into the wheel of the ship. "Ready yourselves, lads and lasses!" he cried out.

A third tentacle punched through the ship. Just as it did, Darrel threw every muscle he had against the wheel, and Briley felt herself tipping sideways. The tentacles immediately left the ship. "Stay strong lads and lasses!" Darrel cried out. "This could become quite ugly right quick!"

Briley sucked in a breath as Darrel then stopped the wheel mid-spin. There was a screeching, horrifying growly moan from outside the ship. It sounded like a hundred trumpets all off tune blown at full blast. The ship shook violently, but no more tentacles appeared. "Steady!" Darrel cried out again. "Ready archers!" he shouted.

Briley was amazed to see several Horgles grabbing bows from little tubes tied to their waists. The bows were somehow folded inside the tubes, with a string hanging on one end, and within seconds the Horgles had their bows strung and arrows nocked. Just when she thought she knew everything about them, Darrel's crew had one more surprise in store.

"Loose!" Darrel cried out.

The archers aimed perfectly, sending arrows through the holes the tentacles had created all about the ship. Some of the arrows just sailed out into the grass beyond, but some struck into the kraken. A monstrous growl surrounded the ship.

"Loose!" Darrel cried again, holding the wheel with all of his might.

More arrows flew out, and the kraken howled in pain. Purple goo rained down onto the deck of the ship through the openings. Then Darrel flung the wheel hard again, and everyone stumbled to the side as the ship broke loose from the kraken's grip. Suddenly, they were traveling through the Green Sea.

"Full speed!" Darrel yelled.

"Aye aye!" The crew rejoiced as their ship sped into the grass. The rush of the Green Sea was so loud through the many holes that Briley needed to hold her hands to her ears.

"I had no idea it was so noisy!" she said to no one in particular.

"Captain!" one of the Horgles cried "What about the other ships, Captain?"

There was a collective gasp from the Horgles, and Briley saw the look of confidence burn away from Darrel's eyes.

"We can't leave them with that beast, Captain!" Dragus

spoke.

"Aye. No, of course we can't," Darrel said with gritted teeth. "But we don't have much way of fighting it either."

"Look, Brother!" Bracken called out. "I don't think we'll need to worry about the other ships! Look!" He pointed out one of the holes in the ship and everyone craned their necks. At first all Briley could see was the thick green grass surrounding the ship, and then she saw a giant purple tentacle lash out.

"It's following us!" Briley shouted.

"I can see that!" Darrel swung the wheel again and the ship took a plunge deeper into the grass. They could only see glimpses here and there, occasional flashes of purple in the distance. Nonetheless, it was easy to tell between one glimpse and the next that the kraken was gaining on them. Their only hope was to outmaneuver it or somehow find a hiding spot.

"Where are the other ships?" Briley asked. It was impossible to see very far into the deep grass.

"I dunno!" Darrel cried out. "Hopefully they are far away from that beast. We'll have to worry about that thing before we can do anything else!"

"Tighten the rigging!" Dragus called out. "Check all your blades and ready for impact!"

"Aye, lads!" Darrel called out. "And ladies too, do as he says!" All around her Horgles were dashing about, tightening ropes. "Hold fast!" Darrel cried out.

He spun the wheel and the ship tilted to its side. Briley leapt for something to hold on to. The ship kept turning through the grass till it was nearly upside down. Luckily everyone had grabbed hold of one of the many ropes spanning the ship. Suddenly Briley understood why they wanted the ship upside down.

"Ready for full reverse on my mark!" Darrel cried out. Briley grabbed hold of a rope and held onto it as tight as she could.

"Reverse?" Bracken called out. "Little brother! Are we going to charge at it?"

"Aye, unless you've got a better idea. If you do you best be spitting it out!"

"We're nearly to the mountain passes. Let's lose it in those. That creature is right at home in the grass. We don't stand a chance taking it head on, but we might lose it in the mountains." Bracken said all of this in one breath.

"That's a fair point," Darrel said. "But I refuse to be kraken snacks today. The creature is nearly upon us. How do you propose stalling it out?"

The whoosh of the grass rushing past was deafening to the point of distraction. Briley had to strain to hear the conversation even though it was being shouted. She definitely favored Bracken's idea. She struggled along her rope, closer to Darrel, straining her ears. As she struggled closer, witches were mounting their brooms and donning their caps. Then as one, they exploded off the deck of the ship, each exiting through one of the many holes in the ship. Briley looked on. Darrel and Bracken still seemed to be arguing. Apparently the witches had a plan of their own.

"Captain!" a booming voice resounded above the din of the voices and the rush of the grass. "Rocks ahead!" the voice cried out.

"Lads and lasses, and the rest of you lot, get ready with anchors!" Darrel cried out. "Ready with hooks. Ready the lines and man the spinners! Don your best most adventurous smile, and stare death in the face today, because—"

Everyone exploded out with, "The fire in my belly it won't go out!"

"That's right, lads and lasses, we've got mountains ahead

and a kraken behind us, the witches have left, and our fleet is all a jumble. I don't have so much a plan as a deep desire to keep the blood in my veins on the inside of my clothes!"

There was a roar of laughter and applause all around. Briley grinned. This was what adventures should be like. Scary and uncertain, but filled with good moments.

"Keep your eyes peeled for a tunnel big enough for our ship, mates!" Darrel called out. "Stay as close as ye can to the rocks without banging the ship! Archers!" he cried. "Be on the lookout for anything purple. If you get the slightest glimpse of a tentacle, I want an arrow in it before you can blink! Get the anchors ready!" he called out. "If we find the right spot to duck down in, we are going for it! And be ready, lads and lasses," he grinned. "More rocks means less grass, so passing through could get pretty tricky. If the ship starts to plummet, don't panic! It'll catch itself on the next batch of grass below us."

Briley's heart pounded in her ears. Everyone scattered as fast as they could, using the ropes to maneuver along the ship. Briley joined the spotters at the front of the ship, and by sticking her eyes up to a tube, she was able to see outside the ship. As she put her eyes to the tube, the green grass around her leapt up to her eyes, magnified. Then she saw a witch whizz by, weaving between blades of grass on her broom. The witch ducked low and moved like a bumblebee between the grasses. She saw two more witches doing the same thing in the distance.

A tentacle lashed out at one of the witches. "Watch out!" Briley cried, instantly realizing there was no way for the witches to hear her. But the witch dodged and the tentacle grabbed onto the grass. The other two witches descended upon it. Ice formed all along the purple tentacle. It quivered for a moment, then broke loose of the ice, and then the body of the kraken came into view. The beast was much darker than its arms, and there were eyeballs all over its body. Each eye looked in a different direction, and they were huge hideous orbs the color of blood. There were arrows and spears sticking out of its hide at all angles, along with pieces of metal and wood. It was like a graveyard of lost pieces and dark eyes. The witches didn't seem to realize how close they were to the body, for they were focused entirely on the tentacles weaving about through the grass. Briley's heart skipped a beat watching the kraken move. It was slow, but it moved through the grass as if it wasn't even there, parting it with ease.

Briley wished there was something she could do other than watch. There was no way the ship or the witches stood a chance against something that massive. Then she felt the ship tilting to the side, and she heard a long scraping noise against the hull.

"Rocks ahead!" one of the spotters shouted.

"Nice bloody warning, you git!" Darrel cried back. "Roll with it, lads! Once we're into the rocks, we'll be on equal footing with that monster!"

Briley couldn't stand watching any more. She had to DO something or she was going to burst like an over filled balloon. She ran away from the spotters, toward the main deck, while the ship tilted to the side. She half ran, half slid along the deck, catching herself against the stairs leading up to the wheel. She vaulted up the stairs to the wheel where Darrel wrestled against it with all of his strength. Dragus stood next to him, pulling levers at the side of the wheel. Usually Darrel handled both the levers and the wheel, but it looked like he was having enough trouble just keeping the wheel steady.

"Full speed! On my mark!" Darrel called out. "Are you ready, Dragus?"

"Aye!" Dragus said, switching between levers. "I still think you're mad though!"

"Of course he's mad!" Briley chimed in, stepping forward. "No sane person would have lived this long!"

Darrel and Dragus laughed together. "Come on, lass!" they shouted as one. "Give us a hand!"

"Aye aye!" Briley jumped up to the wheel, helping Darrel pull it to the side. "Briley the Braverest at your service!"

"Cave mouth six points to starboard!" one of the spotters shouted out.

"Perfect!" Darrel cried out, switching the wheel slightly. Briley helped him push it into position. Moving the wheel was like wrestling with a cobra.

"Ready!" Darrel roared like a lion. His voice filled the ship.

"Aye, Captain!" the crew resounded.

"Mark!" Darrel called out, and Briley helped him hold the wheel steady as Dragus pulled all of the levers down at the same time. The ship shuddered, and the gears below screeched into motion. Briley was thrown backward as the ship shot forward.

"Three points to port!" one of the spotters called out, and Briley hefted the wheel three notches. Then there was a massive THUMP that rocked everyone aboard, and for a split second the ship stopped moving. Everyone lurched about as the ship stopped, and Briley held onto the wheel so as not to pitch across the deck. Then there was a cracking, grating sound and the ship shuddered forward.

"What happened??" Darrel cried out.

"The turn wasn't sharp enough, Captain!" one of the spotters called back. "We struck the tip of some rock, but it's breaking up!"

Briley held onto the wheel with all of her might. It was shaking as the ship shuddered along the rock. Darrel was straining against it as well. It felt like forever that they held onto that wheel, the whole ship vibrating, and then there was a giant CRACK! The ship shot forward and everyone was thrown to the side as the ship tilted.

"Don't let that happen again!" Darrel cried out angrily. "Sharpest eyes, all points!"

"Have you ever done this before?" Briley asked.

"Ah no, lass, never once! But of course, that IS what makes all the best stories to tell!"

Briley grinned, nodding. The grass was thinning out inside the cave, and she wondered in the back of her mind what might happen when they ran out of grass. She wondered too how the other ships were faring and what had happened to the witches, but there was simply nothing they could do about any of that.

"Aye, Captain!" she finally said. "Onward into the best stories then!" Darrel and Dragus laughed heartily, beaming at her.

"The kraken is following, Captain!" one of the spotters shrieked. Everyone turned to the spotter, who was motioning wildly.

The deeper they traveled into the cavern, the darker it got. The crew lit lanterns within the ship, but the spotters couldn't see very far. The grass still grew thick within the cavern.

"Full stop!" Darrel cried out suddenly. Dragus began pulling levers back one by one, and the crew ran about, securing ropes and making preparations.

"What is the plan, Captain?" Dragus asked.

Darrel sighed, shaking his giant head. "I don't know any more, truth be told. We've lost the witches and the other ships."

"But we haven't lost them!" Briley said. "We just don't know where they are!"

"The girl has a point," Dragus grinned.

"Aye, and nerve to spare!" Darrel agreed.

"What do you suggest, lass?" they both asked at once.

Briley grinned. "There's only one thing to do, as far as I can tell."

"What's that?" Darrel asked.

"Well, we can't go back and we can't go forward, so we have to find a way to get up!"

"Up?" Darrel and Dragus were looking at Briley like she had seventeen eyeballs.

"Yeah!" she said. "Get the balloon hoisted! We go up into this mountain as far as we can...find a way out! The cave probably connects to another opening. And there is no way the kraken can climb those rocks. Look at it!" Briley was gathering excitement as she talked. "It was born and bred in the Green Sea! That's all it knows!"

Dragus and Darrel stared at Briley. She swore she could feel another eyeball growing out of the top of her head. She shifted uncomfortably for a second, and then blurted out, "We can do it! The fairies will help us!"

"The fairies?" Darrel and Dragus both laughed. "How in fairyland would they be able to help?"

"They can be our eyes...they glow a little! It's now or never. What do you say? Let the fairies guide us and we can escape the kraken!"

"Uhh, Captain!" one of the crew shouted. "Orders?"

Then there was a massive thump that shook their ship from timber to timber. Briley was thrown to the ground and Darrel caught himself against the wheel. Dragus steadied the captain, but immediately there was another thump, and then another, and Briley heard the sound of creaking wood.

"Archers! Loose! Give it everything you got!" Briley shouted.

"Aim for the eyes if you can!"

Arrows zipped through the holes in the ship, planting themselves into the body of the beast. Purple ooze slopped onto the deck of the ship.

Darrel was back at the wheel, but Briley was the one shouting orders. "Ready the spinners and make haste! Man the pumps... we're going to climb this mountain if it's the last thing we do!"

Some of the crew looked at Briley, and she could feel even more eyeballs growing out of her head. But there was no more time for dawdling.

"Well, you heard the lass!" Darrel called out. "Hop to!"

"Captain?" Dragus asked in a shocked tone.

"I'm not the captain anymore!" Darrel laughed. "I just steer the ruddy boat!" Then Darrel plucked off his massive cap, three times the size of Briley's head, and plopped it on her curly hair. It began to sink over her eyes and then stopped, and Briley could feel it shrinking to fit her just so. Briley smiled so wide, wider than she had ever smiled before. Part of her smile was for Argon, who she knew was connected with this ship. It felt right to be the captain of the ship made out of the Green Land.

"All right, Argonauts!" Briley said aloud, making up the word on the spot. "Prepare to lower the outer shell and loft the balloon! This needs to be seamless! I want the balloon fully pumped and secured before we let her out, so we can take that purple squid face by surprise! Who is with me?"

"I'm with you, Sis!" Harrison could not have chosen a better moment to appear on deck. Briley's mood soared. The kraken was attacking them fiercely, but she knew that if Harrison was by her side, there wasn't anything that could dare stand between them and the best of adventures.

"Harrison!" Briley called out. "How are you feeling, big

brother?"

"Hungry!" he chortled back. "I think I want some kraken back ribs for dinner!"

"Huzzah!" the crew called out. "A fine feast!"

"We're all with you!" Grindel shouted out. The first mate appeared on deck covered in so much soot, the only parts of her that were clean were on the inside. "Captain!" Grindel called out. "There's been more than one fire aboard this boat with all these crazy maneuvers, but there's one fire that won't be put out." She grinned, and even her teeth were black with soot.

"Gather the fairies!" Briley said, standing atop the wooden platform before the wheel. "Gather them all! They are going to be our eyes so we don't run into a ruddy rock and mess up the whole ship!"

"Aye, Captain!" Grindel ran back below decks. Darrel beamed at Briley, and Harrison ran along the deck, helping the crew secure lines. The ship was rocking back and forth as the kraken struggled to maintain its hold. Arrows riddled its enormous body, making it look like a giant purple archery target with arms and eyes. There was no nice way to slice it. The kraken looked a horrible hideous mess all day long and twice on Thursdays.

"Torches to the arrows!" Briley called when the balloon had been assembled on deck. The fairies all hovered around Briley, and Harrison stood atop the platform next to her. "On my mark, we make the thing burn!"

"Huzzah!" many cried.

"Get the bellows a blowin, the ropes a swingin, get the songs as loud and fierce and as proud as you can, because the fire in my belly just won't go out!"

Harrison erupted into song, dancing beside her on the platform. Briley smiled. It was so good to have her brother back.

The fairies buzzed about Briley, glowing slightly. Briley took a minute to absorb this feeling. They were about to attempt something wild, crazy, inexplicable, and amazing. She just hoped she lived through it. She reached out, squeezed Harrison's hand, and cried out, "MARK!"

The arrows swished through the air, trailing little tongues of fire behind them. As the arrows hit the kraken, there was a horrible growl of a screech that filled the cavern. The ship shuddered for a split second, and then the tentacle let loose of the ship.

"Open her up!" Briley cried out. The Horgles pulled at the cranks, lowering the ship's sides. The balloon whooshed up above them, instantly taking the ship up. "All right, my lovely fairies," Briley said, smiling wide. "Please don't let us run into anything!" The fairies all giggled and spun out above the ship, shimmering in the darkness like...well, like only little fairies can.

"It's working!" Harrison clapped her on her shoulder and Briley grinned at her brother. Everyone ran to the sides of the ship, looking below as the ship climbed higher into the cavern.

"It's stuck down there, Captain!" one of the Horgles cried out.

"Good!" Briley said. "Archers to the sides! If that thing comes acallin after us, remind it why it left us alone in the first place!"

Harrison cartwheeled across the railing and Briley jumped for joy. Darrel and Dragus steered the ship as it went higher and higher into the cavern. Grindel oversaw the crew on deck as the ship floated up into the mountain. Every once in a while the fairies would call out to move the ship this way or that, and Darrel and Dragus would pull the lever or move the wheel just so to avoid the rocks around.

Below, the kraken struggled to climb the sides of the rocks.

"Loose arrows!" Briley called out, and the archers sent a

volley down the side of the ship, landing little quills into the beast's purple hide. The beast let out a mighty roar, shaking the cavern around them. The fairies flitted around, avoiding small rocks as they fell from above. Briley looked upward. There was a hint of light far above them. Hopefully it was an opening from the cavern out into the skies above. If they could just make it there without getting destroyed by the falling rocks or eaten alive by the kraken below, they would be able to find the rest of the fleet.

The fairies flitted from side to side, guiding the ship, and Darrel and Dragus followed their movements very adeptly, steering the ship as they climbed.

"Arrows! Arrows! Arrows!" Briley cried out. A giant rock plummeted past the ship, inches from the bow, and Briley cringed. It would only take one of those to take the ship down, dashing any hopes of outrunning the kraken. "Lighten the load!" she cried out. "Dump anything you can over the side!"

The Horgles began dumping bags and goods over the side, dropping whatnots, knick knacks, mish mash, and whatever else they could find. The archers let loose with fury, and Briley could only watch. Harrison was cartwheeling on the railing, whooping encouragement to the crew. Bracken jumped up beside Harrison, encouraging their efforts. Rocks and boulders fell. All around them the cavern shook with fury as they ascended through the cavern.

"Hold fast!" Dragus called out as the fairies moved to the left. Darrel moved the wheel slightly, and another giant rock tumbled from above, crashing into the sides of the cavern as it fell. The kraken below screeched and Briley crossed her fingers, sucked in her breath, and only hoped that they could all make it out alive.

While all of this was going on, some of the Horgles began to hum a sailing song. It sounded familiar and haunting and Briley hummed along, not knowing the words. But soon the sound of the humming fell into the rhythm of the falling rocks, the arrows flying.

Then, as if it burst out of nothing, Briley saw light filling the cavern. "We're nearly there!" she cried out. "Nearly there!"

Dragus pulled hard on the levers and Harrison vaulted from the railing, pulling on the ropes. Darrel steered hard. Bracken leapt into the rigging.

Just as the ship was nearing the opening, the kraken made a final grab for the ship and Briley saw a giant tentacle latch onto the mast, yanking the ship hard to the side. The ship spun suddenly.

"AXES!" Briley shouted in a voice she barely recognized. Harrison leapt from the railing, dashing across the ship with his twin swords flashing. Then another tentacle lashed out about the ship, grabbing the bow. Briley sucked in a breath, watching as the Horgles all rushed to the tentacles, trying to free themselves from the kraken's grip. The fairies were heading back to the ship, and Briley chanced a look backward at the purple beast below. It had a hundred eyes, each dark red, burning with fire, and in each of them she saw a reflection of her own worried face. Every single eye was locked onto her, and Briley screamed at the top of her lungs "Leave us alone!"

The beast either couldn't hear or didn't care, and its great purple arms kept grabbing onto pieces of the ship, pulling them back into the cavern. She knew if they didn't break free soon, the kraken would pull them down into the pit of the cavern. They would all perish. She thought of Argon, how he was part of the ship, like it was his life's blood. She called out to him. "Argon!" she cried. "Argon, wake up! We need your help!"

Argon did not respond. The ship was pulling backward,

and there was nothing she could do. "Help us!" Briley cried out. "Arrows! Fire! Beat it with a stick!" she screamed. She had never felt so desperate, and that was when she realized everyone was staring at her. Harrison's eyes were wide. Darrel and Dragus had stopped moving. Even the fairies floated without movement, each with their eyes locked on her.

Briley looked down at herself, wondering what they were all staring at. She was glowing, softly, like a candle flame or a coal that had once been hot. As she looked down, she saw the glow increasing, and noticed she was hovering ever so slightly off the deck of the ship. Then she felt the glow begin to spread warmth throughout her. The ship was still being pulled back. Briley felt a surge inside of her like a lightning bolt had struck deep in her heart. She closed her eyes and she grew warmer. When she opened her eyes, Briley had changed utterly. Feathery wings grew out of her back and she felt graceful, poised, almost like an angel. She had never before in her life felt as if anything were truly in her control, but in that moment, a perfect storm brewed inside her heart, and Briley leapt from the deck of the ship, straight into the air, spinning, letting her glow surround the ship and enlighten the cavern. She held out her fist toward the kraken and opened her fingers one by one.

As she released her pinky, its eyes dimmed from burning flames to a dull red as if it were lulled toward sleep. She opened her ring finger and the tentacles gripping the ship went slack as if it had been hit by tranquilizers. Her middle finger extended, and the kraken let out a soft purring noise akin to a kitten. Her index pointed toward the beast, and it slithered away from the ship. As she released her thumb, the creature fell asleep.

"Come," she breathed in an ethereal voice her throat had never made before. She flew forward, leading the way out into the dazzling sun. As Briley set her feet down upon the deck of the ship, Harrison hurried over to her with a mirror in his hand.

"That was amazing, Sis!" he grinned. "Look!"

And what she saw nearly stopped her heart. Her normally curly dark hair was now straight and free flowing, the tips fluttering slightly in the breeze. Her skin had turned a light green, like shallow streams, and she could see the veins beneath the skin, a slightly darker green. Small horns decorated her head, and as she smiled, she realized what had happened. "Thank you, Argon," she breathed. Her heart slowed as she realized they were out of danger, and Briley felt her body return to its normal state.

"I didn't know you had it in you!" Darrel grinned at her, finally coming to his senses.

"I didn't!" Briley said in that same ethereal voice. "It was Argon. He's part of me now."

Bracken ran up to her and swallowed her in a giant hug. "My my, kiddo! You certainly put on a show!"

"We need a song to mark this day!" Dragus said. "Ready the drums! Bring out the zithers! Play, Horgles! Play, fairies! Play, today! It was a near and miraculous thing we just witnessed! Let us not forget!"

And soon the ship was bobbing along with the clouds, a melody streaming out of it like none ever heard before. Sweet and slow, the music poured out of the ship, and although the song had never been sung before, everyone knew the words.

It was never afore
She lit up the dark
And took on the beast
With her fire
With her spark!

219

A. Henry Moen

Briley the Braverest!
She conquered this day
Opened her hand
And now the beast doth lay!
Deep in the cavern
Where our fate might have laid
Except that
Briley the Braverest
Has conquered this day!
So gather your courage!
And gather your wits!
Gather, gather and let us all sing!
We draw another breath and with it rejoice!
That Briley the Braverest conquered today!

Chapter Twelve: Reunion

Grace walked with Ann through the twisting tunnels of the cavern until she came to the mouth of the waterfall, where the water splashed onto a ledge underneath it. Grace strode forward, and in the midst of the rushing water was a pedestal with a single egg perched upon it.

"Is this what you wanted me to see?" Grace asked. "Why, that's just an egg!"

"It is not just any egg, though!" Ann said. "Open it."

"Hmmph," was Grace's only reply.

Grace examined the egg before taking hold of it. It was large, about the size of a watermelon. It was blue and green like a river and sea melted together, and yet distinct. She reached out a hand and felt the shell of the egg. It was rough with little bumps all over it. Then Grace took the egg in both her hands and lifted it from the pedestal. The egg became hot in her hands as she moved it from the water.

"Oh my!" Grace exclaimed.

It began to burn her fingers and Grace let go of the egg. It fell to the ground at her feet, and the colors on the shell began to swirl and twist like a storm.

"What's happening?" Grace asked, but again Ann did not answer.

Then there was a hiss and a pop, and the shell of the egg grew a single crack. A tiny black claw wedged out of the shell, and then another, and Grace watched a tiny paw emerge from the egg. The egg twitched and then another black paw stuck out. The shell was thick. Whatever was inside was struggling hard to get out. Grace bent down and put her hands to the crack, pulling the seams apart. She pulled and pulled until finally the egg split open, and there inside was the tiniest black creature Grace had ever seen. It looked like a salamander except it was darker than night, darker than black. Grace picked up the creature and cradled it in her arm, clutching it to her chest.

"Aaarrooo" the creature purred in a tiny voice. "Aaarrrrooo."

"I don't understand, Ann," Grace said, "You took me through all of this for a pet?"

When Grace turned to look back at Ann, the old woman shook her head from side to side. "Oh no," Ann began. "That is not a pet."

Grace nuzzled the creature in the crook of her arm "What is it?"

"Well it's a dragon, of course," Ann chuckled. "Your dragon."

"Mine?" Grace asked. "What do you mean? Enough riddles! Spit it out! I'm tired of these games! Who ARE you!?"

Ann quirked a smile. "Ah. So you want to see?" And then Ann began to change. Her white hair grew longer and darker until it was black like the feathers of a raven. Her simple attire transformed into a dazzling gown that flowed all about her. The cane changed into a scepter with a red ruby sitting atop it, and the next thing Grace knew she was face to face with the Peacock Queen.

Grace backed away, but there was nowhere to go except into the rushing waterfall. Her back went up against the pedestal and water poured all around her as the Peacock Queen advanced.

"Do you know how long I've waited for the person who could open that egg, child?" the queen asked.

"I don't care!" Grace shouted. "Leave me alone! What do you want?"

"Aaarrrooooo," the tiny dragon moaned in Grace's arms. It burrowed deep into the crook of her arm, and Grace realized it must be afraid.

The Peacock Queen smiled at her and stroked the ruby on the top of her scepter. The ruby glowed slightly and then four of her knights came charging into the cavern. There was nowhere to run.

"Where did they come from?" Grace asked in a panic. "How did they get past Patience?"

"Patience is waiting for you, Grace," the Peacock Queen chuckled. "Or rather, he is waiting for the one who holds that dragon."

Grace shook her head. It didn't matter now. The guards were getting closer and her back was up to the pedestal.

"Aaaarrrrrooooooo," the dragon moaned, burying itself into her.

"It'll be all right," Grace whispered to the tiny dragon. She didn't know why it was so important. Perhaps it was the treasure Horace had told her of. At the thought of Horace's betrayal, Grace cringed. He had seemed like such a kind old man. Grace weighed her options. There was no way she was going to fight her way out of this one. Attacking the Peacock Queen was suicide, but if she had worked this hard to get her hands on the baby dragon, Grace definitely did not want her getting ahold of it. Grace closed her eyes. "I'm sorry," she whispered to the dragon.

"Aaaaarrrrooooooo?" it replied. The dragon gave Grace hope, and an idea blossomed in her mind. "I give up!" Grace said aloud. She kneeled to the ground and held the dragon aloft.

"Hold!" the Peacock Queen said aloud as she stroked the ruby on her scepter again. The knights stopped mid-step. The queen smiled at Grace and strode calmly toward her.

"Please forgive me for this," Grace whispered to the dragon.

"Aaaarrrrrooooo," it replied.

The queen was closer now, but not close enough. Grace tensed her muscles. She would only have one chance. The queen just needed to take two more steps.

One.

Two.

Grace flung the dragon high into the air.

"NO!" the queen shouted.

Grace was already moving, her eyes locked on the scepter in the queen's hands. She took hold of it in her left hand while her right hand smacked the queen right in her perfect pale nose. Blood gushed from the queen's nose, and Grace spun away with the scepter in her hand.

"GUARDS!" The queen commanded "Seize her!"

But the guards stood stock still, and Grace was overjoyed that she had guessed correctly; the scepter was the key to controlling the guards! But she couldn't dawdle there. She looked up and saw the dragon plummeting back to the ground, flapping its tiny wings furiously, but they weren't strong enough for flight yet. Grace bolted for the opening, catching the dragon between one

224

step and the next.

"Got you," Grace breathed.

The poor creature was trembling. "Aaaarrrroooo," it moaned.

Grace dashed past the knights for the opening. The tunnels were a maze, but she trusted her heart. Every time she met a crossroads, Grace chose on the instant, running as fast as her legs would carry her. Then up ahead, she saw the door that Patience had been guarding, and she rushed for it. When she dashed through, she saw Patience still sitting there, silently.

"Ah," Patience said. "My time has come."

"OK...," Grace panted. Her heart was beating so fast it felt like it might explode. "That's...just...great.... Can you get me and my friends out of here?"

Patience nodded. "Hold onto me." His voice was a sing song. "You may want to close your ears." Grace put a hand on Patience's arm. She cradled the dragon in her other arm. Then Patience opened his mouth and let out a siren like wail, increasing in pitch. There was no way to plug her ears. Grace felt as if the world were sliding past her. The world trembled and Grace slid as Patience traveled.

Instantly they were back in the cavern. Jaspar, Hamper, and Trick, and the rest of their band, were still gathered on the edge of the lake. Dragons stood on the outside of the lake, guarding the treasure. Patience moved between them as if they were not there. "Come," he whispered. "They will not harm you while I am near. I am the guardian."

"What happened, Grace?" Jaspar asked, looking from Patience to Grace, to the tiny black dragon tucked in her arm.

"I'll tell you all about it later," Grace said. "First, let's get out of here before the queen comes looking for me again!"

Hamper and Trick vaulted to their feet with twin grins on

their faces. "And while we're at it—" Hamper began.

"We might as well grab a pocket of the loot!" Trick finished, scooping coins into the pockets of his pants.

Their small band each took a handful of the treasure. Grace giggled, plucking just one emerald from the pile of gems at her feet. "OK, NOW can we go?" she demanded.

"Yes," Jaspar agreed. "Let's get out of here before these dragons decide they are hungry!"

"They will not as long as I am around, I am—" Patience began.

"We know, we know—" Hamper said.

"You're the guardian!" Trick finished.

Patience's mouth quirked into something suspiciously similar to a grin. "You are right," he said. "Now grab hold of me, each of you."

"And plug your ears if you can," Grace said. "It's really noisy."

They each took hold of Patience. Grace held onto his arm. Jaspar put his hand right next to hers. Hamper and Trick put their hands on his back. The centaur reached out for his hand. The others all gathered around and Patience roared like a siren. Everything spun. Grace felt pulled in a hundred directions at once, and Patience shifted, bringing all of them with him. She felt like she were being folded in half and slammed into walls. It was agony, but it only lasted an instant. Grace clutched hard onto her friends with tears at the corners of her eyes.

***

Grace shuddered as the shifting ended. They were in a castle, but it was not the Crystal Palace. It was made of stone. They stood in a great hall, but it was empty. There were long wooden tables, but they were overgrown with dust and moss covered them. At the end of the hall sat three chairs, also empty and overgrown.

"Where are we?" Grace asked.

"A safe place," Patience whispered. "There is something you should see."

Jaspar started straightening the chairs. Hamper and Trick looked at each other for a split second. A tiny grin landed on Hamper's face. Then Trick laughed aloud. "We'll be back," they said in unison, and then they dashed out of the hall. The rest of the band began helping Jaspar straighten up.

"Come," Patience said, simply. Grace followed him to three seats at the end of the hall. Patience stopped at the bottom of the steps before the chairs. "These," he said, "are thrones of the ancient kings and queens."

Grace looked at the massive chairs. They were made of burnished metal, and while the rest of the castle seemed run down and overgrown, the chairs glistened as if newly polished.

"Was that before the Peacock Queen took over?" Grace asked, unsure why Patience was showing her this.

"Yes," Patience said. "She was born here. Until she became of age, she lived here."

"Why did she leave?" Grace asked.

"Because," Patience said. "Her twin cast her out of the castle."

"Her...what?" Grace gasped. "You mean there's another queen out there?"

"No," Patience said. "Her twin was cast out of our land. The queen performed magic when she was banished from the castle to banish her twin beyond the Hedge."

"So" Grace said, "The Peacock Queen's twin is in my land?"

"Ah." Patience said. "She was."

The baby dragon chose that moment to burrow deeper into Grace's arms. She clutched it closer to her.

"There was one born of light and one born of dark," Patience said. "Both had an affinity for the dragons, for their father was a dragon himself."

"What do you mean, one light and one dark?" Grace asked, almost afraid to hear the answer.

"It is quite literal," Patience said. "While the Peacock Queen has hair darker than night, her twin has hair that glistens like the sun."

"But that can't be—" Grace began.

"It is also true," Patience said, "That while the Peacock Queen desires power, her twin, her counterpart, desires freedom for the fairy folk."

"How do you know all of this?" Grace demanded.

"Because," Patience said simply. "I was her father. Just as I am yours."

"What?" Grace exclaimed. "Me?"

Patience nodded. Then he slid up to one of the chairs and sat upon it. "The dragon in your arms," he said, "Is my grandchild."

This was too much for Grace to take in. "But that's impossible!" she shouted. "I'm only thirteen years old!"

"Ah." Patience smiled at her. "But time does not always tell the truth. Sometimes it lies."

"How can time lie?" Grace asked.

"Here there are many afternoons before morning is done with in your land," Patience said.

"But how do you know it's me and not some other blonde kid from over there?" Grace asked. She kept thinking that this was Briley's adventure, not hers. If anyone was going to be queen of these parts, it would be Briley, while Grace was off exploring and climbing mountains. "All I really want to do is play and explore," Grace shouted. "You're not pinning this kingdom on me! I won't have it! I quit!" Her face felt like it was about to explode.

Patience laughed, and the sound of it filled the hall. Grace didn't think it was the least bit funny.

"If you're her DAD, how come you were locked up? If I'm your daughter, who the heck are the people I grew up with? If this is your grandbaby, how come the Peacock Queen couldn't open the egg?"

"All good questions," Patience said. "The answers to which you will get in good time. But first," he said, "Sit next to me. Hold my hand. Let me show you."

Grace looked up to Patience. The throne he sat in was conformed as if created for his body, with indentations for his tail and scales. Then she looked down to the little dragon in her arms.

"Are you?" it asked her.

"What?" Grace said, staring deep into its pitch black eyes.

"Are you my mother?" it said.

"Is that what you've been trying to ask?" Grace asked it. "When you were saying aroo?"

The dragon nodded. Grace felt a tear falling down her cheek. "No," she said. "I am not your mother. I am something better than that."

The dragon's jaws creaked into a smile. It had no teeth yet, and Grace smiled back at it. Her heart warmed to the creature. Suddenly she knew what it was to care more about something than even your own self.

"All right," Grace looked up to Patience. "Show me."

With that, she sat in the chair next to Patience and reached out her hand. When their fingers touched, Grace gasped and was thrown backward through time. She saw herself holding the dragon, then she saw their party arriving in the hall all holding onto Patience. She watched for minutes as nothing happened.

The moss and dust all cleared off the tables. The overgrown doors became clean, and then without warning, the hall was filled with life. The tables were filled with fairy folk, and music was in the air. The hall was no longer dark, but bright and cheery, with candelabras burning brightly overhead. Grace looked to her left and saw Patience still holding her hand. She looked to her right. The Peacock Queen was sitting next to her.

Grace almost screamed until she realized the queen was a younger version. She looked to be about ten years old, and almost looked happy. Then she smiled at Grace, and she almost blanched. Grace forced a smile onto her lips.

"Good morning, sister," the queen said.

"Good morning," Grace gulped. Patience squeezed her hand and Grace looked over to him.

"What you are about to see is what changed the course of not only your life, Grace, but life for all of us on this side of the Hedge." He grimaced. "Are you ready?"

"Well, I don't see what difference it makes how ready I am," Grace said. "You're going to show me anyway. Am I right?"

Patience laughed so hard that the chair he was in shook with the force of it. "Ah, it is good to be in your company again. And yes, you are quite right."

Grace took in a deep breath. "OK," she said. "Then show me."

"Hold onto me," Patience said.

Then Grace watched as the people in the hall sped into motion, becoming blurs she couldn't keep track of. The sun came up, then set. Parties were thrown, decrees made, plays were performed, all in the blink of an eye. Then the activity stopped again, and Grace gasped. "I do not think I will ever get used to that sensation."

"Ah," Patience said. "Neither do I."

Grace looked to her right, but her sister was not sitting next to her. The hall was empty except for herself and Patience. Then the doors at the end of the hall burst open and several of the crocodile guards Grace had encountered earlier entered. They walked in unison, each carrying a heavy iron spear, and in the fist of each there was a chain. More and more of the creatures entered, each dragging a chain. Grace started to get up, but Patience held her hand firmly. "Do nothing," he said. "Watch."

Then the hall was filled with the crocodiles, and they began to pull the chains forward, putting all of their weight into it. Whatever they were hauling had to be tremendously strong. Then silver glistened beyond the doorway, and the guards kept hauling until they pulled in a dragon like liquid living silver, and it struggled against the chains. It was Patience, except the version of Patience Grace was looking at was anything but fatherly. It snarled. It thrashed. It tried to bite.

Then one of the crocodiles strode to the stairs before the thrones. "We have come for our reward!" it snarled.

Grace watched a much more refined version of herself come running out of a doorway behind the thrones.

"What is the meaning of this?" her other self demanded. "Release my father at once!"

Then the Peacock Queen came behind her. She was dressed in one of her eye blurring gowns, and carried the scepter with the ruby atop it. "Let them speak, Sister."

"We have done as you requested, majesty," the head crocodile snarled. "Now grant us the land you promised!"

Then something jolted inside Grace's heart and her mind became one with her other self. "Oh Sister!" she cried. "What have you done?"

"It is none of your concern," the queen said. "Go, before I order them to capture you as well!"

"But what can you gain from this?" Grace asked, shocked to the core.

"Everything." There was a gleam in the queen's eyes. "The seas. The skies. The dragons. The faeries. This castle. I can gain… everything!"

Grace looked to her father as he continued to wrestle against the chains. "You won't," she said.

"Ah, you are too late to stop this!" the queen said.

"No," Grace said. "I'm not."

"Seize her!" the queen shouted.

But Grace was already moving. She did not have the same powers her sister had. She did not have powerful magic or the aid of the goblins and crocodiles. But there was one kind of magic that Grace knew better than anyone. "Grow," she breathed, reaching inward. The crocodiles were coming for her and Grace smiled at her father. "Grow," she said, feeling the pulse of the land about her.

Then Patience broke loose from his chains, thrashing with his tails and his claws, scattering the crocodiles like green sticks.

"Grow!" Grace commanded.

She was not speaking about Patience, though. Patience had broken loose all on his own. Soon the earth shook and Grace watched her sister's eyes widen.

"No," the queen said.

"Yes," Grace said. Then she shouted out in fury, "Every blade, every leaf, every tree! Grow! Swallow it up! Grow!" she cried out. "Every pebble, every piece, every seed!" The walls around them shook. "Grow! Grow! Grow!"

The Peacock Queen ran to Grace and gripped her arm in her

hands, but it was too late. It had used every ounce of magic Grace had within her, but the spell had already taken hold.

The queen looked into Grace's eyes. "Goodbye, Sister."

Suddenly Grace was spinning away, far far away. She was flying not only from the castle, but from the very land she had lived in. The world blurred and twisted. Rain slashed. Thunder cracked. She cried out. She looked up. Looking down on her was a face she did not recognize, except that Grace did recognize it. She had grown up with that face. It was the face of the woman who had raised her in Piedmont, and she was smiling. It was too much to take all at once.

"Stop!" she cried out. All at once, Grace was slammed back into the present with a jarring sensation. She rubbed her temples. "I don't understand," Grace said. "I don't have magic."

Patience chuckled. "Ah, but you do," he said. "Everyone has magic. Some just know how to use it better than others."

"So.... I...grew the Green Sea?" Grace asked. Patience nodded. "But what did it accomplish?" Grace asked. "It didn't stop her."

"Ah," Patience grinned. "Perhaps not, but you most certainly slowed her down. What used to take a day to travel now takes weeks. The Green Sea hides many wonders, and swallowed still others."

"I'm just a girl. I'm not a princess," Grace said. "I don't want to be queen."

"Then don't," Patience said. "Stay down here while she rules above."

Grace did not need to consider that for more than a few seconds before answering. "I can't do that," she said. "You know that I can't."

"Just so," Patience said.

Just then Hamper and Trick bounded through the doors. "OK!" they said in unison. "This is officially the most boring abandoned castle we've ever explored!" They were covered from head to foot in spider webs and dust. Hamper's face was so dirty she could barely see his eyes. Grace laughed, looking to Jaspar and the rest.

"Well then," she said as regally as she could muster. "Who's ready to go take on the queen?" Everyone strode toward the thrones. "Can you take us back to the Crystal Palace, Patience?" Grace asked. "I think there are some dragons who need persuading."

"Why yes," Patience grinned. "Yes, of course I can."

They all took hold of Patience and he was shifting again. Grace gritted her teeth and they spun away from the undersea castle.

***

Briley awoke from a dream. Argon had come to her in it, vaguely, like an outline of his former self. If she concentrated, Briley could feel the thrum of him inside her heart. Somehow he had given himself not only to the ship, but to her specifically. She could also feel the river of power he had opened up inside her like a poisonous flower. Argon had passed from real life, and she missed him. She dressed and went to the deck of the ship with a tear in her eye.

The sun was high above them. Darrel and Dragus were singing a chanty, steering the ship. Harrison was amidst a group of Horgles in the center of the ship, dancing to their great victory. Briley still wore the captain's hat, and some of the Horgles even saluted her as she passed. Briley couldn't help but chuckle at that. They were deep in the mountains now, likely getting closer to the Peacock Queen's castle than any of them liked.

She was just about to ask about finding the rest of the fleet when in the background she heard the music. Briley shielded her eyes with her hand and turned to see black specks on the horizon. She smiled to herself, not caring how the witches had managed to find them. The witches zoomed closer and closer with their little fleet of ships near at hand, and Briley's heart began to beat more fiercely.

"I can feel them!" she cried out, clutching a hand to her chest. "I mean, I can really, really feel them!"

The Horgles cheered as Harrison bounded up to her. "Sis!" he chuckled. "We're all taking bets on when you're going to turn back into that green angel. That was amazing!" His eyes met hers and Briley hugged her brother close, bringing him against her.

"I love you, Harrison" she said. He was squirming against her, trying to break free, but she wouldn't let him out of the hug. "I still am the angel," Briley chuckled, squeezing him tighter. It smacked Briley hard how much they needed to rely on each other. "You're all I have left, Brother!"

"Aww, stop it, Sis. Everything will be fine. You'll see." He was still trying to break away. "We'll rescue Grace and fix Wendell, and then we'll get back home just like in all the proper fairy stories. This one will end great!"

He tried to break away from her hug, but she wouldn't let him. A tear formed in the corner of Briley's eye. "That's not how it's going to end, Harrison."

The witches began landing on the deck of the ship, their eyes shining like stars. Some landed beside Darrel and Dragus, but they just grinned and pointed in her direction. "Not the captain anymore," she heard Darrel say. "I just steer the thing. Talk to her!"

Briley smiled, removing the captain's hat from her head and

bowing to the witches. Harrison was off like a shot the second she let him go.

"Thank you," Briley said. "For keeping the fleet in one piece."

"What of the beast?" one of the witches asked.

"Contained for now. Far from here." Briley found her voice catching a little. It had been an emotional journey from the beginning. "We almost lost the ship...." Briley choked back a tear. "But we are safe now."

The witches gathered around Briley, each taking a turn to lay their hands upon her brow or her back.

"You have changed," one of them finally said. "We felt it. It's how we were able to find you. Your magic called to us."

Briley opened her mouth, but the witches weren't finished speaking.

"And if we could sense it, you know what that means." The witch speaking looked straight into Briley's eyes, and she finished the sentence.

"It means we need to hurry. The Peacock Queen knows too."

The witches all nodded.

Briley swallowed back a sob. It was so much pressure on such a small thing.

"Full speed!" Briley cried out. "We run straight for the throat!"

"What do we do when we get there?" Dragus asked her. "Have you come up with a plan?"

"I haven't!" Briley smiled at him. "But I do have an idea!"

Just then two more witches came zipping down from the sky. They flew about the ship, creating a kind of shield. If something or someone was going to attack the fleet, the witches would handle it first. They passed through a bank of clouds, and one of the Horgles above shouted out, "Castle ahoy!"

Briley Van Campton

Briley squinted into the distance, and there, perched atop one of the highest mountains, was the Crystal Palace, the home of the Peacock Queen, who everyone dreaded. Fear pricked her heart, and as she cast her eyes about, she saw many quailing now that their destination was so near...as if it had actually become real for the first time. Briley wasn't about to let her crew cower. She started shouting commands. "Sing!" Briley commanded. "Dance!" She called out. "Make music and merry!"

She laughed out as the witches next to her grinned and kicked off the ship, entwining the ships with their songs. The fleet made its way through the mountains surrounded by a wave of celebration, and Briley grinned, watching Harrison dance. There was no doubt that the Peacock Queen would see them coming. Briley only hoped she could see the smile on each of their faces.

"We are drawing near!" Grindel said, coming up to her.

"Aye!" Dragus said. "Whatever we are going to do, we best be doing it soon."

"You do have a plan, don't you?" Grindel asked.

Briley shook her head. "No." She hesitated for only a moment. "But onward we go! The witches are with us! The Horgles are here! The Green Land is with us, and I've got Argon on my side!" Then she stood and climbed up next to the wheel. She shouted out as loud as she could. "Onward!" Briley squeezed Harrison's hand as the Crystal Palace appeared on the horizon. The sun was setting, turning the palace amazing shades of red as the sun crept down.

Harrison looked over to her and grinned, squeezing her hand back. "This is the best adventure yet, Sis!" he chuckled. "You're going to have to work really hard to top this one!"

"I hope I won't have to!" Briley laughed back at him. "This one's been big enough for ten adventures combined!"

"Ah! You young'uns ain't seen nothing yet!" Darrel chortled. "Still plenty of stories to tell!"

"Aye!" Dragus clapped a hand on each of their backs. "Now, as for this plan you have? I'd love to hear it."

"Yeah." Harrison looked to her knowingly. "What's the plan, Sis?"

Briley sucked in a deep breath. "Joy is my plan." Everyone in ear shot stopped moving. They had all been waiting or hoping that Briley knew some secret they didn't. "This is how we win, everyone!" she cried out. "With laughter and vigor and the fires in our bellies! We go in singing! Witches, gather your drums! Horgles, grab your fiddles!" She spun in circles, twirling her hat in the air. "Fairies, raise your voices! Harrison!" She grinned at her older brother.

"Yeah, Si.... I mean, Captain?" he blushed slightly.

"Lead us in the jig! Let 'em hear us coming for miles around, and make no mistake that the fire in our bellies won't go out!"

There was a loud HUZZAH from the crew, and soon enough the air was filled with even more merriment and laughter, and song burst forth as the sun slid under the horizon. The stars all peeked out as if it were a sparkling audience gathered in black seats. They twinkled in rhythm, and Briley smiled as the ships grew closer. They were all singing joyfully. Hope filled the air. There was pleasure on everyone's faces, but they were also waiting for.... Dragons? An army? Something?

"We are almost to the castle!" Bracken called out. Everyone gathered by the railing to look.

The Crystal Palace reflected the light of the night, sparkling in return and glittering like a thousand diamonds. Briley squinted at the palace. There was no way they didn't know they were approaching, and yet there was no resistance at all as of yet. Then she spotted a speck standing atop the tallest tower. Slowly the speck gained shape as they neared, and Briley saw the Peacock Queen standing alone, smiling in a shimmering golden dress that flowed far past her legs. The Peacock Queen spread out her arms and the folds of the dress blew out into the breeze. She was both beautiful and fearsome to behold.

"WELCOME." The voice filled the air. Even though their ships were blasting music, the voice still penetrated the night. The Peacock Queen's dress continued to grow in the breeze, and it glowed brightly against the dark sky. It was almost as if she were growing in size.

The witches wasted no time advancing toward her, and Briley cringed inwardly as the queen swept her cape to her side. A gust of wind rushed from between the folds of the golden fabric, tossing the witches about like a box of black needles. The witches were swept aside, but they were also adept flyers and corrected quickly, dispersing outward.

"You don't have to fight us!" Briley cried out. "We just want fairy land to be as it once was!"

The Peacock Queen looked to her, chuckling to herself as the golden gown continued to overwhelm the darkness. "Little girl," the queen laughed. "Go home!" The Peacock Queen shifted her arm, pointing a long lacquered fingernail straight at Briley, and it felt as if liquid fire were trying to burrow into her heart.

Perhaps long ago, or yesterday, Briley might have died from such an attack. But it was just as she had known when Harrison had said they would all go home. Briley knew how the story had to end. Argon had shown her the way. Become one with her. Right from the start.

Briley let a tear fall from her eye, and then she tapped again into the ancient power all around her. The trees on the mountaintops became her hair. The wind became her voice. She could feel the wings sprouting from her back again, could feel the thrust of Argon's legacy filling her heart. Somewhere back in Piedmont, there was an oak tree she had carved her initials in long ago. Briley's soul tethered itself there, and Briley smiled as she watched the Peacock Queen's eyes grow large.

"But you're just...," the Peacock Queen began.

Briley didn't let her finish. While the queen glowed golden, Briley flashed green all over the sky, sweeping her hand across the mountain, lifting up the rivers, lifting up the song.

"I'm Briley the Braverest!" she called out in a voice nothing like her own. "I will never go out!"

Briley flew upward, growing just as the Peacock Queen grew in size.

"You should have come at us with your army," Briley whispered. As she did, ravens launched from the trees all around them. Briley could feel their feathers as if they were her own fingers. The ravens flew toward the queen as well. "You should have come at us with your dragons!" Briley's voice became a sing song melody. As she spoke, the wind calmed. The witches surrounded the ship, regaining their formation.

The queen hovered in front of her, speechless, motionless. Then she smiled.

Briley hovered before her, feeling invulnerable and amazing.

The Peacock Queen lifted her arm, and into the sky rose the dragons.

Briley had read stories, seen movies, and heard descriptions of what a dragon looked like. They were all wrong. These were not beautiful creatures crafted out of fantasy. They were beasts. Rude and cruel with vicious eyes, they were heavily muscled beasts. Their scales were not symmetrical. They did not glisten like the stars.

The dragons were caked in mud and grime, as if they had been unearthed from an infernal place. Briley counted four of them, then eleven, then there were more than twenty. They flew, their giant ungainly wings flapping steadily and slowly. Each flap flung more mud and grime from the wings. The Peacock Queen smiled and said, "Flame."

As one the dragons opened their mouths. Briley clutched her chest in horror, and jets of red and orange lit through the night, desperate lances seeking anything they could burn.

The witches all dispersed like black hornets kicked from a nest. One of the ships caught fire and immediately began to fall through the sky. Briley's heart began to sink. Argon had given her power, but she was no match for the Peacock Queen and the dragons combined. She closed her eyes, reaching deeper inside herself for Argon's hidden power. "For the Grove," she whispered.

The Horgles began separating their ships from one another, forming a ring around the Peacock Queen. The witches changed their tactics as well, maneuvering in packs of three or four, leading the dragons away from the ships. In their smaller packs, the witches were able to outmaneuver the dragons and confuse them. The dragons had flames and strength, but the witches were able to duck and dodge the attacks.

Then one of the larger dragons came straight for Briley, and she launched herself high into the air to avoid it. The dragon zipped past where she had been and was barreling toward the ship. There were no witches close enough to divert it, and the Horgles couldn't maneuver the ship fast enough. The dragon slammed into the side of the ship, its massive claws grabbing onto the railing. It opened its mouth and Briley saw the flame

241

gathering between its jaws. Horgles ran to the side of the ship with their swords raised, but they weren't going to be fast enough either. It seemed that all would soon be lost.

Briley knew that if that ship went aflame, she would lose her touch with Argon's power as well. Somehow he was invested both in her and in the ship. They were one. They were all one. Suddenly Briley understood. The Ship. Argon. Herself. Her brother, Harrison. The Horgles. Even Piedmont. The science project, the witches. Even the Peacock Queen. It was all ONE thing. Everything was connected.

Then the dragon let loose its flame, and Briley's heart nearly burst in two. She could FEEL the people aboard it, feel their agony. Her brother! Where was Harrison? If she lost him, she.... She couldn't even finish the thought.

But as quickly as the pain came, it ceased. Briley took a breath before daring to open her eyes. Had she died? she wondered. But no. As she opened her eyes, she understood what Argon had meant about her not being the one. For there, atop that mighty dragon's neck, perched Grace.

Although Briley had been transformed by this adventure, Grace had been shaped by it. She looked more mature, even wise. In her arms she clutched a tiny black dragon, and behind her, another molten silver dragon held onto Grace's waist.

The momentum of the battle suddenly stopped raging. The dragons, one by one, came to join the one Grace was riding.

"NO!" the Peacock Queen screeched out. "I will not have this!"

"Sister," Grace said in a far more serene voice. "I have the ruby scepter. I have the dragons. I have finally set free our father, who you imprisoned so long ago. Let it end!"

"You have nothing!" the Peacock Queen cried out. And then

a storm rose in the mountains, slashing rain crisscrossed with lightning. The Peacock Queen laughed gleefully as mountain tops erupted, flinging snow and rocks and rubble into the air.

Briley looked to the queen. Her normally pale and controlled face was contorted with anger and malice. Briley smiled as the Peacock Queen clenched her fists. The dragons all began to fly in a circle, creating a loop around the Crystal Palace.

The dragons swarmed around the queen, but she was not done. The queen raised her hands above her and began to transform. Her golden dress became scales, her lips grew into a ferocious mouth. Her pale skin darkened, blending with the dress until she was no longer anything like a queen at all, but a giant gold plated dragon as large as the moon. She opened her mouth, aiming straight for Briley, and created flames, splattering the skies with crimson and bathing the night in molten midnight.

There was no way for Briley to escape the blast. It caught her, lighting her from head to toe with heat and pain. She could feel her skin erupting in agony. She knew Argon could feel it too. The Grove could feel it. In that instant, it seemed the whole world was on fire, and for Briley it was. Luckily, the pain only lasted an instant. Several of the witches zipped through the air, dashing between Briley and the queen, weaving their spells and diverting the fire.

Briley's heart thudded in her chest. Tears flowed from her eyes as the memory of all of that burning pain still lingered inside. She forced herself to focus her eyes and focus her powers. She watched as the witches zipped in the cylinder around the Crystal Palace, with the queen at the center. At first they had little effect, but just like a storm, each time a witch cast a spell, it built on the previous one.

They spiraled around the dragons, around the queen. Briley

243

held her breath, waiting for what she knew would come. There was a moment of clarity. She knew that the queen had become too powerful to simply defeat. Even if they did cast her out today, she would return years from now, perhaps even more powerful. They had to do more than simply beat her. They needed a cage and a lock and a key. And Briley knew what the cage was. She knew what the lock was.

Argon had shown her. Perhaps without meaning to.

Briley knew what would come next, and she was ready for it.

She chose her moment, expanding not in size, but in spirit. She felt out with ephemeral fingers touching the sky, pricking herself on the stars.

The witches buzzed, ever circling, ever circling, creating a cyclone that whipped trees from their roots. The wind inside the cylinder slammed the fire to the edges. Then the dragons breathed fire too, adding to the cyclone, melting the moment and bathing the queen in liquid heat. The palace below began to shake from its foundation. Pieces of crystal came loose, flying up into the fiery cyclone. Then one of the towers began to separate, and Briley knew her moment was coming to hand. She could still feel the queen within that mass of crystal, fire, and wind. She was still fighting for control.

Another tower, then another came loose, and still the witches raced faster and faster, their magic whipping into full force, creating a storm of impossible ferocity.

Briley gathered herself amongst the night sky, draping herself above the storm. She was small in frame, but her spirit touched the roots and the rocks and the evergreens.

Then the Crystal Palace broke, shattering at its foundation. Every parapet, every beam and bar, every piece of crystal launched into the cyclone. There were flashes of gold amidst the crystal and fire. Briley chanced a look back at her brother, and a tear glistened on her cheek.

"Goodbye, my brother," she said. "Never forget to dance, Harrison."

Then Briley dove downward through the cyclone. She brought all the magic Argon had left her, and slammed it into the center of the storm. It rebounded off the crystal, which had a magic all its own. There were so many forces at work, reverberating and condensing into one singular place. She felt her body falling for a fleeting second, but her spirit was no longer within.

The storm erupted, spread, tossing the witches aside as if they were tinder twigs. The ships of the fleet were pushed away, each struggling to remain airborne in the massive force of the wind all about them. The storm raged outward, through the Green Sea, through all of the land of the fairy folk. It touched every root, every heart. The storm burst like laughter, reshaping the land.

The storm formed rivers, fields, created a new Green Land where the fairy folk would always be safe. Forgotten cities were revealed, their buildings long ago forgotten amongst the Green Sea. The soldiers of the Peacock Queen's army all blinked as one, dropping their enchanted shields and blinking against the night.

Briley could still feel the Peacock Queen within the storm. There was no magic strong enough to defeat her forever. But Argon's gift had been strong enough to direct it, keep it in check. The Green Land was the cage. Briley had become the lock.

Briley's heart beat all throughout the fairy land.

Each flower that bloomed was hers.

Every acorn.

Every squirrel.

Every song belonged to her.

***

245

Harrison crouched beside his sister, crying. Darrel and Dragus were both right next to him, each with a hand on his back.

"Is she dead?" Harrison asked through choked tears.

Briley had fallen so far, so fast to the deck of the ship, that no one had been able to catch her. At least there was no blood that he could see. At least there was that much.

"She saved us...." Darrel put a hand on his shoulder. "But it cost her life."

Harrison couldn't stand to see his sis like this. They had gone through so much.

The ships landed where the Crystal Palace had once stood. The mountain had been shaken down to its base when the palace had fallen apart.

Harrison didn't know who to blame. The queen? The witches? Himself? He clutched the body of his sister. He knew he was crying, and for the first time in his life he didn't care who saw. Darrel put a hand on his shoulder.

"Why did you do it, Sis?" Harrison sobbed.

"She had to." an unfamiliar voice broke in.

"But...." Harrison glanced up and saw that several witches were gathered around him.

"She knew the Peacock Queen would come back otherwise," Isabell said.

"I want my sister back!" Harrison demanded. "Do something!"

The witches all took a step back, shaking their heads.

"You've got to be able to...do...SOMETHING!" Harrison rounded on the witches.

"She is not gone," Isabell said. "She has transformed."

"I don't believe you!" He felt like fighting all the witches at once.

246

"Lad, don't do this." Darrel tried to restrain Harrison, but he was too fast.

Just as Harrison was about to draw his sword, the breeze shifted and the sails all beat in unison.

Tap Tap…Tap Tap Tap…Tap…Tap Tap

There was no mistaking their secret code. It said. *Dance, Brother. Dance and live free.*

Harrison stopped mid stride, wide eyed, his eyes glistening with tears and fury filling his veins. There were so many things he didn't understand.

Then the wind shifted the other direction and the sails beat out again.

Tap Tap…Tap Tap…Tap…Tap Tap

The Fire in my Belly was all it said.

Harrison collapsed to the ground, sobbing uncontrollably. "Oh, Bri!" he cried. "How can I ever dance again?"

The ships had landed around the edge of what had once been a mountain. Harrison looked to the center, piled high with rocks and debris as if nothing had ever or would ever be there.

Then one of the rocks shifted slightly.

Then another.

He saw a hand reach out through the cracks of the rocks and he jumped to his feet. How could anything have survived that much destruction?

The arm slowly reached up, followed by another, and soon Horgles were racing over to grab hold of who or whatever was trying to get out.

They pulled up a young man, and then another hand shot out from a different spot.

Soon all the crew was busy helping bodies out of the rubble and clearing away the boulders and little crystal chips, which were scattered like glitter atop the ground.

There were two fellows who looked like half spiders, and a woman with a horse's torso.

They took out bags of treasure too. It all seemed so far away. In a matter of minutes, where once there had been just rocks and nothing, there was a growing mountain of gold and jewels. Decorated shields, ancient swords. Emeralds, rubies, piled high upon high. And there were eggs too, Harrison saw. Oddly shaped, tiny things, hundreds of them, and each one a different color from the next.

"Dragons' eggs!" someone shouted out, reaffirming Harrison's dread.

"Smashem!" a Horgle cried out.

But before anyone could raise a hand to do away with the eggs, Grace landed next to the eggs, still astride the monstrous dragon. Grace dismounted and stepped amongst the rocks as if they were no more than pebbles, her gait so calm and her skin so bedazzling that all other activity stopped. She laid a hand upon one of the dragons' eggs and stroked it.

Harrison watched as the egg began to crack. A seam developed along it and then out shot a tiny little claw. Grace helped break the egg and let the creature climb up her arm to rest on her shoulder. Grace strode to the center of the area, right next to the amassed treasure and gems, and brought one of the men they had rescued into a fierce hug.

"Jaspar!" she called aloud. "Oh, you wouldn't believe what happened to me!"

The man laughed. "Ah, or you I!"

They both blushed when they realized everyone was watching, and then Grace's eyes hit upon Harrison's and she smiled. Her teeth glistened like sunlight in the deep dark, and she ran for him with the tiny black dragon on her shoulder.

Harrison stood, brushing the dirt from his trousers, unable to fathom everything going on. They hugged fiercely, and at her touch, Harrison's tears melted into happiness.

"Briley, she...."

"Briley is everywhere now," Grace said.

"But she...," Harrison choked back a sob.

"I know," Grace said, stroking his arm.

Soon the Horgles and witches had all gathered around the middle of the mountain, and Grace removed herself from Harrison's arms.

"The dragons' eggs will not be harmed!" she called out. "Their menace has melted with the passing of the queen!"

Something miraculous had happened to Grace that Harrison couldn't contemplate.

"We're not going home, are we, Sis?" Harrison asked as he looked down to Briley's unmoving body.

And although she didn't answer him, he felt the wind stir about him, felt the rocks around him shift, only subtly, as if just for him.

There was no tapping this time, but the air around Harrison warmed. It was as if Briley was giving him the only kind of hug she knew how to give.

"We will take her body to a safe place." Isabel stepped forward with two other witches. The three witches wove their fingers around and Harrison watched his sister's body float up through the air.

"There is hope for her yet" Isabel said cryptically before the three witches launched into the air on their brooms.

"Wait!" Harrison called out to one of the witches "Wait, take me with you! I want to forget!"

"Not today," the witch said. "Today is a day to be remembered."

The fairies jangled in song and people hugged one another. There would be many celebrations, and with each one a song.

The sails slapped together. Tap Tap...Tap...Tap Tap

Dance the wind whispered it.

Dance the rivers bubbled with it.

Dance, Harrison, Briley cooed out the only way she knew how.

Harrison nodded, choking back a sob. He moved first one foot, then the next. He wiped away a tear and took Grace by the hand.

"For Briley the Braverest, I will!" Harrison cried out.

The music played, the fairies glittered, the Horgles sang out, and Harrison danced.

***

"Darrel the Brave!" Grace called out.

All eyes turned to her. Grace stood at the edge of the debris. It was impossible to deny her regal nature. Darrel went up to her with Dragus and Grindel at his side, and all three kneeled.

"I have two favors to ask you," Grace said.

Darrel rose from his bow and wrung his hands together. "Aye, m'lady. And what is it you want of us?"

"My brother Wendell. Can you...try to bring him to me?" Tears were forming in her eyes. "I don't know what the goblins did to him, but he deserves so much...more."

"Aye!" Dragus and Grindel cried out, rising. "It's as good as done."

"And search for Briley," Grace pleaded. "The witches said she might not be lost forever!"

"I'm coming with you!" Harrison bounded up to them. "Whether you like it or not!"

"Oh, aye, lad!" Darrel laughed. "I'd have tied you to the mizzen mast if you hadn't volunteered!"

Everyone laughed at that. Then Grace turned to the others around her. "Jaspar, Hamper, Trick, all my good fellows!" she called to them. "It appears I am supposed to clean up this mess that another queen has made!" She chuckled. "No need for names. I will need a court to help me, and I find none finer than those gathered in front of me."

"But what kind of—?" Trick began

"I'm not much for courting!" Hamper finished.

The centaur kneeled to Grace and Jaspar bowed his head.

"I will find a use for the two of you, I am sure," Grace said, looking both Hamper and Trick in the eye. "I have a feeling you'd be very good at seeking out the hidden places of this land."

"On that you can count!" Hamper and Trick said in unison.

"And Harrison," Grace said with a tear in her eye.

Harrison stumbled toward her, feeling awkward. That is to say, he felt awkward until Grace wrapped him in a warm hug.

"I am so sorry," she whispered into his ear. "I will find a way to get her back, no matter the cost."

There was a choking noise deep in the back of Harrison's throat. Then it slipped between his lungs and rattled around his ribs for a minute. Finally, Harrison buried his face in Grace's shoulders, crying uncontrollably. Then there were more hands and arms surrounding him. The Horgles, Hamper and Trick, even the dragons all gathered around, and Harrison let loose a storm of tears.

"Enough of that," Harrison said finally, breaking away and wiping his eyes. "I am going to dance today!" he said aloud.

Everyone cheered. Then Harrison said, "We will rescue your brother if I have to fight every goblin myself!"

"And I am going to see what I can do about all of this grass," Grace replied.

"You think you can do something about it?" Darrel chimed in hopefully.

"I can do many things," Grace said cryptically. "All it requires is...." She looked to the silvered dragon, who was beginning to take flight. "Patience."

Then Grace mounted the dragon. She brought a hand to her lips and blew them all a kiss before the beast took flight. As the dragon vaulted from the ground, everyone except Darrel the Brave was struck by the sight of her.

"Hey, your holy fairy queen whatsit!" Darrel called out. "What about all these gems and gold and such?"

Grace was a silhouette against the rising sun, barely visible, but there was an echo that resounded off the mountains, making it to all the ears gathered below.

"Keep it!" the echo resounded. "And buy yourself a new hat!"

The end.

About the Author

A. Henry Moen is originally from Illinois. The son of two librarians, he grew up with his nose stuck in books. His favorite stories are the ones that can transport a reader to another world and tries to do that with his writing. Henry is very multifaceted. He enjoys board games, theatre, playing guitar, and hiking in the beautiful Colorado mountains that are now his home. He and his family are always on the lookout for a fun trip or new adventure. "Everything is a Story" he says. "You just have to know how to tell it."

CPSIA information can be obtained
at www.ICGtesting.com
Printed in the USA
FSHW02n0006270618
49641FS